THE LITERATURE OF
DEATH AND DYING

THE LITERATURE OF DEATH AND DYING

DEATH
AND SENSUALITY

A Study of Eroticism
and the Taboo

BY GEORGES BATAILLE

AYER COMPANY, PUBLISHERS, INC.
SALEM, NEW HAMPSHIRE 03079

Reprints Editions, 1992
Ayer Company, Publishers, Inc.
Salem, New Hampshire 03079

Reprinted by permission of
Les Editions de Minuit

Reprinted from a copy in the University
of Michigan Library

THE LITERATURE OF DEATH AND DYING
ISBN for complete set: 0-405-09550-3
See last pages of this volume for titles.

Manufactured in the United States of America

———◆———

Library of Congress Cataloging in Publication Data

Bataille, Georges, 1897-1962.
    Death and sensuality.

    (The Literature of death and dying)
    Reprint of the ed. published by Walker, New York.
    Bibliography: p.
    Includes index.
    1. Erotic literature. I. Title. II. Series.
[HQ462.B3 1977]   301.41   76-19560
ISBN 0-405-09556-2

BY GEORGES BATAILLE

DEATH
AND SENSUALITY

A Study of Eroticism
and the Taboo

Walker and Company

New York

First published in the United States
of America in 1962 by Walker and
Company, a division of Publications
Development Corporation.
Printed in Poland

CONTENTS

FOREWORD

The human spirit is prey to the most astounding impulses. Man goes constantly in fear of himself. His erotic urges terrify him. The saint turns from the voluptuary in alarm; she does not know that his unacknowledgeable passions and her own are really one.

The cohesion of the human spirit whose potentialities range from the ascetic to the voluptuous may nevertheless be sought.

The point of view I adopt is one that reveals the co-ordination of these potentialities. I do not seek to identify them with each other but I endeavour to find the point where they may converge beyond their mutual exclusiveness.

I do not think that man has much chance of throwing light on the things that terrify him before he has dominated them. Not that he should hope for a world in which there would be no cause for fear, where eroticism and death would be on the level of a mechanical process. But man can surmount the things that frighten him and face them squarely.

In doing so, he can be rid of the curious misunderstanding of his own nature that has characterised him until now. All I am doing, is to follow a path where others have trodden before me.

Long before the publication of the present work, eroticism had become a subject that a serious man could study without forfeiting his good name. For many years men have been discussing eroticism fearlessly and at length, so what I have to say in my turn is familiar enough. My sole intention has been to seek for cohesion amid the variety of given facts. I have tried to give a clear picture of a group of behaviour patterns.

By seeking to present a coherent whole I am working in contradiction to scientific method. Science studies one question by itself. It accumulates the results of specialised

7

research. I believe that eroticism has a significance for mankind that the scientific attitude cannot reach. Eroticism
cannot be discussed unless man too is discussed in the
process. In particular, it cannot be discussed independently
of the history of religions.

Hence the chapters of this book do not all deal with the
facts of sex directly. I have neglected other questions besides
that will sometimes seem no less important than those I have
discussed.

I have subordinated all else to the search for a standpoint
that brings out the fundamental unity of the human spirit.

The present work consists of two parts. In the first I have
made a systematic survey of the various interdependent
aspects of human life as they appear from the standpoint of
eroticism.

In the second I have brought together a number of
independent studies where the same assertion is considered,
namely, that the unity of the whole is indisputable. The aim
is the same in both parts. The chapters of the first part
and the various independent studies forming the second
have been under way concurrently from the end of the war
to the present time (1957). This method has one drawback,
however; I have not been able to avoid repetition. More
particularly in the first part I have sometimes reviewed from
a different point of view themes dealt with in the second part.
This procedure is excusable in that it reflects the general tone
of the work, since each separate issue entails consideration
of the whole question. One way of looking at this book is
to regard it as a general view of human life seen from constantly changing standpoints.

With the presentation of this over-all picture as my
starting point, nothing has intrigued me more than the idea
of once more coming across the image that haunted my adoles-
cence, the image of God. This is certainly not a return to
the faith of my youth. But human passion has only one
object in this forlorn world of ours. The paths we take
towards it may vary. The object itself has a great variety of

aspects, but we can only make out their significance by seeing how closely they are knit at the deepest level.

Let me stress that in this work flights of Christian religious experience and bursts of erotic impulses are seen to be part and parcel of the same movement.

I should not have been able to write this book if I had had to work out the problems confronting me on my own. I should like to mention here that my own endeavours have been preceded by *Le Miroir de la Tauromachie* by Michel Leiris, in which eroticism is envisaged as an experience wedded to life itself; not as an object of scientific study, but more deeply, as an object of passion and poetic contemplation. This book is dedicated to Michel Leiris particularly because of this book of his, the *Miroir*, written just before the war. I wish to thank him besides for the help he gave me when I was ill and unable myself to seek out the photographs which accompany my text.

May I also say how touched I have been by the earnest and active support of a great many friends who undertook in the same way to find relevant documents for me. In this context I should like to mention Jacques-André Boissard, Henri Dussat, Théodore Fraenkel, Max-Pol Fouchet, Jacques Lacan, André Masson, Roger Parry, Patrick Waldberg and Blanche Wiehn. I do not know personally M. Falk, Robert Giraud nor the fine photographer Pierre Verger to whom I am also indebted for some of the documentation. I am sure that the very subject matter of this work and the feeling of urgency that the book attempts to meet are important reasons for their whole-hearted co-operation.

I have not yet mentioned the name of my oldest friend Alfred Métraux, but I must acknowledge my great debt to him in general as I thank him for his help on this particular occasion. Not only did he introduce me to the field of anthropology and history of religions in the years that followed the first world war, but I have derived infinite assurance from his uncontested authority in my treatment of the fundamental issues of taboo and transgression.

A*

INTRODUCTION

Eroticism, it may be said, is assenting to life up to the point of death. Strictly speaking, this is not a definition, but I think the formula gives the meaning of eroticism better than any other. If a precise definition were called for, the starting-point would certainly have to be sexual reproductive activity, of which eroticism is a special form. Sexual reproductive activity is common to sexual animals and men, but only men appear to have turned their sexual activity into erotic activity. Eroticism, unlike simple sexual activity, is a psychological quest independent of the natural goal: reproduction and the desire for children. From this elementary definition let us now return to the formula I proposed in the first place: eroticism is assenting to life even in death. Indeed, although erotic activity is in the first place an exuberance of life, the object of this psychological quest, independent as I say of any concern to reproduce life, is not alien to death. Herein lies so great a paradox, that without further ado I shall try to give some semblance of justification to my affirmation with the following two quotations:

"Secrecy is, alas, only too easy," remarks de Sade, *"and there is not a libertine some little way gone in vice, who does not know what a hold murder has on the senses . . ."*

And it was the same writer who made the following statement, which is even more remarkable:

"There is no better way to know death than to link it with some licentious image."

I spoke of a semblance of justification. De Sade's notion, indeed, might stem from an aberration. In any case, even if it is true that the tendency it refers to is not uncommon in human nature, this is a matter of aberrant sensuality. However, there does remain a connection between death and sexual excitement. The sight or thought of murder can give rise to a desire for sexual enjoyment, to the neurotic at any rate. We cannot just pretend that a state of neurosis is the cause of this connection. I personally believe that there is a truth revealed in de Sade's paradox. This truth extends far beyond the confines of vice; I believe that it may even be the basis of our images of life and death. I believe, in fact, that we cannot reflect on existence without reference to this truth. As often as not, it seems to be assumed that man has his being independently of his passions. I affirm, on the other hand, that we must never imagine existence except in terms of these passions.

Now I must apologise for using a philosophical consideration as a starting-point for my argument.

Generally speaking, philosophy is at fault in being divorced from life. But let me reassure you at once. The consideration I am introducing is linked with life in the most intimate way: it refers to sexual activity considered now in the light of reproduction. I said that reproduction was opposed to eroticism, but while it is true that eroticism is defined by the mutual independence of erotic pleasure and reproduction as an end, the fundamental meaning of reproduction is none the less the key to eroticism.

Reproduction implies the existence of *discontinuous* beings.

Beings which reproduce themselves are distinct from one another, and those reproduced are likewise distinct from each other, just as they are distinct from their parents. Each being is distinct from all others. His birth, his death, the events of his life may have an interest for others, but he alone is directly concerned in them. He is born alone. He dies alone. Between one being and another, there is a gulf, a discontinuity.

This gulf exists, for instance, between you, listening to me, and me, speaking to you. We are attempting to communicate, but no communication between us can abolish our fundamental difference. If you die, it is not my death. You and I are *discontinuous* beings.

But I cannot refer to this gulf which separates us without

feeling that this is not the whole truth of the matter. It is a deep gulf, and I do not see how it can be done away with. None the less, we can experience its dizziness together. It can hypnotise us. This gulf is death in one sense, and death is vertiginous, death is hypnotising.

It is my intention to suggest that <u>for us, discontinuous beings that we are, death means continuity of being. Reproduction leads to the discontinuity of beings, but brings into play their continuity; that is to say, it is intimately linked with death.</u> I shall endeavour to show, by discussing reproduction and death, that death is to be identified with continuity, and both of these concepts are equally fascinating. This fascination is the dominant element in eroticism.

I am about to deal with a basic disturbance, with something that turns the established order topsy-turvy. The facts I shall take as a starting-point, will at first seem neutral, objective, scientific and apparently indistinguishable from other facts which no doubt do concern us, but remotely, and without bringing to bear any factors which touch us closely. This apparent insignificance is misleading but I shall take it first at its face value, just as if I did not intend to let the cat out of the bag the next minute.

You know that living creatures reproduce themselves in two ways; elementary organisms through asexual reproduction, complex ones through sexual reproduction.

In asexual reproduction, the organism, a single cell, divides at a certain point in its growth. Two nuclei are formed and from one single being two new beings are derived. But we cannot say that one being has given birth to a second being. The two new beings are equally products of the first. The first being has disappeared. It is to all intents and purposes dead, in that it does not survive in either of the two beings it has produced. It does not decompose in the way that sexual animals do when they die, but it ceases to exist. It ceases to exist in so far as it was discontinuous. But at one stage of the reproductive process there was continuity. There is a point at which the original

one becomes two. As soon as there are two, there is again discontinuity for each of the beings. But the process entails *one
instant* of continuity between the two of them. The first one
dies, but as it dies there is this moment of continuity between
the two new beings.

The same continuity cannot occur in the death of sexual
creatures, where reproduction is in theory independent of
death and disappearance. But sexual reproduction, basically
a matter of cellular division just like asexual reproduction,
brings in a new kind of transition from discontinuity to
continuity. Sperm and ovum are to begin with discontinuous
entities, but they *unite*, and consequently a continuity comes
into existence between them to form a new entity from the
death and disappearance of the separate beings. The new
entity is itself discontinuous, but it bears within itself the
transition to continuity, the fusion, fatal to both, of two
separate beings.

Insignificant as these changes may seem, they are yet
fundamental to all forms of life. In order to make them clear,
I suggest that you try to imagine yourself changing from the
state you are in to one in which your whole self is completely
doubled; you cannot survive this process since the doubles
you have turned into are essentially different from you. Each
of these doubles is necessarily distinct from you as you are
now. To be truly identical with you, one of the doubles
would have to be actually continuous with the other, and not
distinct from it as it would have become. Imagination
boggles at this grotesque idea. If, on the other hand, you
imagine a fusion between yourself and another human being
similar to that between the sperm and the ovum, you can
quite easily picture the change we are talking about.

These broad conceptions are not intended to be taken as
precise analogies. It is a far cry from ourselves with our
self-awareness to the minute organisms in question. I do
warn you, however, against the habit of seeing these tiny
creatures from the outside only, of seeing them as things
which do not exist inside themselves. You and I exist inside

ourselves. But so does a dog, and in that case so do insects and creatures smaller still. However far we may go down the scale of organisms from complex to primitive we cannot draw a line between those which exist inside themselves and those which do not. This inside existence cannot be a result of greater complexity. If the tiniest creatures did not have their own kind of inside existence to begin with, no increase in complexity could endow them with it.

The distance between these diminutive beings and ourselves is nevertheless considerable, and the bewildering feats of imagination I proposed could never hold any precise meaning. All I meant was to give a clear idea through a kind of *reductio ad absurdum* of those infinitesimal changes at the very foundations of our life.

On the most fundamental level there are transitions from continuous to discontinuous or from discontinuous to continuous. We are discontinuous beings, individuals who perish in isolation in the midst of an incomprehensible adventure, but we yearn for our lost continuity. We find the state of affairs that binds us to our random and ephemeral individuality hard to bear. Along with our tormenting desire that this evanescent thing should last, there stands our obsession with a primal continuity linking us with everything that is. This nostalgia has nothing to do with knowledge of the basic facts I have mentioned. A man can suffer at the thought of not existing in the world like a wave lost among many other waves, even if he knows nothing about the division and fusion of simple cells. But this nostalgia is responsible for the three forms of eroticism in man.

I intend to speak of these three type of eroticism in turn, to wit, physical, emotional and religious. My aim is to show that with all of them the concern is to substitute for the individual isolated discontinuity a feeling of profound continuity.

It is easy to see what is meant by physical or emotional eroticism, but religious eroticism is a less familiar notion. The term is ambiguous anyway in that all eroticism has a sacramental character, but the physical and the emotional are to be met with outside the religious sphere proper, while the quest for continuity of existence systematically pursued beyond the immediate world signifies an essentially religious intention. In its familiar Western form religious eroticism is bound up with seeking after God's love, but the East, intent on a similar quest, is not necessarily committed to the idea of a personal God. This idea is absent from Buddhism in particular. I wish now to stress the significance of what I have been trying to say. I have been insisting on a concept that at first glance may have seemed inappropriate and unnecessarily philosophical, that of continuity of being as opposed to discontinuity of being. At the point we have now reached I insist again that without this concept the broader meaning of eroticism and the unity underlying its forms would escape us.

My aim in sidetracking into a disquisition on the discontinuity and continuity of minute organisms engaged on reproductive activity has been to pierce the darkness that has always beset the vast field of eroticism. Eroticism has its own secrets and I am trying to probe them now. Would that be possible without first getting at the very core of existence?

I had to admit just now that it might seem irrelevant and pointless to consider the reproduction of minute organisms. They lack the feeling of elemental violence which kindles every manifestation of eroticism. In essence, the domain of eroticism is the domain of violence, of violation. But let us ponder on the transitions from discontinuity to continuity of these minute organisms. If we relate such transitions to our own experience, it is clear that there is most violence in the abrupt wrench out of discontinuity. The most violent thing of all for us is death which jerks us out of a tenacious obsession with the lastingness of our discontinuous being. We blench at the thought that the separate individuality within us must suddenly be snuffed out. We do not find it easy to link the feelings of tiny creatures engaged in reproduction with our own, but however minute the organisms may be,

we cannot visualise their coming into existence without
doing violence to our imagination: existence itself is at stake
in the transition from discontinuity to continuity. Only
violence can bring everything to a state of flux in this way,
only violence and the nameless disquiet bound up with it.
We cannot imagine the transition from one state to another
one basically unlike it without picturing the violence done to
the being called into existence through discontinuity. Not
only do we find in the uneasy transitions of organisms engaged in reproduction the same basic violence which in
physical eroticism leaves us gasping, but we also catch the
inner meaning of that violence. What does physical eroticism
signify if not a violation of the very being of its practitioners?
—a violation bordering on death, bordering on murder?

The whole business of eroticism is to strike to the inmost
core of the living being, so that the heart stands still. The
transition from the normal state to that of erotic desire presupposes a partial dissolution of the person as he exists in the
realm of discontinuity. Dissolution—this expression corresponds with *dissolute life*, the familiar phrase linked with
erotic activity. In the process of dissolution, the male partner
has generally an active role, while the female partner is
passive. The passive, female side is essentially the one that is
dissolved as a separate entity. But for the male partner the
dissolution of the passive partner means one thing only: it is
paving the way for a fusion where both are mingled, attaining
at length the same degree of dissolution. The whole business
of eroticism is to destroy the self-contained character of the
participators as they are in their normal lives.

Stripping naked is the decisive action. Nakedness offers a
contrast to self-possession, to discontinuous existence, in
other words. It is a state of communication revealing a quest
for a possible continuance of being beyond the confines of
the self. Bodies open out to a state of continuity through
secret channels that give us a feeling of obscenity. Obscenity
is our name for the uneasiness which upsets the physical
state associated with self-possession, with the possession of a

recognised and stable individuality. Through the activity of
organs in a flow of coalescence and renewal, like the ebb and
flow of waves surging into one another, the self is dispos-
sessed, and so completely that most creatures in a state of
nakedness, for nakedness is symbolic of this dispossession
and heralds it, will hide; particularly if the erotic act follows,
consummating it. Stripping naked is seen in civilizations
where the act has full significance if not as a simulacrum of
the act of killing, at least as an equivalent shorn of gravity.
In antiquity the destitution (or destruction) fundamental to
eroticism was felt strongly and justified linking the act of love
with sacrifice. When I come to religious eroticism which is
concerned with the fusion of beings with a world beyond
everyday reality I shall return to the significance of sacrifice.
Here and now, however, I must emphasise that the female
partner in eroticism was seen as the victim, the male as the
sacrificer, both during the consummation losing themselves
in the continuity established by the first destructive act.

This comparison is partially invalidated by the slight
degree of destruction involved. It would be only just true to
say that if the element of violation, violence even, which
gives it its destructive character is withdrawn, this erotic
activity reaches its climax far less easily. If it were truly
destructive, though, if a killing actually took place, the
quality of the erotic act would be no more enhanced thereby
than through the roughly equivalent procedure just described. When the Marquis de Sade in his novels defines
murder as a pinnacle of erotic excitement, that only implies
that the destructive element pushed to its logical conclusion
does not necessarily take us out of the field of eroticism
proper. Eroticism always entails a breaking down of established patterns, the patterns, I repeat, of the regulated social
order basic to our discontinuous mode of existence as defined
and separate individuals. But in eroticism less even than in
reproduction our discontinuous existence is not condemned,
in spite of de Sade; it is only jolted. It has to be jarred and
shaken to its foundations. Continuity is what we are after,

but generally only if that continuity which the death of discontinuous beings can alone establish is not the victor in the long run. What we desire is to bring into a world founded on discontinuity all the continuity such a world can sustain. De Sade's aberration exceeds that limit. Some few people find it tempting and occasionally some even go the whole way. But for the general run of normal men such irrevocable acts only indicate the extremes of practices in the first stages in which everyone must to some extent indulge. The stirrings within us have their own fearful excesses; the excesses show which way these stirrings would take us. They are simply a sign to remind us constantly that death, the rupture of the discontinuous individualities to which we cleave in terror, stands there before us more real than life itself.

Physical eroticism has in any case a heavy, sinister quality. It holds on to the separateness of the individual in a rather selfish and cynical fashion. Emotional eroticism is less constrained. Although it may appear detached from material sensuality it often derives from it, being merely an aspect made stable by the reciprocal affection of the lovers. It can be divorced from physical eroticism entirely, for the enormous diversity of human kind is bound to contain exceptions of this sort. The fusion of lovers' bodies persists on the spiritual plane because of the passion they feel, or else this passion is the prelude to physical fusion. For the man in love, however, the fervour of love may be felt more violently than physical desire is. We ought never to forget that in spite of the bliss love promises its first effect is one of turmoil and distress. Passion fulfilled itself provokes such violent agitation that the happiness involved, before being a happiness to be enjoyed, is so great as to be more like its opposite, suffering. Its essence is to substitute for their persistent discontinuity a miraculous continuity between two beings. Yet this continuity is chiefly to be felt in the anguish of desire, when it is still inaccessible, still an impotent, quivering yearning. A tranquil feeling of secure happiness can only mean the calm which follows the long storm of suffering, for it is more likely that lovers will not meet in such timeless fusion than that they will; the chances are most often against their contemplating in speechless wonder the continuity that unites them.

The likelihood of suffering is all the greater since suffering alone reveals the total significance of the beloved object. Possession of the beloved object does not imply death, but the idea of death is linked with the urge to possess. If the lover cannot possess the beloved he will sometimes think of killing her; often he would rather kill her than lose her. Or else he may wish to die himself. Behind these frenzied notions is the glimpse of a continuity possible through the beloved. Only the beloved, so it seems to the lover—because of affinities evading definition which match the union of bodies with that of souls—only the beloved can in this world bring about what our human limitations deny, a total blending of two beings, a continuity between two discontinuous creatures. Hence love spells suffering for us in so far as it is a quest for the impossible, and at a lower level, a quest for union at the mercy of circumstance. Yet it promises a way out of our suffering. We suffer from our isolation in our individual separateness. Love reiterates: "If only you possessed the beloved one, your soul sick with loneliness would be one with the soul of the beloved." Partially at least this promise is a fraud. But in love the idea of such a union takes shape with frantic intensity, though differently perhaps for each of the lovers. And in any case, beyond the image it projects, that precarious fusion, allowing as it does for the survival of the individual, may in fact come to pass. That is beside the point; this fusion, precarious yet profound, is kept in the forefront of consciousness by suffering as often as not, by the threat of separation.

We ought to take account of two conflicting possibilities. If the union of two lovers comes about through love, it involves the idea of death, murder or suicide. This aura of death is what denotes passion. On a lower level than this implied violence—a violence matched by the separate individual's sense of continuous violation—the world of habit and shared egotism begins, another mode of discontinuity, in fact. Only in the violation, through death if need be, of the individual's solitariness can there appear that image of the beloved object which in the lover's eyes invests all being with significance. For the lover, the beloved makes the world transparent. Through the beloved appears something I shall refer to in a moment in speaking of religious or sacred eroticism, to wit, full and limitless being unconfined within the trammels of separate personalities, continuity of being, glimpsed as a deliverance through the person of the beloved. There is something absurd and horribly commixed about this conception, yet beyond the absurdity, the confusion and the suffering there lies a miraculous truth. There is nothing really illusory in the truth of love; the beloved being is indeed equated for the lover,—and only for him no doubt, but what of that?—with the truth of existence. Chance may will it that through that being, the world's complexities laid aside, the lover may perceive the true deeps of existence and their simplicity.

Apart from the precarious and random luck that makes possession of the loved one possible, humanity has from the earliest times endeavoured to reach this liberating continuity by means not dependent on chance. The problem arises when man is faced with death which seems to pitch the discontinuous creature headlong into continuity. This way of seeing the matter is not the first that springs to mind, yet death, in that it destroys the discontinuous being, leaves intact the general continuity of existence outside ourselves. I am not forgetting that the need to make sure of the survival of the individual as such is basic to our desire for immortality but I am not concerned to discuss this just now. What I want to emphasise is that death does not affect the continuity of existence, since in existence itself all separate existences originate; continuity of existence is independent of death and *is even proved by death.* This I think is the way to interpret religious sacrifices, with which I suggest that erotic activity

can be compared. Erotic activity, by dissolving the separate
beings that participate in it, reveals their fundamental continuity, like the waves of a stormy sea. In sacrifice, the
victim is divested not only of clothes but of life (or is
destroyed in some way if it is an inanimate object). The
victim dies and the spectators share in what his death reveals.
This is what religious historians call the element of sacredness. This sacredness is the revelation of continuity through
the death of a discontinuous being to those who watch it as
a solemn rite. A violent death disrupts the creature's discontinuity; what remains, what the tense onlookers experience in the succeeding silence, is the continuity of all
existence with which the victim is now one. Only a spectacular killing, carried out as the solemn and collective
nature of religion dictates, has the power to reveal what
normally escapes notice. We should incidentally be unable to
imagine what goes on in the secret depths of the minds of
the bystanders if we could not call on our own personal
religious experiences, if only childhood ones. Everything
leads us to the conclusion that in essence the sacramental
quality of primitive sacrifices is analagous to the comparable
element in contemporary religions.

I said just now that I was going to talk about religious
eroticism. *Divine love* would have been a phrase more
easily understood. The love of God is a concept more
familiar and less disconcerting than the idea of the love of a
sacred element. I did not use this term because eroticism
geared to an object beyond immediate reality is far from
being the equivalent of the love of God. I thought it better
to be less easily understood and more accurate.

Sacred and divine are essentially identical notions, apart
from the relative discontinuity of God as a person. God is a
composite being possessed of the continuity I am talking
about on the affective plane in a fundamental way. God is
nevertheless represented by biblical and rational theology
alike as a personal being, as a creator distinct from the
generality of things created. I will say just this about con-

tinuity of existence: it is not in my opinion knowable, but it can be experienced in such fashions, always somewhat dubious, as hazard allows. Only negative experience is worthy of our attention, to my thinking, but this experience is rich enough. We ought never to forget that positive theology is matched by a negative theology founded on mystical experience.

Although clearly distinct from it, mystical experience seems to me to stem from the universal experience of religious sacrifice. It brings to a world dominated by thought connected with our experience of physical objects (and by the knowledge developed from this experience) an element which finds no place in our intellectual architecture except negatively as a limiting factor. Indeed, mystical experience reveals an absence of any object. Objects are identified with discontinuity, whereas mystical experience, as far as our strength allows us to break off our own discontinuity, confers on us a sense of continuity. The means it uses are different from those of physical or emotional eroticism. To be more precise, it does not use means independent of our wills. Erotic experience linked with reality waits upon chance, upon a particular person and favourable circumstances. Religious eroticism through mystical experience requires only that the subject shall not be disturbed.

Generally speaking, though not invariably, in India the succession of the different forms I have mentioned is envisaged with great simplicity. Mystical experience is reserved for the ripeness of old age, when death is near, when circumstances favourable to experience of reality are in default. Mystical experience linked with certain aspects of the positive religions is occasionally opposed to that assenting to life up to the point of death that I take to be in the main the fundamental meaning of eroticism.

But this opposition is not intrinsic. Assenting to life even in death is a challenge to death, in emotional eroticism as well as physical, a challenge to death through indifference to death. Life is a door into existence: life may be doomed but the continuity of existence is not. The nearness of this continuity and its heady quality are more powerful than the thought of death. To begin with, the first turbulent surge of erotic feeling overwhelms all else, so that gloomy considerations of the fate in store for our discontinuous selves are forgotten. And then, beyond the intoxication of youth, we achieve the power to look death in the face and to perceive in death the pathway into unknowable and incomprehensible continuity—that path is the secret of eroticism and eroticism alone can reveal it.

If this train of thought has been closely followed the significance of the sentence already quoted will be abundantly clear in the light of the oneness of the various modes of eroticism:

"*There is no better way to know death than to link it with some licentious image.*"

What I have been saying enables us to grasp in those words the unity of the domain of eroticism open to us through a conscious refusal to limit ourselves within our individual personalities. Eroticism opens the way to death. Death opens the way to the denial of our individual lives. Without doing violence to our inner selves, are we able to bear a negation that carries us to the farthest bounds of possibility?

To finish with, I should like to help you to realize fully that the point I have brought you to, however unfamiliar it may have seemed at times, is none the less the meeting of the ways for violent impulses at the very heart of things.

I spoke of mystical experience, not of poetry. I could not have talked about poetry without plunging into an intellectual labyrinth. We all feel what poetry is. Poetry is one of our foundation stones, but we cannot talk about it. I am not going to talk about it now, but I think I can make my ideas on continuity more readily felt, ideas not to be fully identified with the theologians' concept of God, by reminding you of these lines by one of the most violent of poets, Rimbaud.

> Elle est retrouvée.
> Quoi ? L'eternité.
> C'est la mer allée
> Avec le soleil.

Poetry leads to the same place as all forms of eroticism—
to the blending and fusion of separate objects. It leads us to
eternity, it leads us to death, and through death to continuity.
Poetry is eternity; the sun matched with the sea.

PART ONE

TABOOS AND TRANSGRESSIONS

CHAPTER I

EROTICISM IN INNER EXPERIENCE

Eroticism, an immediate aspect of inner experience as contrasted with animal sexuality

Eroticism is one aspect of the inner life of man. We fail to realise this because man is everlastingly in search of an object *outside* himself but this object answers the *innerness* of the desire. The choice of object always depends on the personal taste of the subject; even if it lights upon a woman whom most men would choose, the decisive factor is often an intangible aspect of this woman, not an objective quality; possibly nothing about her would force our choice if she did not somehow touch our inner being. Even if our choice agrees with that of most other people, in fact, human choice is still different from that of animals. It appeals to the infinitely complex inner mobility which belongs to man alone. The animal itself does have a subjective life but this life seems to be conferred upon it like an inert object, once and for all. Human eroticism differs from animal sexuality precisely in this, that it calls inner life into play. In human consciousness eroticism is that within man which calls his being in question. Animal sexuality does make for disequilibrium and this disequilibrium is a threat to life, but the animal does not know that. Nothing resembling a question takes shape within it.

However that may be, eroticism is the sexual activity of man to the extent that it differs from the sexual activity of animals. Human sexual activity is not necessarily erotic but erotic it is whenever it is not rudimentary and purely animal.

The decisive importance of the transition from animal to man

We know little about the transition from animals to men but its importance is fundamental. The events taking place during this transition are probably hidden from us for ever yet we are better equipped to consider it than it might seem at first sight. We know that men made tools and used them in order to survive, and then, quite quickly no doubt, for less necessary purposes. In a word they distinguished themselves from the animals by work. At the same time they imposed restrictions known as taboos. Quite certainly these taboos were primarily concerned with the dead. Probably at the same time, or nearly so, they were connected with sexual activity. We know the early date of the attitudes towards death through the numerous discoveries of bones gathered together by contemporary men. In any case, Neanderthal man, who was not quite a true man, who had not yet adopted exclusively an upright posture and whose skull was not so different as ours from that of the anthropoids, did often bury his dead. Sexual taboos certainly do not date from these remote times. We may say that they appeared as humanity appeared, but nothing tangible supports this view in so far as we ought to draw conclusions from prehistoric data. Burying the dead leaves traces, but nothing remains to give us the slightest hint about the sexual restrictions of earliest man.

We can only admit that they worked, since we have their tools. Since work, as far as we can tell, logically gave rise to the reaction which determined the attitude towards death, it is legitimate to believe that the taboo regulating and limiting sexuality was also due to it, and the generality of behaviour that is essentially human—work, awareness of death, sexual continence—goes back to the same remote past.

Traces of work appear in the Lower Paleolithic era and the earliest burial we know of goes back to the Middle Paleolithic. Of course we are talking about eras which lasted hundreds of thousands of years according to our present calculations;

these interminable millenia correspond with man's slow shaking-off of his original animal nature. He emerged from it by working, by understanding his own mortality and by moving imperceptibly from unashamed sexuality to sexuality with shame, which gave birth to eroticism. Man proper, whom we call our fellow, who comes on the scene at the time of the cave paintings (Upper Paleolithic), is determined by these changes as a whole; they are religious by nature and he must have felt them as a background to his life.

The inner experience of eroticism; the degree of objectivity connected with the discussion of it; the historical perspective in which this must be seen

There is one disadvantage in talking of eroticism in this way. If I call it a direct activity peculiar to man, this is an objective definition. Yet the objective study of eroticism, however interesting I find it, remains for me a secondary consideration. My purpose is to see in eroticism an aspect of man's inner life, of his religious life, if you like.

I said that I regarded eroticism as the disequilibrium in which the being consciously calls his own existence in question. In one sense, the being loses himself deliberately, but then the subject is identified with the object losing his identity. If necessary I can say in eroticism: *I* am losing myself. Not a privileged situation, no doubt. But the deliberate loss of self in eroticism is manifest; no one can question it. I intend to discuss the theme of eroticism quite deliberately from the subjective point of view, even if I bring in objective considerations at the start. But if I do refer to erotic manifestations in an objective way, I must stress that it is because inner experience is never possible untainted by objective views, but is always bound to some or other indisputably objective consideration.

Eroticism is primarily a religious matter and the present work is nearer to "theology" than to scientific or religious history

I repeat: if I sometimes speak as a man of science I only

seem to do so. The scientist speaks from outside, like an anatomist busy on a brain. (That is not quite true; religious history cannot deny the *inner experience*, past or present, of religion. But that is not important as long as it is forgotten as much as possible.) My theme is the subjective experience of religion, as a theologian's is of theology.

True, the theologian talks about *Christian* theology while religion in the sense I mean it is not just *a* religion, like Christianity. It is religion in general and no one religion in particular. My concern is not with any given rites, dogmas or communities, but only with the problem that every religion sets itself to answer. I take this problem for my own as a theologian does theology. The Christian religion I lay aside. If it were not for the fact that Christianity is a religion after all, I should even feel an aversion for Christianity. That this is so is demonstrated by the subject of the present work. That subject is eroticism. I am making my position clear from the outset. It goes without saying that the development of eroticism is in no respect foreign to the domain of religion, but in fact Christianity sets its face against eroticism and thereby condemns most religions. In one sense, the Christian religion is possibly the least religious of them all.

I should like to make my position perfectly clear.

In the first place I want to rid myself of preconceived notions as rigorously as possible. Nothing binds me to a particular tradition. Thus in occultism or esoteric cults I cannot fail to see preconceived ideas that interest me because they reflect our religious nostalgia, but I must shun them just the same because they represent a given belief. I may add that outside the assumptions of Christianity those of occultism are the most awkward in that they deliberately deny scientific principles in a world where these are dominant. Thus they turn anyone who accepts them into the sort of person who knows that arithmetic exists but who refuses to correct his own mistakes in addition. Science does not blind me (if I were dazzled by science I would conform inadequately to its demands), and arithmetic does not worry me either. Tell me two and two make five if you like, but if I am doing accounts with someone with a clear end in view, I shall forget that you claim two and two equal five. I do not see how anyone can put the problem of religion from the standpoint of gratuitous solutions denied by stringent scientific method. I am not a scientist, in the sense that what I am talking about is indirect experience, not objective material, but as soon as I do talk objectively I do so with the inevitable rigour of the scientists.

I would go so far as to say that for the most part in the religious attitude there is such a thirst for slick answers that religion has come to mean mental facility, and that my first words may make the unwary reader think that we have in mind some intellectual adventure and not the ceaseless search which carries the spirit, beyond philosophy and science if necessary, but by way of them, after every potentiality that can open out before it.

Everyone, however, will admit that neither philosophy nor science can answer the questions that religious aspirations have set us. But everyone will also admit that in the conditions that have hitherto obtained these aspirations have only been able to express themselves in indirect ways. Humanity has never been able to pursue what religion has always pursued except in a world where the quest has depended on dubious factors connected if not with stirrings of material desires at least with chance passions; it may have sturggled against these desires and passions or it may have served them, but it has not been able to remain indifferent to them. The quest begun and pursued by religion, like scientific research, must not be thought of separately from the chance events of history. Not that man has not been wholly dependent on these vicissitudes at some time or other, but that is true for the past. The time is coming, uncertainly enough perhaps, when with any luck we shall no longer need to wait for the decision of other people (in the guise of dogma) before attaining the experience we seek. So far we can freely communicate the results of this experience.

I can concern myself with religion in this sense not like a

schoolteacher giving a historical account of it, mentioning the Brahmin among others, but like the Brahmin himself. Yet I am not a Brahmin or indeed anything at all; I have to pick my way along a lonely path, no tradition, no ritual to guide me, and nothing to hinder me, either. In this book of mine I am describing an experience without reference to any special body of belief, being concerned essentially to communicate an inner experience—religious experience, as I see it—outside the pale of specific religions.

My inquiry, then, based essentially on inner experience, springs from a different source from the work of religious historians, ethnographers, and theologists. No doubt men working in these fields did have to ask whether they could assess the data under their consideration independently of the inner experience which on the one hand they share with their contemporaries and on the other resulted to some degree from their personal experiences modified by contact with the world constituting their fields of study. But in the case of such research workers we can state almost axiomatically that the less their own experience is brought into play the more authentic are their findings. I do not say: the less experience they have, but the less it is brought into play. Indeed I am convinced of the advantages of deep experience for the historian but if he does have a profound experience, since he has it, in fact, the best thing is for him to try and forget it and look at the facts objectively. He cannot forget it entirely, he cannot pare down his knowledge exactly to what he knows from the outside, and that is all to the good, but ideally this inner knowledge should influence his thinking in spite of himself, in so far as that source of knowledge is stubbornly there, in so far as talking about religion without reference to our intimate knowledge of religion would lead to a lifeless accumulation of inert facts churned out in no sort of intelligible order.

On the other hand, if I look at the facts in the light of my personal experience I know what I am discarding when I discard scientific objectivity. To begin with, as I have said, I can impose an arbitrary ban on knowledge acquired by impersonal methods. My experience still implies knowledge of the facts I am dealing with (in eroticism, of bodies; in religion, of the ritual forms without which collective religious practices could not exist). We cannot consider these forms except as illuminated by historical perspective with the erotic value they have acquired. We cannot separate our experience of them from their external aspect and their historical significance. With eroticism, the modifications undergone by our bodies in response to the vigorous stirring within us are themselves linked to the delightful and surprising aspects of sexual creatures. Not only is it impossible to regard this precise data, garnered from many sources, as denying the corresponding inner experience, but it actually assists the experience to stand out from what is individual and fortuitous. Even if it were tied to the objectivity of the outside world, private experience is bound to have an arbitrary flavour and without its universality would be impossible to discuss. Similarly without private experience we could discuss neither eroticism nor religion.

The conditions of an impersonal inner experience; the contradictory experiences of taboos and transgressions

It is in any case necessary to make a clear distinction between a study which calls on personal experience as little as possible and one which draws boldly on such experience. We must admit further that if the former had not been attempted in the first place, the latter would remain condemned to a gratuitousness we are familiar with. More, the conditions which make the present viewpoint possible have not long been in existence.

Whether we are discussing eroticism or religion in general a clear inner experience would have been out of the question at a time when the equilibrium between prohibitions and transgressions, regulating the play of both, did not stand out clearly defined and understood. Knowing that this balance exists is not in itself enough. Knowledge of eroticism or of religion demands an equal and contradictory personal experience of prohibitions and transgressions.

This dual experience is rare. Erotic or religious images draw forth behaviour associated with prohibitions in some people, the reverse in others. The first type is traditional. The second is common at least in the guise of a so-called back-to-nature attitude, the prohibition being seen as unnatural. But a transgression is not the same as a back-to-nature movement; it suspends a taboo without suppressing it.[1] Here lies the mainspring of eroticism and of religion too. I should be anticipating if I were to spend too long now on the profound complicity of law and the violation of law. But if it is true that mistrust (the ceaseless stirrings of doubt) is necessary to anyone trying to describe the experience I am talking about, this mistrust must also meet the demands I will at this stage formulate. Let us say first that our feelings tend to give a personal twist to our opinions. This difficulty is a general one, though it is relatively simple for me to imagine in what way my own inner experience coincides with that of other people and in what way it enables me to communicate with them. This is not usually admitted, but the vague and general nature of this proposition of mine prevents me from emphasising it. Leaving that aside, the obstacles opposed to the communication of experience seem to me to be quite another kettle of fish: they are connected with the taboo on which they are based and this duplicity I mentioned, the reconciling of what seems impossible to reconcile, respect for the law and violation of the law, the taboo and its transgression.

One thing or the other: either the taboo holds good, in which case the experience does not occur, or if it does, only furtively, outside the field of awareness; or it does not hold good; and of the two cases this is the more undesirable. Most frequently, as far as science is concerned, the taboo is

---

[1] There is no need to stress the Hegelian nature of this operation which corresponds with the dialectic phase described by the untranslatable German "aufheben": transcend without suppressing.

not justified, it is pathological, neurotic. Hence it is seen from outside: even if we have our own personal experience, in so far as we see it as a neurotic phenomenon we regard it as an outside mechanism intruding on our consciousness. This way of looking at it does not do away with the experience but it does minimise its significance. Hence if taboos and transgressions are described at all they are described objectively, by the historian, the psychiatrist or the psychoanalyst.

Eroticism as seen by the objective intelligence is something monstrous, just like religion. Eroticism and religion are closed books to us if we do not locate them firmly in the realm of inner experience. We put them on the same level as things known from the outside if we yield albeit unwittingly to the taboo. Unless the taboo is observed with fear it lacks the counterpoise of desire which gives it its deepest significance. The worst of it is that science whose procedures demand an objective approach to taboos owes its existence to them but at the same time disclaims them because taboos are not rational. Inside experience alone can supply the overall view, from which they are finally justifiable. If we undertake a scientific study indeed, we regard objects as exterior to ourselves; we are subjects: in science the scientist himself becomes an object exterior to the subject, able to think objectively (he could not do this if he had not denied himself as a subject to begin with). This is all very well as long as eroticism is condemned, if we reject it in advance, if we rid ourselves of it in this way, but if (as it often does) science condemns religion (ethical religion) which is patently fundamental to science, we are no longer justified in opposing eroticism. If we do not oppose it we must no longer consider it objectively as something outside ourselves.[1] We must envisage it as the stirrings of life within ourselves.

If the taboo conserves its full force there is a difficulty.

[1] This is valid for the whole of psychology, but without eroticism and religion psychology is nothing but an empty shell. I know that for the moment I am playing on an equivocal aspect of religion and eroticism, but only for the sake of the argument of the present work.

Taboos acted on behalf of science in the first place. They removed the object of the taboo from our consciousness by forbidding it, and at the same time deprived our consciousness—our full consciousness, at any rate—of the movement of terror whose consequence was the taboo. But the rejection of the disturbing object and the disturbance itself were necessary for the clarity, the untroubled clarity, of the world of action and of objectivity. Without the existence of prohibitions in the first place, man would not have achieved the lucid and distinct awareness on which science is founded. Prohibitions eliminate violence, and our violent impulses (those which correspond with sexual impulsions can be counted among them) destroy within us that calm ordering of ideas without which human awareness is inconceivable. But if this awareness is to bear precisely on those disturbed impulses of violence, that implies that it has first been able to set itself beyond the reach of taboos: this presupposes that we can direct the light of the questioning intelligence on to these taboos themselves, without whose existence it would never have functioned in the first place. The aware intelligence cannot in this case look on them as a mistake we are victims of, but as the outcome of the fundamental emotion on which humanity depends. The truth of taboos is the key to our human attitude. We must know, we can know that prohibitions are not imposed from without. This is clear to us in the anguish we feel when we are violating the taboo, especially at that moment when our feelings hang in the balance, when the taboo still holds good and yet we are yielding to the impulsion it forbids. If we observe the taboo, if we submit to it, we are no longer conscious of it. But in the act of violating it we feel the anguish of mind without which the taboo could not exist: that is the experience of sin. That experience leads to the completed transgression, the successful trangression which, in maintaining the prohibition, maintains it in order to benefit by it. The inner experience of eroticism demands from the subject a sensitiveness to the anguish at the heart of the taboo no less great than the desire which leads him to infringe it. This is religious sensibility, and it always links desire closely with terror, intense pleasure and anguish.

Anybody who does not feel or who feels only furtively the anguish, nausea and horror commonly felt by young girls in the last century is not susceptible to these emotions, but equally there are people whom such emotions limit. These emotions are in no sense neurotic; but they are in the life of a man what a chrysalis is compared with the final perfect creature. Man achieves his inner experience at the instant when bursting out of the chrysalis he feels that he is tearing himself, not tearing something outside that resists him. He goes beyond the objective awareness bounded by the walls of the chrysalis and this process, too, is linked with the turning topsy-turvy of his original mode of being.

CHAPTER II

THE LINK BETWEEN TABOOS AND DEATH

The contrast between the world of work or reason and that of violence

In the section which follows, whose subject is eroticism at white heat (the blind moment when eroticism attains its ultimate intensity), I shall consider systematically the relationship between those two irreconcilables already mentioned, taboo and transgression.

Man belongs in any case to both of these worlds and between them willy-nilly his life is torn. The world of work and reason is the basis of human life but work does not absorb us completely and if reason gives the orders our obedience is never unlimited. Man has built up the rational world by his own efforts, but there remains within him an undercurrent of violence. Nature herself is violent, and however reasonable we may grow we may be mastered anew by a violence no longer that of nature but that of a rational being who tries to obey but who succumbs to stirrings within himself which he cannot bring to heel.

There is in nature and there subsists in man a movement which always exceeds the bounds, that can never be anything but partially reduced to order. We are generally unable to grasp it. Indeed it is by definition that which can never be grasped, but we are conscious of being in its power: the universe that bears us along answers no purpose that reason defines, and if we try to make it answer to God, all we are doing is associating irrationally the infinite excess in the presence of which our reason exists with our reason itself. But through the excess in him, that God whom we should like to shape into an intelligible concept never ceases, exceeding this concept, to exceed the limits of reason.

In the domain of our life excess manifests itself in so far as violence wins over reason. Work demands the sort of conduct where effort is in a constant ratio with productive efficiency. It demands rational behaviour where the wild impulses worked out on feast days and usually in games are frowned upon. If we were unable to repress these impulses we should not be able to work, but work introduces the very reason for repressing them. These impulses confer an immediate satisfaction on those who yield to them. Work, on the other hand, promises to those who overcome them a reward later on whose value cannot be disputed except from the point of view of the present moment. From the earliest times[1] work has produced a relaxation of tension thanks to which men cease to respond to the immediate urge impelled by the violence of desire. No doubt it is arbitrary always to contrast the detachment fundamental to work with tumultuous urges whose necessity is not constant. Once begun, however, work does make it impossible to respond to these immediate solicitations which could make us indifferent to the promised desirable results. Most of the time work is the concern of men acting collectively and during the time reserved for work the collective has to oppose those contagious impulses to excess in which nothing is left but the immediate surrender to excess, to violence, that is. Hence the human collective, partly dedicated to work, is defined by taboos without which it would not have become the world of work that it essentially is.

The main function of all taboos is to combat violence

What prevents us from seeing this decisive articulation of human life in its simplicity is the capricious way these taboos are promulgated. They have often had a superficially

---

[1] Work made man what he is. The first traces of man are the stone tools he left behind him. According to recent research it seems as though Australopithecus, still far from the highly developed form which we exemplify, left tools of this sort; Australopithecus lived about a million years before us (while Neanderthal man, whose burial places are the earliest known to us, lived only some few thousand years ago).

insignificant air. The significance of taboos if we take them as a whole, particularly if we take into consideration those which we do not fail religiously to observe, is none the less reducible to a simple element. I will formulate this without demonstrating the truth of it immediately (that I will do systematically later and my generalisation will be seen to be a sound one). Violence is what the world of work excludes with its taboos; in my field of enquiry this implies at the same time sexual reproduction and death.

Only later on shall I be able to establish the profound unity of these apparent opposites, birth and death. However, even at this stage their external connections stand revealed in the universe of sadism, there for anyone who thinks about eroticism to ponder on. De Sade—or his ideas—generally horrifies even those who affect to admire him and have not realised through their own experience this tormenting fact: the urge towards love, pushed to its limit, is an urge toward death. This link ought not to sound paradoxical. The excess from which reproduction proceeds and the excess we call death can each only be understood with the help of the other. But it is clear from the outset that the two primary taboos affect, firstly, death, and secondly, sexual functions.

Prehistoric evidence of taboos connected with death

"Thou shalt not kill"; "Thou shalt not perform the carnal act except in wedlock". Such are the two fundamental commandments found in the Bible and we still observe them.

The first of these prohibitions is the consequence of the human attitude towards the dead.

Let me return to the earliest days of our species, when our destiny was at stake. Even before man presented the appearance that he does today, Neanderthal man, whom pre-historians call 'homo faber', was making various stone instruments, often very elaborately, with the aid of which he hewed stone—or wood. This kind of man living a hundred thousand years before ourselves was already like us but still more like the anthropoid. Although he held himself erect like us his legs were still a little bent; when he walked he leaned more on the ball of the foot than on the outer edge. His neck was not as flexible as ours (although certain men have conserved certain of his simian characteristics). He had a low forehead and a jutting brow. We only know the bones of this rudimentary man; we cannot know the exact appearance of his face; not even if his expression was already a human one. All we know is that he worked and cut himself away from violence.

If we look at his life as a whole, he remained inside the realm of violence. (We have not yet entirely abandoned it ourselves). But he escaped its power to some extent. He worked. We have the evidence of his technical skill left by numerous and various stone tools. This skill was remarkable enough in that if he had not given it his considered attention, going back on and perfecting his first idea, he could not have achieved results that were constant and in the long run greatly improved. His tools are in any case not the only proof of an incipient opposition to violence; the burial places left by Neanderthal man bear witness to this also.

Besides work, death was recognized by this man as terrifying and overwhelming, and indeed as supernatural. Prehistory assigns Neanderthal man to the Middle Paleolithic era; as early as Lower Paleolithic, apparently some hundreds of thousands of years before, fairly similar human beings existed who left traces of their work just as Neanderthal man did: the heaps of bones of these earlier men that have been found encourage us to think that death had begun to disturb them, since they paid some attention to skulls at least. But burial of the dead, still a religious practice for humanity at the present time, appears towards the end of the Middle Paleolithic, a little while before the disappearance of Neanderthal man and the arrival of a man exactly like ourselves whom prehistorians, keeping the name 'homo faber' for the earlier type, call 'homo sapiens'.

The custom of burial is the sign of a taboo similar to ours concerning the dead and death. In a vague form at least the taboo must have arisen before this custom. We can even admit that in one sense, so imperceptibly that no proof could have remained, and doubtless unnoticed by those who lived at the time, the birth of this taboo coincided with the beginnings of work. The essential difference is that between a man's dead body and other objects such as stones. Today the perception of this difference is still characteristic of a human being as opposed to an animal; what we call death is in the first place the consciousness we have of it. We perceive the transition from the living state to the corpse, that is, to the tormenting object that the corpse of one man is for another. For each man who regards it with awe, the corpse is the image of his own destiny. It bears witness to a violence which destroys not one man alone but all men in the end. The taboo which lays hold on the others at the sight of a corpse is the distance they put between themselves and violence, by which they cut themselves off from violence. The picture of violence which we must attribute to primitive man in particular must necessarily be understood as opposed to the rhythm of work regulated by rational factors. Lévy-Bruhl's mistake has long been recognized; he denied primitive man a rational mode of thought and conceded him only the uncertain and indistinct images that result from participation.[1] Work is obviously no less ancient than man himself, and though work is not always foreign to animals, human work as distinct from animal work is never foreign to reason. It supposes that a fundamental identity is accepted between itself and the wrought object, and it supposes the difference, resulting from the work, between its substance and the developed tool. Similarly it implies awareness of the use of the tool, of the chain of cause and effect in which it is about to become involved. The laws which govern the acquired skills which give rise to tools or which are served by

[1] Lévy-Bruhl's descriptions are none the less correct and of indubitable interest. If, as Cassirer did, he had talked about 'mythical thought' and not 'primitive thought', he would not have encountered the same difficulties. 'Mythical thought' may be contemporary with rational thought, though it does not originate in the latter.

them are laws of reason from the outset. These laws regulate the changes which work conceives and effects. No doubt a primitive man could not have made them explicit; his language made him aware of the objects it named for him, but was inadequate to deal with the naming process itself. A workman today, the best part of the time would not be in a position to formulate them; nevertheless he observes them faithfully. Primitive man as Lévy-Bruhl describes him may have thought irrationally some of the time that a thing simultaneously is and is not, or that it can be what it is and something else at the same time. Reason did not dominate his entire thinking, but it did when it was a question of work. So much so that a primitive man could imagine, without formulating it, a world of work or reason to which another world of violence was opposed.[1] Certainly death is like disorder in that it differs from the orderly arrangements of work. Primitive man may have thought that the ordering of work belonged to him, while the disorder of death was beyond him, making nonsense of his efforts. The movement of work, the operations of reason were of use to him, while disorder, the movement of violence, brought ruin on the very creature whom useful works serve. Man, identifying himself with work which reduced everything to order, thus cut himself off from violence which tended in the opposite direction.

The horror of the corpse as a symbol of violence and as a threat of the contagiousness of violence

Violence, and death signifying violence, have a double meaning. On the one hand the horror of death drives us off, for we prefer life; on the other an element at once solemn and terrifying fascinates us and disturbs us profoundly. I shall return to this ambiguity. I can only point out in the first place the essential aspect of

---

[1] The expressions 'profane world' (= world of work or reason) and 'sacred world' (= world of violence) are none the less of great antiquity. *Profane* and *sacred*, though, are words from the vocabulary of irrationalism.

recoil in the face of violence which is expressed by taboos
associated with death.

A man's dead body must always have been a source of
interest to those whose companion he was while he lived,
and we must believe that as a victim of violence those nearest
to him were careful to preserve him from further violence.
Burial no doubt signified from the earliest times, as far as
those who buried the body were concerned, their wish to
save the dead from the voracity of animals. But even if that
wish had been the determining factor in the inauguration of
this custom, we cannot say that it was the most important;
awe of the dead in all likelihood predominated for a long
time over the sentiments which a milder civilization developed. Death was a sign of violence brought into a world
which it could destroy. Although motionless, the dead man
had a part in the violence which had struck him down;
anything which came too near him was threatened by the
destruction which had brought him low. Death presented
such a contrast between an unfamiliar region and the everyday world that the only mode of thought in tune with it was
bound to conflict with the mode of thought governed by
work. Symbolical or mythical thought, erroneously labelled
'primitive' by Lévy-Bruhl, is the only kind appropriate to
violence whose essence is to break the bounds of rational
thought implicit in work. According to this way of thinking,
the violence which by striking at the dead man dislocates the
ordered course of things does not cease to be dangerous once
the victim is dead. It constitutes a supernatural peril which
can be 'caught' from the dead body. Death is a danger for
those left behind. If they have to bury the corpse it is less in
order to keep it safe than to keep themselves safe from its
contagion. Often the idea of contagion is connected with the
body's decomposition where formidable aggressive forces are
seen at work. The corpse will rot; this biological disorder,
like the newly dead body a symbol of destiny, is threatening in itself. We no longer believe in contagious magic,
but which of us could be sure of not quailing at the sight

of a dead body crawling with maggots? Ancient peoples took the drying up of the bones to be the proof that the threat of violence arising at the time of death had passed over. More often than not the dead man himself held in the clutch of violence, as the survivors see it, is part and parcel of his own disorder, and his whitened bones are what at last betoken the pacification of his spirit.

The taboo on murder

The taboo relating to the corpse does not always appear intelligible. In 'Totem and Taboo' Freud, because of his superficial knowledge of ethnographical data, nowadays much less vague, thought that the taboo generally countered the desire to touch. The desire to touch the dead was doubtless no greater in former times than it is today. The taboo does not necessarily anticipate the desire; in the presence of a corpse horror is immediate and inevitable and practically impossible to resist. The violence attendant upon a man's death is only likely to tempt men in one direction: it may tend to be embodied in us against another living person; the desire to kill may take hold of us. The taboo on murder is a special aspect of the universal taboo on violence.

In the eyes of primitive man violence is always the cause of death. It may have acted through magical means, but someone is always responsible, someone is always a murderer. The two aspects of the taboo are interrelated. We must run away from death and hide from the forces that have been unleashed. Other forces like those which have overpowered the dead man and are temporarily in possession of him must not be loosed in ourselves.

As a rule the community brought into being by work considers itself essentially apart from the violence implied by the death of one of its members. Faced by such a death the body politic feels that a taboo is in force. But that is only true for the members of the community. Within it the taboo has full force. Without, where strangers are concerned, the taboo is still felt but it can be violated. The community is made up of those whom the common effort unites, cut off from violence by work during the hours devoted to work. Outside this given time, outside its own limits, the comunity can revert to violence, it can resort to murder in war against another community.

In given circumstances, during a given time, the murder of members of a given tribe is permissible, necessary even. Yet the wildest hecatombs, in spite of the irresponsibility of their instigators, never entirely remove the malediction falling on murder. The Bible commands 'Thou shalt not kill', and this sometimes makes us smile, but we deceive ourselves in regarding the Bible as unimportant. Once the obstacle is overthrown what outlasts the transgression is a flouted taboo. The bloodiest of murderers cannot ignore the curse upon him, for the curse is the condition of his achievement. Transgression piled upon transgression will never abolish the taboo, just as though the taboo were never anything but the means of cursing gloriously whatever it forbids.

In the foregoing proposition there is a basic truth: taboos founded on terror are not only there to be obeyed. There is always another side to the matter. It is always a temptation to knock down a barrier; the forbidden action takes on a significance it lacks before fear widens the gap between us and it and invests it with an aura of excitement. "There is nothing", writes de Sade, "that can set bounds to licentiousness . . . The best way of enlarging and multiplying one's desires is to try to limit them".[1] Nothing can set bounds to licentiousness . . . or rather, generally speaking, there is nothing that can conquer violence.

---

[1] Introduction to 'Les Cent Vingt Journées de Sodome'.

CHAPTER III

TABOOS RELATED TO REPRODUCTION

*The taboo universally found in man as opposed to the sexual
freedom of animals*

Later on I shall return to the complementary relationship
uniting taboos which reject violence with acts of transgression which set it free. These counterbalanced urges have a
kind of unity. From considering the significance of a barrier
at the moment of its being overturned, I already have gone
on to introduce a group of taboos parallel with those called
into existence by death. The taboos centred on sexuality
have now to be considered. We have very old traces of customs concerned with death. Prehistoric evidence on sexuality
is more recent; what is more we can draw no conclusions
from them. There are Middle Paleolithic burial sites but
evidence of the sexual activity of the first men goes no
further back than Upper Paleolithic. Art (representation)
does not appear with Neanderthal man[1] but begins with
homo sapiens, and such images of himself as he has left are
rare anyway. These images are generally ithyphallic. Hence
we know that sexual activity like death was early on a subject
of interest to man, but we cannot deduce any clear indications from such vague data as we can with death. Ithyphallic
pictures obviously show a relative freedom. Nevertheless
they cannot prove that those who traced them believed
in unlimited freedom in this field. All we can say is that as
opposed to work, sexual activity is a form of violence, that
as a spontaneous impulse it can interfere with work. A

---

[1] Neanderthal man knew how to use colouring matter but he left no trace of
drawing at all, while such traces are numerous as soon as homo sapiens comes on
the scene.

community committed to work cannot afford to be at its mercy during working hours, so to speak. We would then be justified in thinking that, from the first, sexual liberty must have received some check which we are bound to call a taboo without being able to say anything about the cases in which it applies. At the most we could assume that initially the time set aside for work determined the limit. The only real reason we have for thinking that a taboo of this sort must be very old indeed is that at all times as in all places as far as our knowledge goes, man is defined by having his sexual behaviour subject to rules and precise restrictions. Man is an animal who stands abashed in front of death or sexual union. He may be more or less abashed, but in either case his reaction differs from that of other animals.

These restrictions vary greatly according to time and place. All peoples do not feel the necessity to hide the sexual organs in the same way; but they do generally conceal from sight the male organ in erection; and usually a man and a woman seek privacy to accomplish the sexual act. In Western civilizations nakedness has become the object of a fairly general and weighty taboo, but our contemporary experience calls into question an assumption that once appeared fundamental. The experience we have of changes that are possible does not show the taboos as arbitrary, though; on the contrary, it proves their deep significance in spite of superficial changes of emphasis on aspects unimportant in themselves. We know now how mutable are the specific patterns which are read into the amorphous prohibition. This prohibition simply imposes the necessity for submitting sexual activity to generally accepted restrictions. But it gives us the certainty that there is a fundamental rule which demands that we submit, and in common, to restrictions of one sort or another. The taboo within us against sexual liberty is general and universal; the particular prohibitions are variable aspects of it.

I am astonished to be the first person to state this so unequivocally. It is ridiculous to isolate a specific 'taboo'

such as the one on incest, just one aspect of the general
taboo, and look for its explanation outside its universal basis,
namely the amorphous and universal prohibitions bearing
on sexuality. Roger Caillois, however, is an exception to this
tendency. He writes: "problems on which a great deal of ink
has been used up, like the prohibition on incest, can only be
given a fair solution if they are considered as special cases of
a system that embraces all religious taboos in a given
society".[1] As I see it, the beginning of Caillois' statement is
perfect, but when he says "a given society" he is still referring to a special case, a given aspect. It is high time we gave
our attention to all religious taboos in all ages and in all
climates. Caillois' remark forces me to state here and now
that this amorphous and universal taboo is constant. Its
shape and its objects do change; but whether it is a question
of sexuality or death, violence, terrifying yet fascinating, is
what it is levelled at.

The taboo on incest

The 'special case' of the taboo on incest is the one that
commands most attention, even as far as replacing on a
general view sexual taboos proper. Everyone knows that a
taboo on sexuality does exist, amorphous and indefinable;
all mankind observes it, but this observance is so varied
according to the time and the place that no-one has found a
formula for it that would allow it to be generally discussed.
The taboo on incest, no less universal, is translated into
well-defined customs always pretty rigorously formulated,
and a single unambiguous word gives a general definition
of it. That is why incest has been the subject of numerous
studies while the general taboo of which it is only a special
case and from which springs an inchoate collection of prohibitions has no place in the minds of people whose business
it is to study human behaviour. So true it is that human
intelligence is moved to consider what is simple and easily
defined to the exclusion of matters that are vague, difficult

---

[1] '*L'homme et le sacré*' 2nd. edition, Gallimard, 1950, p. 71, note 1.

to grasp and variable. Hence the taboo on sex has so far evaded the curiosity of scientists, while the various forms of incest, no less clearly defined than those of animal species, offered them what they liked, puzzles to solve, on which their ingenuity could be exerted.

In archaic societies, classifying persons according to their blood relationships and determining what marriages are forbidden sometimes becomes quite a science. The great merit of Claude Lévi-Strauss is that he found in the endless meanderings of archaic family structures the origin of peculiarities, that cannot derive only from the vague fundamental taboo that made men in general observe laws opposed to animal freedom. In the first place the dispositions concerning incest answered the need to bind with rules a violence that if it had been allowed a free rein might have disturbed the order to which the community desired to submit itself. But independently of this basic requirement fair laws were necessary for the distribution of the women among the men; certain dispositions, strange but precise, are understandable if one takes into consideration the desirability of an ordered distribution. The taboo made it necessary that a rule of some kind should be in force, but the particular rules decided upon could take secondary matters into consideration which had nothing to do with secular violence and its menace to reason and order. If Lévi-Strauss had not shown the origins of a certain aspect of marriage conventions, there would have been no reason not to seek the significance of the taboo on incest there, but that aspect simply met the need to find an answer to the problem of sharing out the available women.

If we insist on reading a significance into the general movement of incest which forbids physical union between close relations, we ought first to consider the strong feeling which has persisted. This feeling is not a fundamental one, but neither were the circumstances which determined the forms of the taboo. It seems natural at first glance to look among apparently ancient customs for a cause. But once this research has gone a fair distance the opposite seems true. The cause we have sought out did not constitute a curtailment of freedom in principle, it could only use that principle for particular ends. We must refer the special case to the "whole body of religious taboos" known to us and to which we are still subject. Is there anything more firmly rooted in us than the horror of incest? (With this also I associate respect for the dead, but I shall not show until later on how all taboos are basically interrelated.) We look on physical union with the mother or father or with a brother or sister as inhuman. The persons with whom we may not have sexual relations are variously defined. Yet without the rule ever having been formulated we may not associate sexually with those who were living in the family home when we were born; this limiting factor would be clearer no doubt if other variable taboos, arbitrary seeming to those not subject to them, were not involved. At the centre, a fairly simple and constant nucleus, surrounded by an arbitrary and variable complex, characterises this fundamental taboo. Nearly everywhere can be found this solid core and simultaneously the surrounding fluidity and mobility. This mobility obscures the significance of the nucleus. The nucleus is not intangible in itself, but considering it we gain a more acute insight into the primal horror whose repercussions are sometimes due to chance and sometimes coincident with social convenience. It is always at bottom a matter of two incompatibles: the realm of calm and rational behaviour and the violence of the sexual impulse. With the passing of the ages, could the rules which spring from this dichotomy have been defined except in variable and arbitrary forms?[1]

Menstruation and loss of blood at childbirth

No less than incest certain other taboos seem to us to spring from the general horror of violence; for instance, the

---

[1] I have left over until the second part of this book (see the fourth study) a more detailed analysis of incest based on Claude Lévi-Strauss' learned work 'Les Structures Élémentaires de la Parenté', Presses Universitaires, 1949, 8vo, 640 pp.

taboos associated with menstruation and the loss of blood at childbirth. These discharges are thought of as manifestations of internal violence; blood in itself is a symbol of violence. The menstrual discharge is further associated with sexual activity and the accompanying suggestion of degradation: degradation is one of the effects of violence. Childbearing cannot be dissociated from this complex of feelings. Is it not itself a rending process, something excessive and outside the orderly course of permitted activity? Does it not imply the denial of the established order, a denial without which there could be no transition from nothingness to being, or from being to nothingness? There may well be something gratuitous about these assessments; moreover the taboos seem almost trivial to us even if we do feel disgust at such unclean processes. They have nothing to do with the firm nucleus of the taboo. They are subsidiary aspects to be reckoned among the mutable elements surrounding that ill-defined central area.

CHAPTER IV

AFFINITIES BETWEEN REPRODUCTION AND DEATH

Death, Corruption and the Renewal of Life

It is clear from the start that taboos appeared in response to the necessity of banishing violence from the course of everyday life. I could not give a definition of violence straight away, nor do I think it necessary to do so[1]. The unity of meaning of these taboos should finally be clear from studies of their various aspects.

We come up against one difficulty at the start: the taboos I regard as fundamental affect two radically different fields. Death and reproduction are as diametrically opposed as negation and affirmation.

Death is really the opposite process to the process ending in birth, yet these opposite processes can be reconciled.

The death of the one being is correlated with the birth of the other, heralding it and making it possible. Life is always a product of the decomposition of life. Life first pays its tribute to death which disappears, then to corruption following on death and bringing back into the cycle of change the matter necessary for the ceaseless arrival of new beings into the world.

Yet life is none the less a negation of death. It condemns it and shuts it out. This reaction is strongest in man, and horror at death is linked not only with the annihilation of the individual but also with the decay that sends the dead

---

[1] But the idea of violence as opposed to reason is dealt with in Eric Weil's masterly work *Logique de la Philosophie* (Vrin). The conception of violence at the basis of Eric Weil's philosophy, moreover, seems to me akin to my own.

flesh back into the general ferment of life. Indeed the deep respect for the solemn image of death found in idealistic civilisation alone comes out in radical opposition. Spontaneous physical revulsion keeps alive in some indirect fashion at least the consciousness that the terrifying face of death, its stinking putrefaction, are to be identified with the sickening primary condition of life. For primitive people the moment of greatest anguish is the phase of decomposition; when the bones are bare and white they are not intolerable as the putrefying flesh is, food for worms. In some obscure way the survivors perceive in the horror aroused by corruption a rancour and a hatred projected towards them by the dead man which it is the function of the rites of mourning to appease. But afterwards they feel that the whitening bones bear witness to that appeasement. The bones are objects of reverence to them and draw the first veil of decency and solemnity over death and make it bearable; it is painful still but free of the virulent activity of corruption.

These white bones do not leave the survivors a prey to the slimy menace of disgust. They put an end to the close connections between decomposition, the source of an abundant surge of life, and death. But in an age more in touch with the earliest human reactions than ours, this connection appeared so necessary that even Aristotle said that certain creatures, brought into being spontaneously, as he thought, in earth or water, were born of corruption.[1] The generative power of corruption is a naive belief responding to the mingled horror and fascination aroused in us by decay. This belief is behind a belief we once held about nature as something wicked and shameful: decay summed up the world we spring from and return to, and horror and shame were attached both to our birth and to our death.

That nauseous, rank and heaving matter, frightful to look upon, a ferment of life, teeming with worms, grubs and eggs,

[1] That is how Aristotle thought of "spontaneous generation", which he believed to take place.

is at the bottom of the decisive reactions we call nausea, disgust or repugnance. Beyond the annihilation to come which will fall with all its weight on the being I now am, which still waits to be called into existence, which can even be said to be about to exist rather than to exist (as if I did not exist here and now but in the future in store for me, though that is not what I am now) death will proclaim my return to seething life. Hence I can anticipate and live in expectation of that multiple putrescence that anticipates its sickening triumph in my person.

Nausea and its general field

When somebody dies we, the survivors, expecting the life of that man now motionless beside us to go on, find that our expectation has suddenly come to nothing at all. A dead body cannot be called nothing at all, but that object, that corpse, is stamped straight off with the sign "nothing at all". For us survivors, the corpse and its threat of imminent decay is no answer to any expectation like the one we nourished while that now prostrate man was still alive; it is the answer to a fear. This object, then, is less than nothing and worse than nothing.

It is entirely in keeping that fear, the basis of disgust, is not stimulated by a real danger. The threat in question cannot be justified objectively. There is no reason to look at a man's corpse otherwise than at an animal's, at game that has been killed, for instance. The terrified recoiling at the sight of advanced decay is not of itself inevitable. Along with this sort of reaction we have a whole range of artificial behaviour. The horror we feel at the thought of a corpse is akin to the feeling we have at human excreta. What makes this association more compelling is our similar disgust at aspects of sensuality we call obscene. The sexual channels are also the body's sewers; we think of them as shameful and connect the anal orifice with them. St. Augustine was at pains to insist on the obscenity of the organs and function of reproduction. "Inter faeces et urinam nascimur", he said—"we are born between faeces and ùrine". Our faecal products are not subject to a taboo formulated by meticulous social regulations like those relating to dead bodies or to menstruation. But generally speaking, and though the relationship defies clear definition, there do exist unmistakable links between excreta, decay and sexuality. It may look as though physical circumstances imposed from without are chiefly operative in marking out this area of sensibility. But it also has its subjective aspect. The feeling of nausea varies with the individual and its material source is now one thing and now another. After the living man the dead body is nothing at all; similarly nothing tangible or objective brings on our feeling of nausea; what we experience is a kind of void, a sinking sensation.

We cannot easily discuss these things which in themselves are nothing at all. Yet they do make their presence felt and often they force themselves on the senses in a way that inert objects perceived objectively do not. How could anyone assert that that stinking mass is nothing at all? But our protest, if we make one, implies our humiliation and our refusal to see. We imagine that it is the stink of excrement that makes us feel sick. But would it stink if we had not thought it was disgusting in the first place? We do not take long to forget what trouble we go to to pass on to our children the aversions that make us what we are, which make us human beings to begin with. Our children do not spontaneously have our reactions. They may not like a certain food and they may refuse it. But we have to teach them by pantomime or failing that, by violence, that curious aberration called disgust, powerful enough to make us feel faint, a contagion passed down to us from the earliest men through countless generations of scolded children.

Our mistake is to take these teachings lightly. For thousands of years we have been handing them down to our children, but they used to have a different form. The realm of disgust and nausea is broadly the result of these teachings.

The prodigality of life and our fear of it

After reading this we may feel a void opening within us. What I have been saying refers to this void and nothing else.

But the void opens at a specific point. Death, for instance, may open it: the corpse into which death infuses absence, the putrefaction associated with this absence. I can link my revulsion at the decay (my imagination suggests it, not my memory, so profoundly is it a forbidden object for me) with the feelings that obscenity arouse in me. I can tell myself that repugnance and horror are the mainsprings of my desire, that such desire is only aroused as long as its object causes a chasm no less deep than death to yawn within me, and that this desire originates in its opposite, horror.

From the outset reflections like these go beyond all reasonableness.

It takes an iron nerve to perceive the connection between the promise of life implicit in eroticism and the sensuous aspect of death. Mankind conspires to ignore the fact that death is also the youth of things. Blindfolded, we refuse to see that only death guarantees the fresh upsurging without which life would be blind. We refuse to see that life is the trap set for the balanced order, that life is nothing but instability and disequilibrium. Life is a swelling tumult continuously on the verge of explosion. But since the incessant explosion constantly exhausts its resources, it can only proceed under one condition: that beings given life whose explosive force is exhausted shall make room for fresh beings coming into the cycle with renewed vigour.[1]

A more extravagant procedure cannot be imagined. In one way life is possible, it could easily be maintained, without

[1] Although this truth is generally ignored, Bossuet expounds it in his Sermon on Death (1662). "Nature" he says "as if jealous of her gifts to us, often declares and makes plain the fact that she cannot leave us for long in possession of the little substance she lends us, which must not remain always in the same hands but must be kept eternally in circulation. She needs it for other forms, she asks for it to be returned for other works. Those continual additions to humankind, the children being born, seem to nudge us aside as they come forward, saying 'Back now; it is our turn'. So as we see others pass ahead of us, others will see us pass, and themselves present the same spectacle to their successors".

this colossal waste, this squandering annihilation at which imagination boggles. Compared with that of the infusoria, the mammalian organism is a gulf that swallows vast quantities of energy. This energy is not entirely wasted if it allows other developments to take place. But we must consider the devilish cycle from start to finish. The growth of vegetable life implies the continuous piling up of dissociated substances corrupted by death. Herbivorous creatures swallow vegetable matter by the heap before they themselves are eaten, victims of the carnivore's urge to devour. Finally nothing is left but this fierce beast of prey or his remains, in their turn the prey of hyenas and worms. There is one way of considering this process in harmony with its nature: the more extravagant are the means of engendering life, the more costly is the production of new organisms, the more successful the operation is! The wish to produce at cut prices is niggardly and human. Humanity keeps to the narrow capitalist principle, that of the company director, that of the private individual who sells in order to rake in the accumulated credits in the long run (for raked in somehow they always are).

On a comprehensive view, human life strives towards prodigality to the point of anguish, to the point where the anguish becomes unbearable. The rest is mere moralising chatter. How can this escape us if we look at it dispassionately? Everything proclaims it! A febrile unrest within us asks death to wreak its havoc at our expense.

We go half way to meet these manifold trials, these false starts, this squandering of living strength in the transition from ageing beings to other younger ones. At bottom we actually want the impossible situation it all leads to: the isolation, the threat of pain, the horror of annihilation; but for the sensation of nausea bound up with it, so horrible that often in silent panic we regard the whole thing as impossible, we should not be satisfied. But our judgments are formed under the influence of recurring disappointments and the obstinate expectation of a calm which goes hand in hand with that desire; our capacity to make ourselves understood is in direct ratio with the blindness we cling to. For at the crest of the convulsion which gives us shape the naive stubbornness that hopes that it will cease can only increase the torment, and this allows life, wholly committed to this gratuitous pattern, to add the luxury of a beloved torment to fatality. For if man is condemned to be a luxury in himself, what is one to say of the luxury that is anguish?

Man's "no" to Nature

When all is said and done human reactions are what speed up the process; anguish speeds it up and makes it more keenly felt at the same time. In general man's attitude is one of refusal. Man has leant over backwards in order not to be carried away by the process, but all he manages to do by this is to hurry it along at an even dizzier speed.

If we view the primary taboos as the refusal laid down by the individual to co-operate with nature regarded as a squandering of living energy and an orgy of annihilation we can no longer differentiate between death and sexuality. Sexuality and death are simply the culminating points of the holiday, nature celebrates, with the inexhaustible multitude of living beings, both of them signifying the boundless wastage of nature's resources as opposed to the urge to live on characteristic of every living creature.

In the long or short run, reproduction demands the death of the parents who produced their young only to give fuller rein to the forces of annihilation (just as the death of a generation demands that a new generation be born). In the parallels perceived by the human mind between putrefaction and the various aspects of sexual activity the feelings of revulsion which set us against both end by mingling. The taboos embodying a single dual-purpose reaction may have taken shape one at a time, and one can even imagine a long time elapsing between the taboo connected with death and the one connected with reproduction (often the most perfect things take shape hesitatingly through successive modifications). But we perceive their unity none the less: we feel we are dealing with an indivisible complex, just as if man had once and for all realised how impossible it is for nature (as a given force) to exact from the beings that she brings forth their participation in the destructive and implacable frenzy that animates her. Nature demands their surrender; or rather she asks them to go crashing headlong to their own ruin. Humanity became possible at the instant when, seized by an insurmountable dizziness, man tried to answer "No".

Man tried? In fact men have never definitively said *no* to violence (to the excessive urges in question). In their weaker moments they have resisted nature's current but this is a momentary suspension and not a final standstill.

We must now examine the transgressions that lie beyond the taboos.

CHAPTER V

TRANSGRESSION

The transgression does not deny the taboo but transcends it and completes it

It is not only the great variety of their subjects but also a certain illogicality that makes it difficult to discuss taboos. Two diametrically opposed views are always possible on any subject. There exists no prohibition that cannot be transgressed. Often the transgression is permitted, often it is even prescribed.

We feel like laughing when we consider the solemn commandment "Thou shalt not kill" followed by a blessing on armies and the Te Deum of the apotheosis. No beating about the bush: murder is connived at immediately after being banned! The violence of war certainly betrays the God of the New Testament, but it does not oppose the God of Armies of the Old Testament in the same way. If the prohibition were a reasonable one it would mean that wars would be forbidden and we should be confronted with a choice: to ban war and to do everything possible to abolish military assassination; or else to fight and to accept the law as hypocritical. But the taboos on which the world of reason is founded are not rational for all that. To begin with, a calm opposite to violence would not suffice to draw a clear line between the two worlds. If the opposition did not itself draw upon violence in some way, if some violent negative emotion did not make violence horrible for everyone, reason alone could not define those shifting limits authoritatively enough. Only unreasoning dread and terror could survive in the teeth of the forces let loose. This is the nature of the taboo which makes a world of calm reason possible but is

63

itself basically a shudder appealing not to reason but to
feeling, just as violence is. (Human violence is the result
not of a cold calculation but of emotional states: anger, fear
or desire.) We have to take into consideration the irrational
nature of taboos if we want to understand the indifference
to logic they constantly display. In the sphere of irrational
behaviour we are reviewing we have to say: "Sometimes an
intangible taboo is violated, but that does not mean to say
that it has ceased to be intangible." We can even go as far as
the absurd proposition: "The taboo is there in order to be
violated." This proposition is not the wager it looks like at
first but an accurate statement of an inevitable connection
between conflicting emotions. When a negative emotion has
the upper hand we must obey the taboo. When a positive
emotion is in the ascendent we violate it. Such a violation
will not deny or suppress the contrary emotion, but justify
it and arouse it. We should not be frightened of violence in
the same way if we did not know or at least obscurely sense
that it could lead us to worse things.

The statement: "The taboo is there to be violated" ought
to make sense of the fact that the taboo on murder, universal
though it may be, nowhere opposes war. I am even convinced that without the prohibition war would be impossible
and inconceivable!

Animals, recognising no taboos, have never progressed
from the fights they take part in to the organised undertaking
of war. War in a way boils down to the collective organisation
of aggressive urges. Like work it is organised by the community; like work it has a purpose, it is the answer to the
considered intention of those who wage it. We cannot say
therefore that war and violence are in conflict. But war is
organised violence. The transgression of the taboo is not
animal violence. It is violence still, used by a creature
capable of reason (putting his knowledge to the service of
violence for the time being). At the very least the taboo is
the threshold beyond which murder is possible; and for the
community war comes about when the threshold is crossed.

If transgression proper, as opposed to ignorance of the taboo, did not have this limited character it would be a return to violence, to animal violence. But nothing of the kind is so. Organised transgression together with the taboo make social life what it is. The frequency—and the regularity—of transgressions do not affect the intangible stability of the prohibition since they are its expected complement—just as the diastolic movement completes a systolic one, or just as explosion follows upon compression. The compression is not subservient to the explosion, far from it; it gives it increased force. This looks like a new idea though it is founded on immemorial experience. But it runs counter to the world of speech from which science is derived and that is why it is found stated only recently. Marcel Mauss, perhaps the most remarkable interpreter of the history of religion, was conscious of it and formulated it in his oral teaching, but his printed work brings it out only in a small number of significant sentences. Only Roger Caillois, following Mauss's teaching and advice, has fully examined this aspect of transgression in his "Theory of Celebrations".[1]

Transgression without limits

Often the transgression of a taboo is no less subject to rules than the taboo itself. No liberty here. "At such and such a time and up to a certain point this is permissible"— that is what the transgression concedes. But once a limited licence has been allowed, unlimited urges towards violence may break forth. The barriers are not merely raised, for it may even be necessary at the moment of transgression to assert their solidity. Concern over a rule is sometimes at its most acute when that rule is being broken, for it is harder to limit a disturbance already begun.

However, in exceptional cases unlimited transgression is conceivable.

---

[1] *L'Homme et le Sacré*, second edition, Gallimard, 1950, chapter 4, *Le Sacré de transgression: théorie de la fête*.

Let me give you a noteworthy instance. It can happen that violence over-reaches the bounds of the taboo in some way. It seems—it may seem—that once the law has become powerless there is nothing to keep violence firmly within bounds in the future. Basically death contravenes the taboo against the violence which is supposedly its cause. Most frequently the subsequent sense of rupture brings in its wake a minor disturbance which funeral rites and festivities with their ordered ritual, setting bounds to disorderly urges, are able to absorb. But if death prevails over a sovereign whose exalted position might seem to be a guarantee against it, that sense of rupture gets the upper hand and disorder knows no bounds.

Caillois has described the behaviour of certain oceanic peoples.

"When social and natural life" he says[1] "are summed up in the sacred person of a king, the hour of his death determines the critical instant and looses ritual licence. This licence corresponds closely with the importance of the catastrophe. The sacrilege has a social nature. It is committed at the expense of the kingship, the heirarchy and the established powers. No hint of resistance is ever offered to the frenzy of the people. This is considered as necessary as obedience to the dead man was. In the Sandwich Islands the people on learning of the king's death commit all the acts looked on as criminal in ordinary times: they set buildings on fire, they loot and they murder, while women are expected to prostitute themselves publically . . . In the Fiji Islands the consequences are even more clearly defined. The death of the chief gives the signal for pillage, subject tribes invade the capital and indulge in every form of brigandage and depredation.

"Yet these transgressions still constitute a sacrilege. They break the rules that were in force yesterday and which will be restored tomorrow, sacred and inviolable. They appear in fact as major acts of sacrilege."

[1] Op. cit. page 151.

It is noteworthy that the disorder takes place during "the critical period of decay and degradation represented by death", during "the time when its active and contagious virulence is in full swing". It "ends when all the rotting flesh has finally disappeared from the royal corpse, when nothing is left of the remains but a hard, clean, incorruptible skeleton."[1]

The mechanism of transgression is manifest when violence is let loose in this way. Man intended to curb nature when he set up taboos in opposition and indeed he thought he had succeeded. When he confined the violent urges of his own nature within bounds he thought he had done the same for the violence in the world outside himself. But when he saw how ineffectual was the barrier he had sought to set up against violence, the rules he had meant to observe himself lost their significance. His suppressed urges were unleashed, thenceforth he killed without hesitation, ceased to control his sexual exuberance and feared no longer to perform publically and unrestrainedly acts which hitherto he had only performed in private. As long as the king's body was given over to an active decomposition the whole of society was under the sway of violence. The barrier that had not saved the king from the ravages of death could not withstand the excesses that constantly endanger the social order.

No well-defined rules order these "major acts of sacrilege" given free rein by the death of the king, but when nothing remains of the dead man but the clean bones this chaotic reign of licence comes to an end. Even in this extreme case transgression has nothing to do with the primal liberty of animal life. It opens the door into what lies beyond the limits usually observed, but it maintains these limits just the same. Transgression is complementary to the profane world, exceeding its limits but not destroying it. Human society is not only a world of work. Simultaneously—or successively—it is made up of the profane and the sacred, its two complementary forms. The profane world is the world of taboos.

[1] Op. cit. page 153.

The sacred world depends on limited acts of transgression. It is the world of celebrations, sovereign rulers and God.

This approach is a difficult one, in that *sacred* simultaneously has two contradictory meanings. Whatever is the subject of a prohibition is basically sacred. The taboo gives a negative definition of the sacred object and inspires us with awe on the religious plane. Carried to extremes that feeling becomes one of devotion and adoration. The gods who incarnate this sacred essence put fear into the hearts of those who reverence them, yet men do reverence them none the less. Men are swayed by two simultaneous emotions: they are driven away by terror and drawn by an awed fascination. Taboo and transgression reflect these two contradictory urges. The taboo would forbid the transgression but the fascination compels it. Taboos and the divine are opposed to each other in one sense only, for the sacred aspect of the taboo is what draws men towards it and transfigures the original interdiction. The often intertwined themes of mythology spring from these factors.

The only clear and comprehensible distinction between these two aspects of the taboo is an economic one. Taboos are there to make work possible; work is productive; during the profane period allotted to work consumption is reduced to the minimum consistent with continued production. Sacred days though are feast days. Then things which usually are forbidden are permitted or even required, though the upheaval is not necessarily as total as that following the death of a king. The values of the workaday world are inverted, as Caillois has pointed out.[1] From an economic standpoint the reserves accumulated during periods of work are squandered extravagantly at feast times. Here is a clear-cut distinction. We are not perhaps justified in asserting that religion is based on breaking the rules rather than on the rules themselves but feast days depend on a readiness to make great inroads upon savings and feast days are the crown of religious activity. Getting and spending are the

[1] Op. cit. IV *Le Sacré de transgression: théorie de la fête*, page 125-168.

two phases of this activity. Seen in this light religion is like a dance where a movement backwards is followed by a spring forward.

Man must combat his natural impulses to violence. This signifies 'an acceptance of violence at the deepest level, not an abrupt break with it; the feeling responsible for the rejection of violence is kept going in the background by this acceptance. Moreover the urge to reject violence is so persistent that the swing of accepted violence always has a dizzying effect. Man is seized first with nausea, then as it passes by a heady vertigo—phases of the paradoxical dance ordained by religious attitudes.

By and large, then, in spite of the complexity of the impulses concerned the meaning is plain enough: religion is the moving force behind the breaking of taboos. Now, religion is founded on feelings of terror and awe, indeed it can hardly be thought of without them, and their existence causes some confusion. The recoil that inevitably follows the forward movement is constantly being presented as the essence of religion. This interpretation is obviously incomplete and the misunderstanding could easily be cleared up but for a misleading inner swing of feeling based on a deep inversion in harmony with the rational or practical world. In universal religions like Christianity or Buddhism terror and nausea are a prelude to bursts of burning spiritual activity. Founded as it is on a reaffirmation of the primary taboos, this spiritual life yet implies a celebration, that is, the transgression, not the observation, of the law. In Christianity and Buddhism ecstasy begins where horror is sloughed off. A sense of union with the irresistible powers that bear all things before them is frequently more acute in those religions where the pangs of terror and nausea are felt most deeply. More than any other state of mind consciousness of the void about us throws us into exaltation. This does not mean that we feel an emptiness in ourselves, far from it; but we pass beyond that into an awareness of the act of transgression.

In order to define the nature and implications of transgression, rather than less complex cases I shall describe the peaks reached by overwhelming religious experience, Christian or Buddhist, where acts of transgression are accomplished. First, however, I must turn to less complex forms of transgression. I shall speak of war and sacrifice and then of physical eroticism.

CHAPTER VI

MURDER, HUNTING AND WAR

Cannibalism

Transgression outside well defined limits is rare; within them taboos may well be violated in accordance with rules that ritual or at least custom dictate and organise.

The alternation of taboo and transgression which otherwise would be hard to grasp is most clearly seen in eroticism. On the other hand a coherent picture of eroticism would be impossible unless this swing from taboo to transgression and back, in the main a religious phenomenon, is taken into account. But first let us consider the associations of death.

It is noteworthy that the taboo surrounding the dead has no complementary desire running counter to the revulsion. At first sight sexual objects excite alternate attraction and repulsion, hence the taboo and its suspension. Freud based his interpretation of the taboo on the primal necessity of erecting a protective barrier against excessive desires bearing upon objects of obvious frailty. If he goes on to discuss the taboo on touching a corpse he must imply that the taboo protected the corpse from other people's desire to eat it. This is a desire no longer active in us, one we never feel now. Archaic societies, however, do show the taboo as alternatively in force and suspended. Man is never looked upon as butchers' meat, but he is frequently eaten ritually. The man who eats human flesh knows full well that this is a forbidden act; knowing this taboo to be fundamental he will religiously violate it nevertheless. There is a significant example in the communion feast following on the sacrifice. The human flesh that is eaten then is held as sacred; we are nowhere near a return to the simple animal ignorance of

71

taboo. The object some undiscriminating animal is after is not what is desired; the object is "forbidden", sacred, and the very prohibition attached to it is what arouses the desire. Religious cannibalism is the elementary example of the taboo as creating desire: the taboo does not create the flavour and taste of the flesh but stands as the reason why the pious cannibal consumes it. This paradox of the attraction of forbidden fruit will be seen again when we come to eroticism.

Duels, feuds and war

We may find the desire to eat human flesh completely alien to us; not so the desire to kill. Not all of us feel it, but who would go so far as to deny that it has as lively, if not as exacting, an existence among the masses as sexual appetite? There is a potential killer in every man; the frequency of senseless massacres throughout history makes that much plain. The desire to kill relates to the taboo on murder in just the same way as does the desire for sexual activity to the complex of prohibitions limiting it. Sexual activity is only forbidden in certain cases, but then so is murder; it may be more roundly and more generally forbidden than sexual activity is, but the taboo, like that on sex, only serves to limit killing to certain specific situations. The formula has a massive simplicity: "Thou shalt not kill." Universal, yes, but obvious exceptions are implied—"except in wartime, and other circumstances allowed, more or less, by the body politic." So there is a nearly perfect analogy between it and the sexual commandment which runs: "Thou shalt not perform the carnal act except in matrimony alone." To this should obviously be added "or in certain cases hallowed by custom".

A man may kill another in a duel, in a feud, and in war. Murder is criminal. Murder implies that the taboo is either not known or not heeded. Duels, feuds and war do violate an accepted taboo, but according to set rules. In the duel of today with its complicated procedure the sense of something forbidden is dominant. Not so with primitive peoples; with them the taboo could only be violated with a religious intent, and duels cannot have been the confrontation of mere individuals as they were from the Middle Ages onwards. In the first place the duel was a form of war; the two sides pinned their faith on the valour of their champions who met in single combat after a challenge duly given and received, fighting it out in front of the masses intent on mutual destruction.

Feuds are a kind of war where the antagonists belong to a tribe rather than to a territory. Like duels, like war, they are ordered with detailed precision.

The hunt and the expiation of the animal's death

In feuds and duels, and in war, which we shall consider later, it is a man's death that occurs, although the law forbidding killing is earlier than the distinction felt by man between himself and the larger animals. Indeed, this distinction comes quite late. To begin with man saw himself as like the animals, and this attitude persists to this day in hunting peoples with their primitive customs. Hence the hunting of primitive man is, no less than duels, feuds and war, a form of transgression. Yet there is one significant difference. It seems that murder of a fellow man was unknown in the very earliest times when humanity was closest to the animals.[1]

On the other hand, in those days it must have been usual to hunt other animals. We could maintain that hunting is the outcome of work, made possible only by the fabrication of stone tools and weapons. But even if the taboo were generally a consequence of work, it could not have come into being so swiftly as to rule out a long period during which hunting developed and no taboo on killing animals surrounded it. Anyway we cannot imagine a period dominated by the taboo and then a return to hunting after a deliberate

---

[1] There is no taboo as such on the killing by one animal of another like itself, but in fact such killings are rare in instinctive animal behaviour, whatever difficulties instinct may raise. Even fights between animals of the same species do not necessarily end in a kill.

C*

act of transgression. The taboo on hunting offers the same characteristics as other taboos. I have stressed the fact that broadly speaking there is a taboo on sexual activity, but this can only be readily grasped through a comparison with the taboo on hunting among hunting peoples. Men do not necessarily abstain from the forbidden activity, but take part in it as a conscious infringement of the law. Neither hunting nor sexual activity could be forbidden in practice. The taboo cannot suppress pursuits necessary to life, but it can give them the significance of a religious violation. It imposes limits on them and controls the form that they take. It can exact penance from the guilty. The act of killing invested the killer, hunter or warrior, with a sacramental character. In order to take their place once more in profane society they had to be cleansed and purified, and this was the object of expiatory rituals. Primitive societies give numerous examples of these.

Prehistorians usually ascribe a magical significance to cave paintings. The hunters were after these animals, and they were depicted in the hope that pictorial expression of the wish would make the wish come true. I am not so sure that this was so. Might not the secret and religious atmosphere of the caves have corresponded with the religious nature of transgression which indisputably invested the hunt with significance? Representation would then have followed on transgression. This would be difficult to prove, but if prehistorians were to visualise the alternation of taboo and transgression and perceive clearly the religious aura that surrounded the animals as they were done to death, I think we might adopt a standpoint in greater harmony with the importance of religion in the earliest development of humanity in preference to the magical image theory which has something poor and unsatisfying about it. The cave drawings must have been intended to depict that instant when the animal appeared and killing, at once inevitable and reprehensible, laid bare life's mysterious ambiguity. Tormented man refuses life, yet lives it out as he miraculously transcends his own refusal. This hypothesis rests on the fact that expiation regularly follows upon the killing of an animal among peoples whose way of life is probably similar to that of the cave artists. Its great merit is to suggest a coherent interpretation of the Lascaux pit painting where a dying bison faces the man who has probably killed it and whom the painter shows as a dead man. The subject of this famous picture, which has called forth numerous contradictory and unsatisfactory explanations, would therefore be murder and expiation.[1]

This view has at least the virtue of replacing the magical (and utilitarian) interpretation of cave pictures with its obvious insufficiency by a religious one more in keeping with notions of the ultimate in human experience that are usually the concern of art and are here echoed by these prodigious paintings come down to us from the depths of the past.

The earliest record of war

Hunting must be considered as a primitive form of transgression apparently earlier than war which seems to have been unknown to the men of the "Franco-cantabrian" painted caves living during the Upper Paleolithic period. At any rate war would not have had the primary importance it attained later for these our earliest fellow men; indeed they put us in mind of the Eskimos who up to our own day have lived mostly ignorant of war.

War was first depicted by the men of the rock paintings of eastern Spain. Their pictures seem to date partly from the end of the Upper Paleolithic, partly from the succeeding period. Towards the end of the Upper Paleolithic ten or fifteen thousand years ago, the transgression of the taboo forbidding originally the killing of animals, considered as essentially the same as man, and then the killing of man himself, became formalised in war.

[1] See G. Bataille, *Lascaux ou la naissance de l'art*, Skira 1955, page 139-140, where I have listed and criticised the various explanations then current. Others no more satisfactory have been published since. By 1955 I had relinquished the idea of putting forward my own hypothesis.

Just like the taboos surrounding death, the transgression
of these taboos has left far reaching signs, as we shall see. I
have remarked earlier that any certain knowledge of sexual
taboos and transgressions dates only from historical times.
There are several reasons in a work on eroticism for tackling
first transgression in general and that of the taboo on murder
in particular. It would be impossible to grasp the significance
of eroticism without reference to the general pattern;
eroticism is disconcerting and difficult to comprehend if its
contradictory effects have not first been seen more clearly
and earlier in time in another domain.

All that the Spanish Levant paintings show is how long
ago two groups of adversaries first met in war. But archae-
ological evidence on war is in general abundant. The struggle
between two groups demands in itself a few essential rules.
The first obviously concerns the marking off of hostile
groups and a declaration of hostilities before the combat.
We have definite knowledge of the rules for a declaration of
war among primitive peoples. The aggressors' own private
decision might suffice, and then the adversary was taken by
surprise. But it seemed more frequently within the spirit of
the transgression to give him a ritual warning. The war that
followed might itself develop according to rules. Primitive
war is rather like a holiday, a feast day, and even modern
war almost always has some of this paradoxical similarity.
The taste for showy and magnificent war dress goes very
far back, for originally war seemed a luxury. It was no
attempt to increase the peoples' or rulers' riches by conquest:
it was an aggressive and extravagant exuberance.

The distinction between ritual and calculated forms of war

Military uniforms have carried on this tradition right up
to modern times; the preponderant consideration now, however, is to avoid attracting the enemy's fire. But this concern
to minimise losses is foreign to the earliest spirit of war.
Transgressing the taboo was first and foremost an end in
itself, though secondarily it may have served some other

purpose. There are grounds for believing that war was first another outlet for the feelings that are given expression in ceremonial rites. The evolution of war in feudal China, long before our own date, is described thus: "A baron's war began with a challenge. Warriors sent by their lord would come and die heroically by their own hand before the rival lord, or else a war chariot would hurl itself insultingly towards the adversaries' city gates. Then the chariots engage in a mêlée and the lords make conventional charges at each other before the fight to the death begins in earnest."[1] The archaic aspects of the Homeric wars have a universal character. It was really a game, but the results were so serious that very soon calculated action superseded obedience to the rules of the game. The history of China makes this plain:." . . . as time goes on, these chivalrous customs lapse. What was once a war of chivalry degenerates into a pitiless struggle, into a clash of peoples and the entire population of a province would be hurled against its neighbours."

War has in fact always oscillated between giving primary importance to adherence to the rules when war is an end in itself and setting a premium on the hoped for political result. Even in our own day there are two opposite schools of thought among military specialists. Clausewitz took his stand against exponents of the tradition of chivalry and emphasised the need to destroy the enemy's forces without pity. "War," he writes "is an act of violence, and there is no limit to the manifestation of this violence."[2] There is no doubt that broadly speaking his tendency has slowly come to the fore in the modern world, superseding the ritual practices of the past with their hold on the older generation. We must be careful not to confuse the humanisation of war and its fundamental tradition. Up to a certain point the necessities of war have left room for the development of individual rites. The spirit of traditional rules may have favoured this

[1] Rene Grousset and Sylvie Regnault-Gatier, in *l'Histoire universelle de la Pléiade*, Gallimard, 1955, Volume 1, page 1552-1553.
[2] Karl von Clausewitz, *On War*, London, Clowes, 1909 (translated A. M. E. Maguire).

development but the rules themselves never correspond with our contemporary concern to limit losses or the suffering of combatants. Limits were set to the breaking of the taboo, but they were formal ones. The aggressive impulse did not hold undisputed sway. Conditions were laid down, rules were meticulously observed, but once the frenzy was loosed it knew no bounds.

Cruelty and organised war

War was different in kind from animal violence and it developed a cruelty animals are incapable of, especially in that the fight, frequently followed by a massacre of the enemy, was as often as not a prelude to the torture of the prisoners. This cruelty is the specifically human aspect of war. I take the following frightful details from Maurice Davie: "In Africa, war captives are often tortured, killed, or allowed to starve to death. Among the Tshi-speaking peoples 'prisoners of war are treated with shocking barbarity.' Men, women and children—mothers with infants on their backs and little children scarcely able to walk—are stripped and secured together with cords round the neck in gangs of ten or fifteen; each prisoner being additionally secured by having the hands fixed to a heavy block of wood, which has to be carried on the head. Thus hampered, and so insufficiently fed that they are reduced to mere skeletons, they are driven after the victorious army for month after month, their brutal guards treating them with the greatest cruelty; while, should their captors suffer a reverse, they are at once indiscriminately slaughtered to prevent recapture. Ramseyer and Kühne mention the case of a prisoner, a native of Accra, who was 'kept in log', that is, secured to the felled trunk of a tree by an iron staple driven over the wrist, with insufficient food for four months, and who died under this ill-treatment. Another time they saw amongst some prisoners a poor, weak child, who, when angrily ordered to stand upright, 'painfully drew himself upright showing the sunken frame in which every bone was visible.'

Most of the prisoners seen on this occasion were mere living skeletons. One boy was so reduced by starvation, that his neck was unable to support the weight of his head, which, if he sat, drooped almost to his knees. Another equally emaciated, coughed as if at the last gasp; while a young child was so weak from want of food as to be unable to stand. The ashantis were much surprised that the missionaries should exhibit any emotion at such spectacles; and, on one occasion when they went to give food to some starving children, the guards angrily drove them back." Both the regular army and the levies in Dahomey show an equal callousness to human suffering. "Wounded prisoners are denied all assistance, and all prisoners who are not destined to slavery are kept in a condition of semi-starvation that speedily reduces them to mere skeletons . . . The lower jaw-bone is much prized as a trophy . . . and it is very frequently torn from the wounded and living foe". . . . The scenes that followed the sack of a fortress in Fiji "are too horrible to be described in detail." That neither age nor sex were spared was the least atrocious feature. Nameless mutilations inflicted sometimes on living victims, deeds of mingled cruelty and lust, made self-destruction preferable to capture. With the fatalism that underlies the Melanesian character many would not attempt to run away, but would bow their heads passively to the club stroke. If any were miserable enough to be taken alive their fate was awful indeed. Carried back bound to the main village, they were given up to young boys of rank to practice their ingenuity in torture, or stunned by a blow they were laid in heated ovens, and when the heat brought them back to consciousness of pain, their frantic struggles would convulse the spectators with laughter."[1]

Violence, not cruel in itself, is essentially something organised in the transgression of taboos. Cruelty is one of its forms; it is not necessarily erotic but it may veer towards other forms of violence organised by transgression. Eroticism, like cruelty, is premeditated. Cruelty and eroticism are

[1] M. R. Davie, *The Evolution of War*, Yale University Press, 1929, page 298-299.

conscious intentions in a mind which has resolved to trespass into a forbidden field of behaviour. Such a determination is not a general one, but it is always possible to pass from one domain to another, for these contiguous domains are both founded on the heady exhilaration of making a determined escape from the power of a taboo. The resolve is all the more powerful because the return to stability afterwards is at the back of the mind, and without that the outward surge could not take place. It is as if the waters should over-flow and yet be certain to subside again at the same time. The transition from one state to another may be made as long as the basic framework is not risked.

Cruelty may veer towards eroticism, and similarly a massacre of prisoners may possibly end in cannibalism. But a return to animality where all limits are removed is inconceivable in war. There are always some reserves made which stress the human character of even un-bridled violence. Athirst for blood, the warriors still do not turn on each other in their frenzy. Here is an intangible rule which regulates fury at its roots. Similarly the taboo on cannibalism generally persists even when the most inhuman passions are raging.

We must point out that the most sinister forms are not necessarily linked with primitive savagery. Organised war with its efficient military operations based on discipline, which when all is said and done excludes the mass of the combatants from the pleasure of transgressing the limits, has been caught up in a mechanism foreign to the impulsions which set it off in the first place; war today has only the remotest connection with war as I have described it; it is a dismal aberration geared to political ends. Primitive war itself can hardly be defended: from the outset it bore the seeds of modern warfare, but the organised form we are familiar with today, that has travelled such a long way from the original organised transgression of the taboo, is the only one that would leave humanity unsatisfied.[1]

---

[1] If its machinery were to be set going, that is.

CHAPTER VII

MURDER AND SACRIFICE

The suspension of the taboo surrounding death for religious reasons; sacrifice; and animals regarded as sacred beings

The unleashed desire to kill that we call war goes far beyond the realm of religious activity. Sacrifice though, while like war a suspension of the commandment not to kill, is the religious act above all others.

True, sacrifice is looked on basically as an offering, not necessarily as a bloody affair. Notice that most often the victims are animals, often slain as substitutes for men, for as civilisation developed the sacrifice of a human being seemed horrible. But this was not in the first place the reason for sacrificing animals. Human sacrifice is a recent thing, and the victims of the earliest sacrifices known to us were animals. It looks as though the gulf that now separates man and beast came after the domestication of animals, and that occurred in neolithic times. Certainly taboos tended to separate beast from man, as only man observes them. But primitive man saw the animals as no different from himself except that, as creatures not subject to the dictates of taboos, they were originally regarded as more sacred, more god-like than man.

The most ancient gods were largely animals, immune to the taboos which set fundamental limits to man's sovereignty. To begin with, the killing of an animal may well have aroused a powerful feeling of sacrilege, and performed collectively, would consecrate the victim and confer a sort of godhead on it.

As an animal, the victim was an object of superstition

already because of the curse laid upon violence, for animals never forsake the heedless violence that is the very breath of their life. But as the first men saw it, animals must know the basic laws; they could not fail to be aware that the mainspring of their being, their violence, was a violation of that law: they broke it deliberately and consciously. But in death violence reaches its climax and in death they are wholly and unreservedly in its power. Such a divinely violent manifestation of violence elevates the victim above the humdrum world where men live out their calculated lives. Compared with these death and violence are a sort of delirium; they cannot stop at the limits traced by respect and custom which give human life its social pattern. To the primitive consciousness, death can only be the result of an offence, a failure to obey. Again, death turns the rightful order topsy-turvy.

Death puts the finishing touch to the sinfulness that characterises animals. It penetrates to the very depth of the animal's being, and the bloody ritual reveals these secret depths.

Let us return now to the thesis suggested in the introduction, that "for us as discontinuous beings death implies the continuity of being".

On sacrifice, I wrote: "The victim dies and the spectators share in what his death reveals. This is what religious historians call the sacramental element. This sacramental element is the revelation of continuity through the death of a discontinuous being to those who watch it as a solemn rite. A violent death disrupts the creature's discontinuity: what remains, what the tense onlookers experience in the succeeding silence, is the continuity of all existence with which the victim is now one. Only a spectacular killing carried out as the solemn and collective nature of religion dictates has the power to reveal what normally escapes notice. We should incidentally be unable to imagine what goes on in the secret hidden depths of the minds of the bystanders if we could not call on our own personal religious experiences, if only childhood ones. Everything leads us to the conclusion that in essence the sacramental quality of primitive sacrifices is analogous to the comparable element in contemporary religions."[1]

To relate that to my present argument I should say that divine continuity is linked with the transgression of the law on which the order of discontinuous beings is built. Men as discontinuous beings try to maintain their separate existences, but death, or at least the contemplation of death, brings them back to continuity.

This is of primary importance.

As taboos came into play, man became distinct from the animals. He attempted to set himself free from the excessive domination of death and reproductive activity (of violence, that is) under whose sway animals are helpless.

But under the secondary influence of transgression man drew near to the animals once more. He saw how animals escape the rule of taboos and remain open to the violence (the excess, that is) that reigns in the realms of death and reproduction. It appears that this secondary accord between man and the animals, this rebound, as it were, belongs to the era of the cave paintings, to human beings as we know them, coming after Neanderthal Man who was still close to the anthropoids. These men left the wonderful pictures of animals familiar to us today. But they rarely depicted themselves, and if they did, they disguised themselves first so to speak; they hid behind the features of some animal or other with whose mask they covered their own face. The more accurate drawings of men have this curious characteristic, at any rate. Humanity must have been ashamed of itself at that time, not of its underlying animality, as we are. It did not reverse its earlier fundamental decisions: Upper Paleolithic man had upheld the taboos relating to death, he had gone on burying the bodies of those near to him; and we have no reason to doubt besides that he was no stranger to sexual taboos probably known to Neanderthal

Man (the taboos bearing on incest and menstruation that are at the bottom of all our behaviour patterns). But the accord with animal nature made the unilateral form of a taboo impossible to observe. It would be hard to point to a well-defined difference in structure between the Middle Paleolithic, the time of Neanderthal Man, and the Upper Paleolithic, when rituals of transgression must have begun to spread, as we know both from the habits of primitive peoples and from documentary evidence of antiquity. We are in the realms of hypothesis, but we are entitled to believe that if the hunters of the painted caves did practice sympathetic magic as is generally admitted, they felt at the same time that animal nature was sacred. This quality implies the observation of the oldest taboos and at the same time a limited degree of transgression, comparable with that which occurred later. As soon as human beings give rein to animal nature in some way we enter the world of transgression forming the synthesis between animal nature and humanity through the persistence of the taboo; we enter a sacred world, a world of holy things. What shapes this change assumed we do not know, nor where the sacrifices took place,[1] nor a great deal about erotic life in those far-off days. (All we can do is refer to the frequent ithyphallic representations of man.) But we do know that this newborn world held animal nature as divine and must have been stirred by the spirit of transgression from the very beginning. The spirit of transgression is the animal god dying, the god whose death sets violence in motion, who remains untouched by the taboos restraining humanity. Taboos do not in fact concern either the real animal sphere or the field of animal myth; they do not concern all-powerful men whose human nature is concealed beneath an animal's mask.

---

[1] The model of the headless bear, though, in the Montespan Cave (H. Breuil, *Quatre Cent Siècles d'Art Pariétal*, Montignac 1952, page 236-238) might well suggest a ceremony something like the sacrifice of a bear, belonging to the late Upper Paleolithic. The ritual killing of a captive bear amongst Iberian hunters or the Aino of Japan has a very primitive character, I feel. They may well be compared with whatever the Montespan modelling implies.

The spirit of this early world is impossible to grasp at first; it is the natural world mingled with the divine; yet it can be readily imagined by anybody whose thought is in step with the processes[1], it is the human world, shaped by a denial of animality or nature[2], denying itself, and reaching beyond itself in this second denial, though not returning to what it had rejected in the first place.

The world seen in these terms is certainly not that of the Upper Paleolithic. To assume that it was the world of the men of the painted caves makes that period and its products easy to understand, but we cannot be sure that it came into existence until a later date known to us through earliest history, and its existence is confirmed by the findings of ethnography, the modern scientific observation of primitive peoples. To Greeks and Egyptians of historical times the animals had suggested a sovereign existence and given them the first images of their gods exalted by death and sacrifice.

These images must be seen as part of an extension of the picture I have already tried to give of the world of the early hunters. I was bound to mention this world first, for then animal nature formed a cathedral, as it were, within which human violence could be centred and condensed. The animality of the cave paintings and the domain of animal sacrifice cannot in fact be understood one without the other. What we know of animal sacrifice opens a way to an understanding of the painted caves, and they help us to comprehend animal sacrifice.

Beyond anguish

The feeling of anguish responsible for the earliest taboos showed man's refusal or withdrawal in face of the blind surge of life. The first men, their conscience awoken by work, felt uneasy before the dizzy succession of new birth and inevitable death. Looked at as a whole, life is the huge

---

[1] Or if the reader prefers: whose thought is dialectic, capable of developing through the reconciling of opposites.

[2] To put it precisely: shaped by work.

movement made up of reproduction and death. Life brings forth ceaselessly, but only in order to swallow up what she has produced. The first men were confusedly aware of this. They denied death and the cycle of reproduction by means of taboos. They never contained themselves within this denial, however, or if they did so it was in order to step outside it as quickly as possible: they came out as they had gone in, with brusque determination. Anguish is what makes humankind, it seems; not anguish alone, but anguish transcended and the act of transcending it. Life is essentially extravagant, drawing on its forces and its reserves unchecked; unchecked it annihilates what it has created. The multitude of living beings is passive in this process, yet in the end we resolutely desire that which imperils our life.

We are not always strong enough to will this. We come to an end of our resources and sometimes desire is impotent. If the danger is too great, if death is inevitable, then the desire is generally inhibited. But if good luck favours us, the thing we desire most ardently is the most likely to drag us into wild extravagance and to ruin us. Different people stand up in different ways to great losses of energy or money or to a serious threat of death. As far as they are able (it is a quantitative matter of strength) men seek out the greatest losses and the greatest dangers. We tend to believe the opposite because men's strength is usually slight. But if a good measure of strength does fall to them they immediately want to spend themselves and lay themselves bare to danger. Anyone with the strength and the means is continually spending and endangering himself.

By way of illustrating these assertions valid in a general sense I shall leave very early times and primitive customs for the moment. I should like to put forward for consideration a familiar phenomenon experienced by the great mass of humanity among whom we live. I refer to the commonest form of literature, popular detective novels. These books are usually about the misfortunes of the hero and the threats which besiege him. Without his difficulties and his fears there would be nothing in his life to hold and excite the reader and make him identify himself with the hero as he peruses his adventures. The gratuitous nature of the novels and the fact that the reader is anyway safe from danger usually prevent him from seeing this very clearly, but we live vicariously in a way that our lack of energy forbids us in real life. Without too much personal discomfort we experience the feeling of losing or of being in danger that somebody else's adventures supply. If we had infinite moral resources we should like to live like this ourselves. Which of us has not dreamed of himself as the hero of a book? Prudence—or cowardice—is stronger than this wish, but if we think of our deepest desires which frailty alone forbids us to realise, the stories we read so eagerly will show us their nature.

Following upon religion, literature is in fact religion's heir. A sacrifice is a novel, a story, illustrated in a bloody fashion. Or rather a rudimentary form of stage drama reduced to the final episode where the human or animal victim acts it out alone until his death. Ritual ceremonies are certainly dramatic versions repeated on a certain date, of a myth, of the death of a god. There is nothing here that should surprise us. In a symbolic form this happens every day at the sacrifice of the mass.

Anguish always works in the same way. The greatest anguish, the anguish in the face of death, is what men desire in order to transcend it beyond death and ruination. But it can be overcome like this on one condition only, namely, that the anguish shall be appropriate to the spirit of the man who desires it.

Anguish is desired in sacrifice to the greatest possible extent. But when the bounds of the possible are over-reached, a recoil is inevitable.[1] Human sacrifice often takes the place of animal sacrifice, no doubt as the distance between man

---

[1] The Aztecs, to whom sacrifice was a familiar thing, imposed fines on those who could not bear to see children being led to their death and turned their heads away from the procession.

and animal increases and the death of an animal partly
loses its power to disturb and terrify. Later, on the other
hand, as civilisation grew, animal victims would sometimes
replace human ones as a less barbarous sacrifice. Quite late
the bloody sacrifices of the Israelites were felt to be repugnant, and Christians have only ever known symbolic sacrifice. Man had to move in harmony with an extravagance of
nature ending in the profusion of death, but he still had
to have the strength to do this. Otherwise a feeling of
nausea would gain the upper hand and reinforce the taboos.

CHAPTER VIII

FROM RELIGIOUS SACRIFICE
TO EROTICISM

Christianity, and the sacred nature of transgression misunderstood

In the Introduction I discussed the similarity perceived by man in ancient times between the act of love and sacrifice. They felt the immediacy of sacrifice more strongly than we do, for we never perform a sacrifice. The sacrifice of the mass is a reminder but it only rarely makes a deep impression on our sensibility. However obsessive we find the symbol of the Cross, the mass is not readily identified with the bloody sacrifice.

The main difficulty is that Christianity finds law-breaking repugnant in general. True, the gospels encourage the breaking of laws adhered to by the letter when their spirit is absent. But then the law is broken because its validity is questioned, not in spite of its validity. Essentially in the idea of the sacrifice upon the Cross the very character of transgression has been altered. That sacrifice is a murder of course, and a bloody one. It is a transgression in the sense that it is of course a sin, and of all sins indeed the gravest. But in transgression as I have described it sin, if sin there is, and expiation, if expiation there is, are the consequence of a resolute and intentional act. The intentional nature of the act is what makes the primitive attitude hard for us to understand; our thinking is outraged. The idea of deliberately transgressing the law which seems holy makes us uneasy. But the sin of the crucifixion is disallowed by the priest celebrating the sacrifice of mass. The fault lies in the blindness of the authors of the deed and we are bound to think that they would not have committed it if only they had known. True, the Church sings Felix Culpa—happy fault! So there is a point of view which accepts the necessity of the deed. The echoing liturgy is in harmony with the deeps of primitive human thought but strikes a false note in the logic of Christian feeling. Misunderstanding the sanctity of transgression is one of the foundations of Christianity, even if at its peaks men under vows reach the unthinkable paradoxes that set them free, that over-reach all bounds.

The ancient comparison of sacrifice and erotic intercourse

The harmony perceived by men of old has been made meaningless by this failure to grasp the nature of transgression. If transgression is not fundamental then sacrifice and the act of love have nothing in common. If it is an intentional transgression sacrifice is a deliberate act whose purpose is a sudden change in the victim. The creature is put to death. Before that it was enclosed in its individual separateness and its existence was discontinuous, as I said in the Introduction.[1] But this being is brought back by death into continuity with all being, to the absence of separate individualities. The act of violence that deprives the creature of its limited particularity and bestows on it the limitless, infinite nature of sacred things is with its profound logic an intentional one. It is intentional like the act of the man who lays bare, desires and wants to penetrate his victim. The lover strips the beloved of her identity no less than the blood-stained priest his human or animal victim. The woman in the hands of her assailant is despoiled of her being. With her modesty she loses the firm barrier that once separated her from others and made her inpenetrable. She is brusquely laid open to the violence of the sexual urges set loose in the organs of reproduction; she is laid open to the impersonal violence that overwhelms her from without.

Doubtless early men would hardly have been able to

[1] See above p. 16.

expound an analysis in detail; only familiarity with large-scale thinking on the subject has made that possible since. The original experience and the development of numerous threads are both necessary if the similarities between two profound experiences are to be accurately mapped out. But the inner experience of piety in sacrifice and in un-trammelled eroticism might by chance befall one person. That would make possible, if not a clear, analogy at least a feeling that there was a resemblance. This possibility vanished with Christianity where piety eschewed the desire to use violent means to probe the secrets of existence.

The flesh in sacrifice and in love

The external violence of the sacrifice reveals the internal violence of the creature, seen as loss of blood and ejaculations. The blood and the organs brimful of life were not what modern anatomy would see; the feeling of the men of old can only be recaptured by an inner experience, not by science. We may presume that they saw the fulness of the blood-swollen organs, the impersonal fullness of life itself. The individual discontinuous existence of the animal was succeeded in its death by the organic continuity of life drawn into the common life of the beholders by the sacrificial feast. There remains something slightly bestial about consuming this meat in an atmosphere of surging carnal life and the silence of death. Now the only meat we eat is prepared for the purpose, inanimate, removed from the organic seething of life where it made its first appearance. The sacrifice links the act of eating with the truth of life revealed in death.

It is the common business of sacrifice to bring life and death into harmony, to give death the upsurge of life, life the momentousness and the vertigo of death opening on to the unknown. Here life is mingled with death, but simultaneously death is a sign of life, a way into the infinite. Nowadays sacrifice is outside the field of our experience and imagination must do duty for the real thing. But even if sacrifice and its religious meaning escape us we cannot fail to know the reactions concerned with certain elements in the spectacle, namely nausea. We have to imagine a sacrifice as something beyond nausea. But if the divine transfiguration does not take place, taken separately the different aspects may finally induce a feeling of nausea. Cattle being slaughtered or cut up often makes people sick today, but there is nothing in the dishes served at tables to remind them of this. So one might say of contemporary experience that it inverts pious conduct and sacrifice.

This inversion is meaningful if we now consider the similarity between the act of love and the sacrifice. Both reveal the flesh. Sacrifice replaces the ordered life of the animal with a blind convulsion of its organs. So also with the erotic convulsion; it gives free rein to extravagant organs whose blind activity goes on beyond the considered will of the lovers. Their considered will is followed by the animal activity of these swollen organs. They are animated by a violence outside the control of reason, swollen to bursting point and suddenly the heart rejoices to yield to the breaking of the storm. The urges of the flesh pass all bounds in the absence of controlling will. Flesh is the extravagance within us set up against the law of decency. Flesh is the born enemy of people haunted by Christian taboos, but if as I believe an indefinite and general taboo does exist, opposed to sexual liberty in ways depending on the time and the place,[1] the flesh signifies a return to this threatening freedom.

The flesh, decency and the taboo on sexual freedom

When I first discussed the general taboo on sexual activity I evaded the issue being unable—or unwilling—to define it. Truth to tell, in that it is never easy to discuss it defies definition. Decency is a chance matter of time and place and standards vary continually, even with individuals. That is why I have confined myself to taboos that could be defined, connected with incest or menstruation, and have postponed

[1] See above p. 53.

consideration of the more general malediction attached to sexuality. I shall not turn my attention to this until later, and I shall examine the transgressions of this amorphous taboo before I try to define it.

First I should like to go back some way.

If a taboo exists, it is a taboo on some elemental violence, to my thinking. This violence belongs to the flesh, the flesh responsible for the urges of the organs of reproduction.

Through an objective consideration of the activity of those organs I shall try to get at the fundamental inner experience transcending the flesh. I want first to turn your attention to the inner experience of the plethora which I said was revealed in the death of the sacrificial victim. Underlying eroticism is the feeling of something bursting, of the violence accompanying an explosion.

CHAPTER IX

SEXUAL PLETHORA AND DEATH

Reproductive activity seen as a form of growth

Eroticism taken as a whole is an infraction of the laws of taboos: it is a human activity. But although it begins when purely animal nature ends, its foundation is animal none the less. Human nature may turn from that foundation in horror but allows it to persist at the same time, and so effectively that the expression "bestiality" is continually linked with eroticism. It is false to imagine that breaking the sexual taboos means a return to nature as exemplified in the animals, and yet the behaviour forbidden by the taboos is like that of animals. Physical sexuality, always accompanying eroticism, is to it what the brain is to the mind; physiology remains the material basis of thought in just the same way. We must include the animal's sexual function with the rest of the data if we are to put our inner experience of eroticism in its proper place in objective reality, and even give it our first attention. Indeed, the sexual functions of animals have aspects which bring us close to the inner experience as we consider them attentively.

In order, then, to get at the inner experience, we shall now discuss physical conditions.

In the fields of objective reality life always brings into play, except when there is impotence, an excess of energy which must be expended, and this super-abundance is in fact either used up in the growth of the unity envisaged or it is quite simply wasted.[1] Hence sexuality has a certain

[1] All this is clear if we look at society's economic activity. The organism's activity is more elusive: there is always a connection between growth and the development of sexual functions both dependent on hypophysis. We cannot measure the calory expenditure of the organism regularly enough to be sure

ambiguity. Even sexual activity independent of its genetic ends is no less essentially concerned with growth. Taken together the gonads grow. To have a clear picture of this process we must go back to scissiparity, the simplest mode of reproduction. The scissiparous organism does grow, but once it has grown the single organism will one day or another split into two. Let us call the original cell *a*, the two cells it turns into *aa* and *aaa*, then the transition from the first state to the second is not independent of the growth of *a*, as *aa* + *aaa*, compared with the earlier states represented by *a*, signifies the growth of the latter.

What we must note is that *aa*, although other than *aaa*, is not, any more than the latter, other than *a*. Something of *a* persists in *aa*, something of *a* persists in *aaa*. I shall return to the disconcerting nature of a growth which calls the unity of the growing organism in question, but for the present let us note this, that reproduction is nothing but a form of growth. In general this is clear from the multiplication of individuals, the most obvious result of sexual activity. But growth of the species in sexual reproduction is only one aspect of reproduction in primitive scissiparity, in the sphere of asexual reproduction. Like all the cells of the individual organism, sexual gonads are scissiparous. At bottom every living unity grows. If in growing it attains a state of plethora it can divide, but growth or plethora is the condition of that division which in the world of living things we call reproduction.

The growth of the whole and the contribution of individuals

Objectively, making love is a question of reproduction.

Hence, following our reasoning, it is growth, but not our growth. Neither sexual activity nor scissiparity provide for the growth of the being itself engaged on reproduction

which of two ends it serves, growth or genetic activity. But hypophysis appropriates energy now for the development of sexual functions and now for growth. So gigantism impedes sexual functioning and precocious puberty might coincide with arrested growth, though this is open to doubt.

whether it copulates or more simply divides. Reproduction brings about an impersonal growth.

The fundamental contrast referred to in the first place between loss and growth can therefore be seen in terms of another difference, where impersonal growth as opposed to sheer loss stands against personal growth. There is no basic, selfish growth unless the individual grows without changing. If the growth is for the benefit of a being or a group beyond the individual it is no longer a growth but a contribution, and for the individual making it, it is a loss of his substance The giver will find himself again in the gift, but he must give first of all; he must first of all renounce more or less completely whatever is needed for the growth of the whole.

Death and continuity in asexual and sexual reproduction

We must first take a close look at the situation brought about by division.

Within the asexual organism *a* there was continuity.

When *aa* and *aaa* appeared, the continuity was not immediately done away. Whether it vanished at the beginning or the end of the crisis is unimportant, but there was a moment of suspense. At that moment, that which was not yet *aa* was continuous with *aaa*, but the plethora was threatening this continuity. The plethora is what initiates the glide towards the division of the organism, but it divides at the very moment, the moment of the glide, the critical moment when these two beings about to become separate at any minute are still not yet so. The crisis of separation springs from the plethora; it is not separation yet but a state of ambiguity. In the plethora the organism passes from the calm of repose to a state of violent agitation, a turbulent agitation which lays hold of the total being in its continuity. But the violence of agitation which at first takes place within the being's continuity calls forth a violence of separation from which discontinuity proceeds. Calm returns when the separation is complete and two distinct beings exist side by side.

The plethora of the cell which leads in these circumstances to the creation of one, of two new beings is rudimentary compared with the plethora of the male and female organs ending in the climax of sexual reproduction.

But both crises have essential aspects in common. Both originate in super-abundance. Both are bound up with the growth of the group of beings reproducing and reproduced. And in both there is the disappearance of the individual.

Immortality is wrongly ascribed to dividing cells. Cell *a* survives in neither *aa* nor *aaa*, *aa* is not the same as *a* or *aaa;* in fact during the division *a* ceases to be, *a* disappears, *a* dies. It leaves no trace, no corpse, but die it does. The plethora of the cell ends in creative death, in the solution of the crisis in which appears the continuity of the new beings (*aa* and *aaa*), originally one and the same and now escaping into their final separation from each other.

The significance of this last aspect common to both modes of reproduction is of cardinal importance.

The overall continuity of beings is pushed to the limit in both cases. (Objectively speaking, this continuity is given by one being to another and by each to the totality of the others in the transitions of the reproductive process.) But death is always fatal to individual discontinuity and it appears whenever a deep continuity is revealed. Asexual reproduction conceals it at the same time as it invites it; here the dead individual disappears in death, is spirited away. In this sense asexual reproduction is death's ultimate truth; death proclaims the fundamental discontinuity of beings (and of existence itself). The discontinuous being alone dies, and death lays bare the falsehood of discontinuity.

A return to inner experience

In sexual types of reproduction individual discontinuity is a more robust affair. The discontinuous being does not disappear altogether when he dies but leaves traces that may even last for ever. A skeleton may last millions of years. At the highest level the sexual being is tempted, indeed obliged, to believe in the immortality of his separate existence. He looks upon his "soul", his discontinuity, as the deepest truth of his own being, for he is taken in by the survival of his physical being although this may be only partial and its constituent parts may decompose. Since bones are so durable he has even invented the "resurrection of the body". On the day of judgment the bones are to come together and the resuscitated bodies bring the soul back to its original state. Here is an exaggeration of a physical condition in which continuity, no less fundamental in sexual reproduction, is lost: the genetic cells divide and from one to another it is possible to have an objective understanding of the initial unity. Continuity underlying each scissiparous division is always obvious.

On the level of the discontinuity and the continuity of beings the only new element in sexual reproduction is the fusion of the two minute entities, tiny cells, the male and female gametes. But the fusion makes the fundamental continuity finally plain; it shows that lost continuity can be found again. The discontinuousness of sexual beings gives rise to a dense and heavy world where individual separateness has terrifying foundations; the anguish of death and pain has bestowed on this wall of separation the solidity of prison walls, dismal and hostile. Yet within this unhappy world lost continuity can be found again if fertilisation takes place: fertilisation, fusion, that is, would be unthinkable if the apparent discontinuousness of the simplest animated beings were not an illusion.

Only the discontinuousness of complex creatures seems intangible to begin with. We do not seem able to conceive of their discontinuity being reduced to a single unity or of being doubled (or called in question). The moments of plethora when animals are in the grip of sexual fever are critical ones in their isolation. Then fear of death and pain is transcended, then the sense of relative continuity between animals of the same species, always there in the background as a contradiction, though not a serious one, of apparent discontinuity, is suddenly heightened. Curiously enough, this does not happen under exactly similar conditions between individuals of the same sex. It would seem that only a secondary difference has the power to bring a deep-seated identity which might have lain concealed to the surface of consciousness. Similarly a loss is felt more intensely just as it takes place. The sex difference seems to stimulate this undefined sense of continuity due to similarity of race while at the same time betraying it and making it hurtful. Perhaps one should not compare the reactions of animals with man's inner experience after thus discussing objective data. Science sees it in a simple light: animal reaction is determined by physiological facts. Similarity of species is indeed a physiological fact for the observer, and difference of sex is another. But the notion of a similarity made more obvious by a difference is founded on some inner experience. All I can do is stress this change of emphasis in passing. It is characteristic of this work. I believe that a study with man as its subject is bound to make changes like this in places. A study that sets out to be scientific minimises the part played by subjective experience, while I on the other hand am methodically minimising that played by objective knowledge. Indeed when I put forward the findings of science on reproduction, at the back of my mind I intended to transpose them. I know that I cannot undergo the inner experience of animals, still less of animalcula; no more can I imagine it. But animalcula have an inner experience just as complex animals do: the transition from existence in-itself to existence for-itself cannot be assigned exclusively to complex creatures or to mankind. Even an inert particle, lower down the scale than the animalcula, seem to have this existence for-itself, though I prefer the words inside or inner experience; none of the terms used to describe it are wholly satisfactory. I cannot fail to know that this inner experience which I can neither undergo myself nor picture in my imagination implies by definition *a feeling of self*. This elementary feeling is not *consciousness of self*. Consciousness of self follows upon consciousness of external objects, only clearly known with humanity. But feeling of self necessarily varies as the self concerned withdraws into its discontinuity. This withdrawal is greater or lesser according to the facilities available for objective discontinuity, in inverse ratio to those available for continuity. The firmness and stability of a conceivable limit are important but the feeling of self varies according to the degree of isolation. Sexual activity is a critical moment in the isolation of the individual. We know it from without, but we know that it weakens and calls into question the feeling of self. We use the word crisis: that is, the inner effect of an event known objectively. As an objective fact of knowledge the crisis is none the less responsible for a basic inner phenomenon.

General facts concerning sexual reproduction

The material basis of the crisis is the plethora; with asexual beings this is clear straight away. There is growth; growth determines reproduction and consequently division and the death of the plethoric individual. It is less clear in the realm of sexual beings but a super-abundance of energy is none the less a starting point for the activity of the sexual organs and just as for the simplest organisms brings death in its train.

Not directly, however. As a general rule, the sexual individual survives the super-abundance and even the excesses into which it leads him. Death is the result of the sexual crisis only in exceptional cases, but the significance of these is admittedly striking, so much so that the exhaustion following the final paroxysm is thought of as a "little death". Humanly speaking, death is always the symbol of the retreating waters after the violence of the storm, but it is not only to be seen as a remote parallel. We must never forget that the multiplication of beings goes hand in hand with death. The parents survive the birth of their offspring but the reprieve is only temporary. A stay is granted, partly for the benefit of the newcomers who need assistance, but the appearance of the newcomers guarantees the disappearance of their predecessors. Death follows reproduction with sexual beings too, at a distance even if not immediately.

Death is the inevitable consequence of super-abundance; only stagnation ensures that creatures shall preserve their discontinuity, their isolation, that is. This discontinuity is a challenge to the pressure that is bound to abolish the barriers keeping separate individuals apart. The forward surge of life may require the barriers temporarily, for without them no complex organisation would be possible, no organisation effective. But life is movement and nothing within that movement is proof against it. Asexual beings die of their own development, of their own impulsion. Sexual ones can put up only a temporary resistance, to their own teeming energies as to the general surge of life. True, occasionally what they succumb to is only the collapse of their own resources and metabolism; there is no doubt about this. Only multiple death can resolve the dilemma of these ever-multiplying existences. The idea of a world where human life might be artificially prolonged has a nightmare quality yet gives no glimpse of anything beyond that slight delay. Death is waiting in the long run, made necessary by multiplying and teeming life.

A comparison of the two elementary aspects as seen objectively and subjectively

Those aspects of life in which reproduction is bound up with death are undeniably and objectively real, but as I have already said, even an elementary form of life has certainly a subjective experience of itself. We can even discuss this rudimentary experience while admitting that it is incommunicable. The crisis of existence is here. The being experiences being in the crisis that puts it to the test, the being's very being is called into question in the transition from continuity to discontinuity or from discontinuity to continuity. We agree that the simplest organism is aware of itself and of its limits. If these limits alter, its basic consciousness is under attack, and this attack is critical for a being having consciousness of self.

In sexual reproduction, I have said that the objective aspects were ultimately the same as in scissiparous division. But when we examine the human experience of this in eroticism we seem to have come a long way from these fundamental aspects and their objective reality. Particularly, in eroticism, our feeling of plethora is not connected with the consciousness of engendering life. One might even say that the fuller the erotic pleasure, the less conscious we are of the children who may result from it. On the other hand, the depression following upon the final spasm may give a foretaste of death, but the anguish of death and death itself are at the antipodes of pleasure. If a reconciliation between the objective reality of reproduction and the subjective experience of eroticism is possible it has some other basis. One thing is fundamental: the objective fact of reproduction calls into question within the subjective consciousness the feeling of self, the feeling of being and of the limits of the isolated being. It questions the discontinuity with which the feeling of self is necessarily bound up because that furnishes its limits; even a vague feeling of self belongs to a discontinuous being. But this discontinuity is never absolute; with sexuality particularly a sense of the existence of others beyond the self-feeling suggests a possible continuity as opposed to the original discontinuity. Other individuals, in sexuality, are continually putting forward the possibility of continuity; others are continually threatening a rent in the seamless garment of the separate individuality. Throughout the vicissitudes of animal life, those others, those fellow creatures, are there just off-stage; they form a background of neutral figures, a simple one perhaps, but one that undergoes a critical change in times of sexual activity. At that moment the other individual does not yet appear positively, it is negatively linked to the disturbed violence of the plethora. Each being contributes to the self-negation of the other, yet the negation is not by any means a recognition of the other as a partner.

This attraction seems to be a matter less of similarity between the two than of the plethora of the other. The violence of the one goes out to meet the violence of the other; on each side there is an inner compulsion to get out of the limits of individual discontinuity. There is a meeting between two beings projected beyond their limits by the sexual orgasm, slowly for the female, but often for the male with fulminating force. At the moment of conjunction the animal couple is not made up of two discontinuous beings drawing close together uniting in a current of momentary continuity: there is no real union; two individuals in the grip of violence brought together by the preordained reflexes of sexual intercourse share in a state of crisis in which both are beside themselves. Both creatures are simultaneously open to continuity. But nothing persists in their imperfect awareness. The crisis over, the discontinuity of each is intact. This crisis is simultaneously the most intense and the least significant.

Fundamental characteristics of the subjective experience of eroticism

During this examination of the animal experience of sexuality I have moved some way from the objective facts of sexual reproduction commented upon a little earlier. I have been endeavouring to see the way clear through the subjective experience of animals starting from a few facts drawn from the life of infinitesimal beings. I have been guided by our human subjective experience and my inevitable awareness of what is lacking in animal experience. To tell the truth I have scarcely added anything to such suppositions as are permissible if a broad foundation is to be laid. Moreover I have been stating the obvious.

I have not given consideration to the objective facts of sexual reproduction in order to ignore them thenceforth, however.

Eroticism is the meeting place where all these considerations crop up again.

With human life we are fairly and squarely inside

subjective experience. The objective elements we perceive
are finally reduced to their subjective terms. I believe that
the transitions from this continuity to continuity in eroticism
are what they are because of the knowledge of death that
from the word go connects the rupture of discontinuity and
the consequent glide towards a potential continuity with
death. We may perceive these characteristics from without,
but if we did not already feel them from within their significance would escape us. There is also a leap to be made
from the objective fact showing us the necessity of death
linked to the super-abundance of life across to the dizzy
confusion which the subjective experience of death brings to
mind. This disturbance, together with a plethora of sexual
activity, brings a profound disquiet in its train. If I had not
already realised from outside that they were identical, how
should I have recognised in the paradoxical experiences of
plethora and swoon bound up with each other, the movement of the individual transcending in death the always
provisional discontinuity of life?

The first obvious thing about eroticism is the way that an
ordered, parsimonious and shuttered reality is shaken by a
plethoric disorder. Animal sexuality brings out this same
plethoric disorder but no barrier of resistance is raised
against it. Animal disorder is freely dissipated in untrammelled violence. The rupture is consummated, the stormy
floods subsides and the solitude of the individual closes in
upon it once more. The only modification of individual
discontinuity possible for the animal is death. Either the
animal dies or else when the tumult has died down its discontinuity remains intact. In human life on the other hand,
sexual violence causes a wound that rarely heals of its own
accord; it has to be closed, and will not even remain closed
without constant attention based on anguish. Primary
anguish bound up with sexual disturbance signifies death.
The violence of this disturbance reopens in the mind of the
man experiencing it, who also knows what death is, the abyss
that death once revealed. The violence of death and sexual

violence, when they are linked together, have this dual significance. On the one hand the convulsions of the flesh are more acute when they are near to a black-out, and on the other a black-out, as long as there is enough time, makes physical pleasure more exquisite. Mortal anguish does not necessarily make for sensual pleasure, but that pleasure is more deeply felt during mortal anguish.

Erotic activity is not always as overtly sinister as this, it is not always a crack in the system; but secretly and at the deepest level the crack belongs intimately to human sensuality and is the mainspring of pleasure. Fear of dying makes us catch our breath and in the same way we suffocate at the moment of crisis.

In principle eroticism seems at first sight the very opposite of this horrifying paradox. It is a plethora of the genital organs. An animal impulse in us is the cause of the crisis. But the organs do not freely enter this state of chance. It cannot take place without the consent of our will. It upsets an ordered system on which our efficiency and reputation depend. In fact the individual splits up and his unity is shattered from the first instant of the sexual crisis. Just then the plethoric life of the body comes up against the mind's resistance. Even an apparent harmony is not enough; beyond consent the convulsions of the flesh demand silence and the spirit's absence. The physical urge is curiously foreign to human life, loosed without reference to it so long as it remains silent and keeps away. The being yielding to that urge is human no longer but, like the beasts, a prey of blind forces in action, wallowing in blindness and oblivion. An indefinite general taboo is set up against that violence, known to us less from outside sources than directly, through the subjective knowledge that its nature is irreconcilable with our basic humanity. There is no formula for this general taboo. In the structure of acceptable behaviours only inessential aspects are seen, varying according to persons and circumstances, not to speak of times and places. What Christian theology says about the sins of the flesh shows as

D*

much through the ineffectualness of the prohibitions proclaimed as through the numerous outspoken comments (in Victorian England for example), the gratuitousness, the inconsistency, the violence answering violence of the reactions against the taboo. Only the actual experience of states of normal sexual activity and the clash between them and socially approved conduct allows us to recognise that this activity has its inhuman side. The organs' plethora induces reactions alien to the normal run of human behaviour. A rush of blood upsets the balance on which life is based. A madness suddenly takes possession of a person. That madness is well known to us but we can easily picture the surprise of anyone who did not know about it and who by some device witnessed unseen the passionate lovemaking of some woman who had struck him as particularly distinguished. He would think she was sick, just as mad dogs are sick. Just as if some mad bitch had usurped the personality of the dignified hostess of a little while back. Sickness is not putting it strongly enough, though; for the time being the personality is dead. For the time being its death gives the bitch full scope, and she takes advantage of the silence, of the absence of the dead woman. The bitch wallows—wallows noisily—in that silence and that absence. The return of the personality would freeze her and put an end to the sensual delight she has abandoned herself to. The loosing of the sexual urge is not always as violent as I have described it but this is none the less a fair picture of the diametrically opposite poles.

The urge is first of all a natural one but it cannot be given free rein without barriers being torn down, so much so that the natural urge and the demolished obstacles are confused in the mind. The natural urge means a barrier destroyed. The barrier destroyed means the natural urge. Demolished barriers are not the same as death but just as the violence of death overturns—irrevocably—the structure of life so temporarily and partially does sexual violence. Indeed Christian theology identifies the moral degradation following the sins of the flesh with death. Inevitably linked with the moment of climax there is a minor rupture suggestive òf death; and conversely the idea of death may play a part in setting sensuality in motion. This mostly adds up to a sense of transgression dangerous to general stability and the conservation of life, and without it the instincts could not run their course unhindered. But transgression is not only objectively necessary to this freedom, for it can happen that unless we see that transgression is taking place we no longer have the feeling of freedom that the full accomplishment of the sexual act demands,—so much so that a scabrous situation is sometimes necessary to a blasé individual for him to reach the peak of enjoyment (or if not the situation itself, an imaginary one lived out like a daydream during interintercourse). Such a situation is not always a terrifying one. Many women cannot reach their climax without pretending to themselves that they are being raped. But deep within the significant break there dwells a boundless violence.[1]

The paradox of the general taboo on sexual freedom, if not on sexuality

The remarkable thing about the sex taboo is that it is fully seen in transgression. It is inculcated partly through education but never resolutely formulated. Education proceeds as much by silence as by muffled warnings. The taboo is discovered directly by a furtive and at first partial exploration of the forbidden territory. At first nothing could be more mysterious. We are admitted to the knowledge of a pleasure in which the notion of pleasure is mingled with mystery, suggestive of the taboo that fashions the pleasure at the same time as it condemns it. The revelation through

[1] There are widespread and staggering possibilities of harmony between erotic urges and violence. I am thinking of a passage from Marcel Aymé (*Uranus*, Gallimard, page 151-152) which has the merit of presenting the incident in all its banality in an immediate and accessible way. Here is the last sentence: "The sight of these two cautious, dismal and mean-spirited specimens of the petty bourgeoisie eyeing the victims from their Renaissance dining-room and titillating each other and jigging up and down in the folds of the curtains, just like dogs . . ." The passage describes the execution of some militia men, preceded by other horrible and bloody incidents, observed by a couple who sympathised with the victims.

transgression has certainly not remained constant throughout the ages. Fifty years ago the irony of sex education was more obvious still. But everywhere—and doubtless from the earliest times—our sexual activity is sworn to secrecy, and everywhere, though to a variable degree, it appears contrary to our dignity so that the essence of eroticism is to be found in the inextricable confusion of sexual pleasure and taboo. In human terms the taboo never makes an appearance without suggesting sexual pleasure, nor does the pleasure without evoking the taboo. The basis is a natural urge and in childhood the natural urge acts alone. But there is never any truly human pleasure at that age and anyway we can never remember it. I can imagine objections and exceptions but they cannot shake such a plain fact.

In the human sphere sexual activity has broken away from animal simplicity. It is in essence a transgression, not, after the taboo, a return to primitive freedom. Transgression belongs to humanity given shape by the business of work. Transgression itself is organised. Eroticism as a whole is an organised activity, and this is why it changes over the years. I shall try to give a picture of eroticism seen in its diversity and its changes. Eroticism first appears in transgression of the first degree, for that is what marriage is when all is said and done. But it is only really present in more complex forms in which the quality of transgression is stressed progressively more and more.

The quality of transgression, or in other words, the sinfulness.

CHAPTER X

TRANSGRESSION IN MARRIAGE AND IN ORGY

Marriage seen as a transgression and the right of entry

Marriage is most often thought of as having little to do with eroticism.

We use the word eroticism every time a human being behaves in a way strongly contrasted with everyday standards and behaviour. Eroticism shows the other side of a façade of unimpeachable propriety. Behind the façade are revealed the feelings, parts of the body and habits we are normally ashamed of. It must be stressed that although this aspect has apparently nothing to do with marriage it has in fact always been present in it.

Marriage in the first place is the framework of legitimate sensuality. "Thou shalt not perform the carnal act except in matrimony alone." In even the most puritan societies marriage is not questioned. But I have in mind the quality of transgression that persists at the very basis of marriage. This may seem a contradiction at first, but we must remember other cases of transgression entirely in keeping with the general sense of the law transgressed. Sacrifice particularly, is in essence, as we have seen, the ritual violation of a taboo; the whole process of religion entails the paradox of a rule regularly broken in certain circumstances. I take marriage to be a transgression then; this is a paradox, no doubt, but laws that allow an infringement and consider it legal are paradoxical. Hence just as killing is simultaneously forbidden and performed in sacrificial ritual, so the initial sexual act constituting marriage is a permitted violation.

Near relations having exclusive rights over sisters and daughters would perhaps relinquish these rights to strangers who, coming from outside, had a kind of irregularity about them that qualified them to undertake that act of transgression which the first act of intercourse in marriage was taken to be. This is only a hypothesis, but if we want to see how marriage fits into the sphere of eroticism such a possibility is not to be neglected. In any case, that there is a feeling of transgression about marriage is a matter of everyday experience; popular wedding celebrations alone make that much clear. Sexual intercourse in marriage or outside it has always something of the nature of a criminal act, particularly where a virgin is concerned, and always to some extent when it takes place for the first time. With this in mind I think it makes sense to talk about a certain power of transgression a stranger would have and a man living in the same community would not possess.

Recourse to a power of transgression not possessed by the first comer seems generally to have been favoured, especially on serious occasions like the violation of the taboo making copulation a shameful thing when it is practised with a women for the first time. That operation would often be entrusted to men who, unlike the bridegroom, had the authority to transgress. They must have had a quality of sovereignty in some way or another that protected them from the taboo valid for mankind in general. The priesthood would be the obvious choice, but in the Christian world it was out of the question to have recourse to God's ministers, and the custom of entrusting the defloration to the local lord grew up[1]. Sexual intercourse or the initial act at least was evidently considered forbidden and dangerous, but the lord or the priest had the power to touch sacred things without too great a risk.

Repetition

The erotic side or, more simply, the transgressional aspect

[1] In any case the *jus primae noctis* which the feudal lord affected as the sovereign power in his own domain was not as has been thought the outrageous privilege of a tyrant who no one dared resist. At least it did not originate in that way.

of marriage often escapes notice because the word *marriage* describes both the act of getting married and the state of being married; we forget the former and just think of the latter. Besides, the economic value of women has long made the state of marriage the most important thing; calculations, expectations and results have focused interest on the state at the expense of the intensity of feeling that characterises the brief moment of the act. It is different in kind from the expectations it raises—the home, the children and the domestic activity which will result.

The most serious thing is that habit dulls intensity and marriage implies habit. There is a remarkable connection between the innocence and the absence of danger offered by repeated intercourse (the first act being the only one to fear) and the absence of value on the level of pleasure generally associated with this repetition. This is no negligible connection: it has to do with the very essence of eroticism. But the full flowering of sexual life is not negligible either. Without the intimate understanding between two bodies that only grows with time conjunction is furtive and superficial, unorganised, practically animal and far too quick, and often the expected pleasure fails to come. A taste for constant change is certainly neurotic, and certainly can only lead to frustration after frustration. Habit, on the other hand, is able to deepen the experiences that impatience scorns to bother with.

With repetition the two opposing viewpoints are complementary. Without a doubt, the aspects, the signs and the symbols which give eroticism its richness demand a certain basic irregularity. Carnal life would be a poor thing not far removed from the animals' heavy-footed endeavours if it had never been indulged in with a fair amount of freedom in response to capricious urges. While it is true that sexual life blossoms with habit, it is hard to say how far a happy life prolongs the sensations roused in the first instance by a troubled impulse or revealed by forbidden explorations. Habit itself owes something to the higher pitch of excitement dependent on disorder and rule-breaking. We can ask whether the deep love kept alive in marriage would be possible without the contagion of illicit love, the only kind able to give love a greater force than that of law.

Ritual orgy

In any case the orderly framework of marriage provides only a narrow outlet for pent-up violence.

Apart from marriage, feast days provided opportunities for rule-breaking and at the same time made possible normal life dedicated to orderly activity. Even the "holiday on the death of a king", that I mentioned, fixed a limit in time to apparently boundless disorder in spite of its prolonged and amorphous nature. Once the royal remains had become a skeleton, disorder and excess ceased to prevail and taboos came into force once more. Ritual orgies often connected with less disorderly feasts allowed for only a furtive interruption of the taboo on sexual behaviour. Often the licence extended only to members of a fraternity, as in the Dionysic Feasts, but it might well have a more precise religious connotation transcending eroticism. We do not know exactly what used to happen: we can always imagine a heavy vulgarity taking the place of frenzy. But it is no use denying the possibility of a state of exaltation composed of the intoxication commonly accompanying the orgy, erotic ecstasy and religious ecstasy.

In the orgy the celebration progresses with the overwhelming force that usually brushes all bonds aside. In itself the feast is a denial of the limits set on life by work, but the orgy turns everything upside-down. It is not by chance that the social order used to be turned topsy-turvy during the Saturnalia, the master serving the slave, the slave lolling on the master's bed. These excesses derive their most acute significance from the ancient connection between sensual pleasure and religious exaltation. This is the direction given to eroticism by the orgy no matter what disorder was involved, making it transcend animal sexuality.

There is nothing of this sort in the rudimentary eroticism of marriage. Transgression, yes, whether violent or not; but transgression in marriage is without consequence, it is independent of other developments, possible ones, no doubt, but not imposed by custom and even frowned on by custom. One might just possibly consider the vogue of dirty jokes in our own day as having something of the marriage ceremony about it at a popular level, but this custom implies an inhibited eroticism turned into furtive sallies, sly allusions and humorous double meanings. Sexual frenzy though, with its religious overtones, is the true stuff of orgies. A very old aspect of eroticism is seen in the orgy. Orgiacal eroticism is by nature a dangerous excess whose explosive contagion is an indiscriminate threat to all sides of life. The original rites made the Maenads devour their own living infants in their ferocious frenzy. Later on this abomination was echoed in the bloody omophagia of kids first suckled by the Maenads.

The orgy is not associated with the dignity of religion, extracting from the underlying violence something calm and majestic compatible with profane order; its potency is seen in its ill-omened aspects, bringing frenzy in its wake and a vertiginous loss of consciousness. The total personality is involved, reeling blindly towards annihilation, and this is the decisive moment of religious feeling. All this occurs within the framework of man's secondary assent in the measureless proliferation of life. The refusal implied by taboos confines the individual within a miserly isolation compared with the vast disorder of creatures lost in each other, whose very violence lays them open to the violence of death. From another standpoint the suspension of taboos sets free the exuberant surge of life and favours the unbounded orgiastic fusion of those individuals. This fusion could in no way be limited to that attendant on the plethora of the genital organs. It is a religious effusion first and foremost; it is essentially the disorder of lost beings who oppose no further resistance to the frantic proliferation of life. That enormous unleashing of natural forces seems to be divine, so high does it raise man above the condition to which he has condemned himself of his own accord. Wild cries, wild violence of gesture, wild dances, wild emotions as well, all in the grip of immeasurably convulsive turbulence. The perdition ahead would demand this flight into the regions where all individuality is shed, where the stable elements of human activity disappear and there is no firm foothold anywhere to be found.

The orgy as an agrarian ritual

The orgies of archaic peoples are usually interpreted in a way that completely by-passes everything that I have tried to show. Before proceeding, then, I must discuss the traditional interpretation which tends to reduce them to rituals of contagious magic. The men who ordained these orgies did indeed believe that they ensured the fertility of the fields. No one doubts that this is so. But the whole story has not been told if practices which far surpass the necessities of an agrarian rite are explained only in terms of that rite. Even if orgies had at all times and everywhere had this meaning one would still be justified in enquiring whether this was their only meaning. To comprehend the agrarian aspect of a custom is indisputably of interest in that it thereby becomes part of the history of agricultural civilisation, but it is ingenuous to see all the actions accounted for by a belief in their efficacy. Work and material utility have certainly determined, or at any rate conditioned, the behaviour, religious as well as profane, of semi-civilised peoples. But that does not mean that an extravagant custom derives specifically from a wish to make plantations fertile. Work set up the distinction between the sacred and the profane. It is the origin of the taboos which made man deny nature. On the other hand, the limits of the working world supported and maintained in the struggle against nature by those taboos also delineated the sacred world. In one way the sacred world is nothing but the natural world persisting in so far as it cannot be entirely reduced to the order laid down by work, profane order, that is. But the sacred world is only the natural world in one sense. In another it transcends the earlier world made up of work and taboos. In this sense the sacred world is a denial of the profane, yet it also owes its character to the profane world it denies. The sacred world is also the result of work in that its origin and significance are to be sought not in the immediate existence of nature's creation but in the birth of a new order of things, brought about in turn by the opposition to nature of the world of purposeful activity. The sacred world is separated from nature by work; it would be unintelligible for us if we did not see how far work determines its nature and existence.

The human mind formed by work would usually attribute to action a usefulness analogous to that of work. In the sacred world the explosion of violence suppressed by a taboo was regarded not only as an explosion but also as an action, and was considered to have some use. Originally such explosions, like war or sacrifice or orgies, were not calculated ones. But as transgressions perpetrated by men they were organised explosions, they were actions whose possible use appeared as a secondary consideration and were not contested.

The effects of war as an act were of the same order as the effects of work. In sacrifice there came into play forces to which consequences were arbitrarily attributed, just as if the force were that of a tool handled by a man. The effects attributed to orgies are of a different order. In human affairs example is catching. A man enters the dance because the dance makes him dance. A contagious action, and this one really is contagious, was thought to affect not only other men but nature as well. So sexual activity, which can be considered by and large as growth, as I have said, was thought to encourage growth in vegetation.

But only secondarily is transgression an action undertaken because of its usefulness. In war, in sacrifice or in orgies, the human mind arranged a convulsive explosion, banking on the real or imaginary result. War is not a political enterprise in origin, nor sacrifice a piece of magic. Similarly the orgy did not orginate in the desire for abundant crops. The origins of war, sacrifice and orgy are identical; they spring from the existence of taboos set up to counter liberty in murder or sexual violence. These taboos inevitably shaped the explosive surge of transgression. All this does not mean that recourse was never had to the orgy—or war, or sacrifice—for the sake of the results rightly or wrongly attributed to them. But in that case it was a secondary and inevitable business of frantic violence hurled in among the wheels of human activity as organised by work.

Violence in these conditions is no longer a purely natural and animal affair. The explosion preceded by anguish takes on a divine significance transcending immediate satisfaction. It has become a religious matter. But in the same movement it also becomes human; it finds its place in the chain of cause and effect that communal efforts have built up upon the foundation of work.

CHAPTER XI

CHRISTIANITY

Licence and the making of the Christian world

The modern view of the orgy must at all costs be rejected. It assumes that those who took part had no sense of modesty at all, or very little. This superficial view implies that the men of ancient civilisation had something of the animal in their nature. In some respects it is true these men do often seem nearer than ourselves to the animals, and it is maintained that some of them shared this feeling of kinship. But our judgments are linked to the idea that our peculiar modes of life best show up the difference between man and animal. Early men did not contrast themselves with animals in the same way, but even if they saw animals as brothers the reactions on which their humanity was based were far from being less rigorous than ours. True, the beasts they hunted lived under material conditions much like their own, but then they erroneously ascribed human feelings to animals. In any case primitive (or archaic) modesty is not always weaker than our own. It is only very different, more formalist, not so automatic and unconscious; no less lively for that, it proceeds from beliefs kept alive by a basic anguish. This is why when we discuss the orgy in a very general way we have no grounds for seeing it as an abandoned practice but on the contrary we should regard it as a moment of heightened tension, disorderly no doubt, but at the same time a moment of religious fever. In the upside down world of feast-days the orgy occurs at the instant when the truth of that world reveals its overwhelming force. Bacchic violence is the measure of incipient eroticism whose domain is originally that of religion.

But the truth of the orgy has come down to us through the Christian world in which standards have been overthrown once more. Primitive religious feeling drew from taboos the spirit of transgression. Christian religious feeling has by and large opposed the spirit of transgression. The tendency which enables a religious development to proceed within Christianity is connected with these relatively contradictory points of view.

It is essential to decide what the effects of this contradiction have been. If Christianity had turned its back on the fundamental movement which gave rise to the spirit of transgression it would have lost its religious character entirely, in my opinion. However, the Christian spirit retains the essential core, finding it in continuity in the first place. Continuity is reached through experience of the divine. The divine is the essence of continuity. Christianity relies on it entirely, even as far as to neglect the means by which this continuity can be achieved, means which tradition has regulated in detail though without making their origin plain. The nostalgia or desire that opened up these paths managed to get partially lost among the details and calculations often dear to traditional piety.

But in Christianity there has been a dual process. Basically the wish was to open the door to a completely unquestioning love. According to Christian belief, lost continuity found again in God demanded from the faithful boundless and uncalculated love, transcending the regulated violence of ritual frenzy. Man transfigured by divine continuity was exalted in God to the love of his fellow. Christianity has never relinquished the hope of finally reducing this world of selfish discontinuity to the realm of continuity afire with love. The initial movement of transgression was thus steered by Christianity towards the vision of violence transcended and transformed into its opposite.

This ideal has a sublime and fascinating quality.

Nevertheless there is another side to the matter: how to adjust the sacred world of continuity to the world of discontinuity which persists. The divine world has to descend among the world of things. There is a paradox in this double intention. The determined desire to centre everything on continuity has its effect, but this first effect has to compromise with a simultaneous effect in the other direction. The Christian God is a highly organised and individual entity springing from the most destructive of feelings, that of continuity. Continuity is reached when boundaries are crossed. But the most constant characteristic of the impulse I have called transgression is to make order out of what is essentially chaos. By introducing transcendence into an organised world, transgression becomes a principle of an organised disorder. Its organised character is the result of the organised ways of its adherents. Such an organisation is founded upon work but also and at the same time upon the discontinuity of beings. The organised world of work and the world of discontinuity are one and the same. Tools and the products of toil are discontinuous objects, the man who uses the tools and makes the goods is himself a discontinuous being and his awareness of this is deepened by the use or creation of discontinuous objects. Death is revealed in relation to the discontinuous world of labour. For creatures whose individuality is heightened by work, death is the primal disaster; it underlines the inanity of the separate individual.

Faced with a precarious discontinuity of the personality, the human spirit reacts in two ways which in Christianity coalesce. The first responds to the desire to find that lost continuity which we are stubbornly convinced is the essence of being. With the second, mankind tries to avoid the terms set to individual discontinuity, death, and invents a discontinuity unassailable by death—that is, the immortality of discontinuous beings.

The first way gives continuity its full due, but the second enables Christianity to withdraw whatever its wholesale generosity offers. Just as transgression organised the continuity born of violence, Christianity fitted this con-

tinuity regarded as supreme into the framework of discontinuity. True, it did no more than push to its logical conclusion a tendency which was already marked. But it accomplished something which had hitherto only been suggested.
It reduced the sacred and the divine to a discontinuous and
personal God, the creator. What is more, it turned whatever
lies beyond this world into a prolongation of every individual
soul. It peopled Heaven and Hell with multitudes condemned with God to the eternal discontinuity of each
separate being. Chosen and damned, angels and demons,
they all became inpenetrable fragments, for ever divided,
arbitrarily distinct from each other, arbitrarily detached
from the totality of being with which they must nevertheless
remain connected.

This multitude of creatures of chance and the individual
creator denied their solitude in the mutual love of God and
the elect—or affirmed it in hatred of the damned. But love
itself made sure of the final isolation. What had been lost in
this atomisation of totality was the path that led from
isolation to fusion, from the discontinuous to the continuous,
the path of violence marked out by transgression. Desire for
harmony and conciliation in love and submission took the
place of the overwhelming wrench of violence, even while
the memory of early cruelty lasted. I spoke earlier[1] of the
Christian evolution of sacrifice. I shall try now to give a
general picture of the changes wrought by Christianity in
sacred matters.

The basic ambiguity: Christianity's reduction of religion to its
benign aspect: Christianity's projection of the darker side of
religion into the profane world

In Christian sacrifice the faithful are not made responsible
for desiring the sacrifice. They only contribute to the
Crucifixion by their sins and their failures. This shatters
the unity of religion. At the pagan stage religion was based
on transgression and the impure aspects were no less divine

[1] See below p. 89.

than the opposite ones. The realm of sacred things is composed of the pure and of the impure[1]. Christianity rejected
impurity. It rejected guilt without which sacredness is
impossible since only the violation of a taboo can open the
way to it.

Pure or favourable sacredness has been dominant since
pagan antiquity. But even if it was nothing but a prelude to
a transcendental act, impure or ill-omened sacredness was
there underneath. Christianity could not get rid of impurity
altogether, it could not wipe out uncleanness entirely. But it
defined the boundaries of the sacred world after its own
fashion. In this fresh definition impurity, uncleanness and
guilt were driven outside the pale. Impure sacredness was
thenceforward the business of the profane world. In the
sacred world of Christianity nothing was allowed to survive
which clearly confessed the fundamental nature of sin or
transgression. The devil—angel or god of transgression (of
disobedience and revolt)—was driven out of the world of
the divine. Its origin was a divine one, but in the Christian
order of things (which prolonged Judaic mythology) transgression was the basis not of his divinity but of his fall. The
devil had fallen from divine favour which he had possessed
only to lose. He had not become profane, strictly speaking:
he retained a supernatural character because of the sacred
world he came from. But no effect was spared to deprive
him of the consequences of his religious quality. The cult
that no doubt still persisted, a survival from the days of
impure divinities, was stamped out. Death by fire was in
store for anyone who refused to obey and who found in sin
a sacred power and a sense of the divine. Nothing could
stop Satan from being divine, but this enduring truth was
denied with the rigours of torment. A cult which had
indisputably upheld certain aspects of religion was now
thought of as nothing but a criminal parody of religion.

[1] See Roger Caillois, *L'Homme et le Sacré* second edition, Gallimard, 1950,
pages 35-72. This text of Caillois is also published in the *Histoire Générale des
Religions*, Quillet, 1948, volume I under the title *L'Ambiguité du Sacré*.

Its very aura of sacredness was considered a profanation.

The principle of profanation is the use of the sacred for profane purposes. Even in the heart of paganism uncleanness could result from contact with something impure. But only in Christianity did the existence of the impure world become a profanation in itself. The profanation resided in the fact that it existed, even if pure things were not themselves sullied. The original contrast between the sacred and the profane world subsided into the background with the coming of Christianity.

One side of the profane allied itself to the pure half, the other to the impure half of the sacred. The evil to be found in the profane world joined with the diabolical part of the sacred and the good joined with the divine. The light of sanctity shone on the good whatever *good* may have meant in practical terms. The word *sanctity* originally meant *sacred things*, but this quality became associated with a life dedicated to Good, to Good and to God at the same time.[1]

Profanation resumed the original meaning of profane contact that it had in pagan religion. But it possessed another implication. Profanation in paganism was essentially unlucky, deplorable from all points of view. Transgression alone in spite of its dangerous nature had the power to open a door on to the sacred world. Profanation in Christianity was neither the same as original transgression, although rather like it, nor the same as early profanation. It most resembled transgression. Paradoxically, Christian profanation, being a contact with something impure, gained access to the essentially sacred, gained access to the forbidden world. But this underlying sacredness was simultaneously profane and diabolic as far as the Church was concerned. In spite of everything there was a sort of formal logic about the Church's attitude. What she regarded as sacred was separated from the profane world by well-defined formal limits that

---

[1] However, the underlying affinity between sanctity and transgression has never ceased to be felt. Even in the eyes of believers, the libertine is nearer to the saint than the man without desire.

had become traditional. The erotic, the impure or the diabolic were not separated from the profane world in the same way: they lacked a formal character, an easily understood demarcation.

In the original world of transgression the impure was itself well-defined, with stable forms accentuated by traditional rites. What paganism regarded as unclean was automatically regarded as sacred at the same time. That which condemned paganism, or Christianity, held to be unclean was no longer, or never became, the subject of a formal attitude. There may have been a formalisation of Sabbaths but it was never stable enough to persist. If sacred formalism would have none of it, the unclean was condemned to become profane.

The merging of sacred uncleanness and the profane seems to have been for some long time contrary to the feeling about the true nature of things persisting in man's memory, but the inverted religious structure of Christianity demanded it. It is perfect in so far as the feeling of sacredness dwindles when it is encased in formal patterns that seem a little out of date. One of the signs of this decline is the lack of heed paid to the existence of the devil these days; people believe in him less and less—I was going to say that they have ceased to believe in him altogether. That means that the dark side of religious mystery, more ill-defined than ever, finally loses all significance. The realm of religion is reduced to that of the God of Good, whose limits are those of light. There is no curse on anything in this domain.

This development had consequences in the domain of science (which is interested in religion from its own profane point of view; but I must say in passing that my attitude personally is not a scientific one. Without committing myself to particular religious forms I regard, or my book regards, religion from a religious point of view.) The connection between the good and the sacred appears in the work, remarkable in its way by a disciple of Durkheim. Robert Hertz rightly insists on the humanly significant differences between left-hand side and right-hand side[1]. A general belief associated good luck with the right-hand side, bad luck with the left-hand side; that is, the right with the pure, the left with the impure. In spite of the premature death of its author[2], the study has remained famous. It anticipated other works on a question which up to then had been rarely tackled. Hertz identified the pure with the holy, the impure with the profane. His work was later than the one which Henri Hubert and Marcel Mauss had devoted to magic[3], in which the complexity of the domain of religion was already obvious but the numerous confirmations of instances witnessing to the "duality of sacredness" was only generally recognised much later.

Witches' Sabbaths

Eroticism fell within the bounds of the profane and was at the same time condemned out of hand. The development of eroticism is parallel with that of uncleanness. Sacredness misunderstood is readily identified with Evil. While it conserved a sacred quality in people's minds the violence of eroticism could cause anguish or nausea, but it was not identified with profane Evil, with the violation of the rules that reasonably and rationally safeguard people and property. These rules, sanctioned by a sense of taboo, are different from those that proceed from the blind functioning of the taboo in that they vary according to their rational utility. With eroticism the preservation of the family was the main consideration, and the sorry plight of fallen women banished from family life was another. But a coherent whole only took shape within Christianity, when the original sacred character of eroticism ceased to be apparent at the same

[1] Hertz, if not a Christian, at least adhered to an ethic very like the Christian one. His study first appeared in the *Revue Philosophique*. It was reprinted in a collection of his writings, *Mélanges de Sociologie religieuse et de Folklore*, 1928.

[2] He was killed in the first world war.

[3] *Esquisse d'une théorie générale de la Magie* in *Année Sociologique* 1902-1903. The cautious position of the authors was opposed to that of Frazer (close to that of Hertz). Frazer regarded magical practices as profane. Hubert and Mauss regard magic as a religious phenomenon, at least *lato sensu*. Magic is often left-handed, unclean, but it raises complex issues that I shall not tackle here.

time as social considerations gained in importance.

The orgy with its emphasis on the sacred nature of eroticism transcending individual pleasure was to become the subject of special attention from the Church. The Church was in general against eroticism, but this opposition was based on the profane evil of sexual activity outside marriage. The feelings roused by the transgression of the taboo had to be suppressed at all costs.

The battle waged by the Church in this matter shows how difficult that was. A world of religion without uncleanness, in which nameless and unrestricted violence was severely condemned, was not accepted straight away.

But we know little or nothing of the nocturnal celebrations of the Middle Ages—or of the beginnings of modern times. The fault may lie to some extent with the cruelty of the repressive measures applied against them. Our sources of information are the confessions dragged by the judges from unfortunates put to the torture. Torture made the victims repeat what the judges' imagination suggested. We can only suppose that Christian vigilance could not prevent the survival of pagan festivals, at least in regions of deserted moorlands. We may well imagine a half-Christian mythology inspired by theology substituting Satan for the divinities worshipped by the yokels of the high Middle Ages. It is not even ridiculous at a pinch to see the devil as a *Dionysos redivivus*.

Certain authors have doubted the existence of witches' sabbaths. In our own day, people have even questioned the existence of the Voodoo cult. That cult exists none the less, even if it has sometimes turned into a tourist attraction. Everything leads us to believe that the cult of Satan, to which the Voodoo offers resemblances, did indeed exist, even if less frequently in reality than in the minds of the judges.

Here is what seems to emerge from readily accessible data.

The Sabbaths, vowed in the lonely night to the secret cult

of the god who was the other face of God, could only make
more marked a ritual based on the topsy-turvydom of the
feast. The judges in the witch trials were no doubt able to
persuade their victims to confess to a parody of Christian
rites. But the masters of the Sabbath may just as well have
thought up these practices themselves as have them suggested by their judges. We cannot tell from one isolated
example whether it belongs to the judge's imagination or
the real cult. But at least we may assume that sacrilege was
the basic principle. The name of Black Mass which appeared
towards the end of the Middle Ages was a general description of the meaning of the infernal feast. The Black Mass
attended by Huysmans, described in *Là-Bas*, is indisputably
authentic. I think it too much to imagine that the recognised
rites of the seventeenth or nineteenth centuries derive from
the tortures of the Middle Ages. These practices may have
exercised their fascination before the judges' interrogations
made them a temptation.

Imaginary or not, the Sabbaths are at any rate in keeping
with a form that the Christian imagination was in a sense
obliged to adopt. They describe the unleashing of passions
implied and contained in Christianity; imaginary or not, it is
the Christian situation that they define. Transgression in
pre-Christian religions was relatively lawful; piety demanded
it. Against transgression stood the taboo, but it could always
be suspended as long as limits were observed. In the
Christian world the taboo was absolute. Transgression
would have made clear what Christianity concealed, that
the sacred and the forbidden are one, that the sacred can
be reached through the violence of a broken taboo. As I
have already said, Christianity proposed this paradox on
the religious plane; access to the sacred is Evil; simultaneously, Evil is profane. But to be in Evil and to be free, to
exist freely within Evil (since the profane world is not subject to the restraints of the sacred world) was not only the
condemnation but also the reward of the guilty. The excessive pleasure of the licentious answered the horror of the

faithful. For the faithful, licence condemned the licentious and showed up their corruption. But corruption, or Evil, or Satan, were objects of adoration to the sinner, man or woman, and dear to him or to her. Pleasure plunged deep into Evil. It was essentially a transgression, transcending horror, and the greater the horror the deeper the joy. Imaginary or not, the stories of the Sabbaths mean something: they are the dream of a monstrous joy. The books of de Sade expand these tales; they go much further but still in the same direction. It is always a matter of defying the taboo. If this was not done according to rules, an enormous possibility opened up towards profane liberty: the possibility of profanation. Transgression was organised and limited. Even yielding to the temptation of ritual procedure, profanation bore within itself the entry into limitless potentialities, indicating now the richness of boundless possibilities and now their disadvantages—rapid exhaustion and death to follow.

Pleasure and the certainty of doing wrong

Just as the simple taboo created eroticism in the first place in the organised violence of transgression, Christianity in its turn deepened the degree of sensual disturbance by forbidding organised transgression.

The monstrous practices of those Sabbath nights, real or imaginary, or of the lonely prison where de Sade wrote the *Cent vingt Journées*, had a general form. Baudelaire stated a universally valid truth when he wrote[1]: "I say the unique and supreme pleasure of love lies in the certainty of doing *evil*[2]. And men and women know from birth that all pleasure is to be found in evil". I said first that pleasure was bound up with transgression. But Evil is not transgression, it is transgression condemned. Evil is in fact sin. Sin is what Baudelaire means. The accounts of Sabbaths in their turn correspond with this desire to sin. De Sade denied

[1] In *Fusées*, I!I.
[2] Baudelaire's italics.

Evil and sin. But he had to introduce the notion of irregularity to account for the bursting of the sensual climax. He even had frequent recourse to blasphemy. He sensed the silliness of profanation if the blasphemer denied the sacred nature of the Good that Blasphemy was intended to despoil. Yet he went on blaspheming. The necessity and the impotence of de Sade's blasphemy are significant, however. The Church had denied the sacred nature of erotic activity as part of transgression in the first place. Reacting against this, "free thinkers" denied in general what the Church held to be divine. By her denial the Church finally almost lost the power to evoke a sacred presence, especially in so far as the devil, the unclean one, ceased to stir up a deep-seated trouble in man's mind. At the same time free thinkers ceased to believe in Evil. They were thus on the way to a state of affairs in which, since eroticism was no longer a sin and since they could no longer be certain of doing wrong, eroticism was fast disappearing. In an entirely profane world nothing would be left but the animal mechanism. No doubt the memory of sin might persist; it would be like feeling that there was a trap somewhere!

When a situation is transcended there is no going back to the starting point. In liberty, liberty is impotent; yet liberty still means the decision how to use oneself. Undertaken with lucidity and in spite of this impoverishment, physical activity might be influenced by the conscious memory of an endless metamorphosis whose various stages would still be possible. But anyway we shall see that black eroticism returns by a devious route. And finally emotional eroticism—the most ardent kind, after all—might gain what physical eroticism has almost lost.[1]

[1] I cannot dwell any longer within the framework of this book upon the significance of a memory of black eroticism in emotional eroticism, which transcends it. I will just say, though, that black eroticism can be resolved in the awareness of a couple in love. The significance of black eroticism is seen in this awareness in a shadowy form. The possibility of sin arises, only to disappear again; it cannot be grasped but it does arise. The memory of sin is not the aphrodisiac that sin itself once was, but with sin everything finally vanishes; a sense of catastrophe or disillusion follows on the heels of enjoyment. In emotional eroticism the beloved can

CHAPTER XII

THE OBJECT OF DESIRE: PROSTITUTION

The erotic object

I have discussed the Christian position with regard to sacred eroticism and the orgy. I have described the latest stage in which eroticism has become sin and has been hard put to it to survive in a world of freedom whence sin has vanished.

I must now go back beyond this stage. The orgy was not the farthest point reached by eroticism in the pagan world. The orgy is the sacred aspect of eroticism in which the continuity of beings beyond solitude is most plainly expressed. Only in one way, however. In the orgy continuity cannot be laid hold of; individuals lose themselves at the climax, but in mingled confusion. The orgy is necessarily disappointing. Theoretically it is the complete negation of the individual quality. It presupposes, it even demands equality among the participants. Not only is individuality itself submerged in the tumult of the orgy, but each participant denies the individuality of the others. All limits are completely done away with, or so it seems, but it is impossible for nothing to remain of the differences between individuals and the sexual attraction connected with those differences.

The final aim of eroticism is fusion, all barriers gone, but

no longer escape, he is held fast in the vague memory of the successive possibilities which have made their appearance as eroticism has evolved. The clear realisation of these diverse possibilities written into that long development leading up to the power of profanation is above all able to show the unity of the ecstatic moments which make a sense of the continuity of all being accessible to discontinuous creatures. An ecstatic lucidity is thereafter possible, bound up with the knowledge of the limits of being.

its first stirrings are characterised by the presence of a desirable object.

In the orgy this object does not stand out by itself, for sexual excitement occurs through an uncontrolled urge, the opposite of habitual reserve. But everybody has this urge. It is objective but it is not perceived as an object; the person who perceives it is at the same time animated by it. On the other hand, excitement is normally roused by something distinct and objective. In the animal kingdom, the odour of the female often sets the male after her. The songs and displays of birds bring into play other kinds of perception that tell the female that the male is near and the sexual shock is at hand. Smell, hearing, sight and even taste are objective signals distinct from the activity they incite. They are signals to announce the crisis. In the world of man these messages have an intense erotic value. A pretty girl stripped naked is sometimes an erotic symbol. The object of desire is different from eroticism itself; it is not eroticism in its completeness, but eroticism working through it.

Even in the animal world these outward signs make the differences between individuals perceptible. In our own world, beyond the orgy, they make the differences obvious, and as individuals are unequally equipped with them according to their talents, state of mind and wealth, they stress the difference. The development of these signs has the following consequence: eroticism which is a fusion, which shifts interest away from and beyond the person and his limits, is nevertheless expressed by an object. We are faced with the paradox of an object which implies the abolition of the limits of all objects, of an *erotic object*.

Women, the privileged objects of desire

Theoretically a man may be just as much the object of a woman's desire as a woman is of a man's desire. The first step towards sexual intercourse, however, is usually the pursuit of a woman by a man. Men have the initiative, and women have the power of exciting desire in men. It would be quite wrong to say that women are more beautiful or even more desirable than men. But with their passive attitude they try by exciting desire to bring about the conjunction that men achieve by pursuing them. They are no more desirable, but they lay themselves open to be desired.

They put themselves forward as objects for the aggressive desire of men.

Not every woman is a potential prostitute, but prostituion is the logical consequence of the feminine attitude. In so far as she is attractive, a woman is a prey to men's desire. Unless she refuses completely because she is determined to remain chaste, the question is at what price and under what circumstances will she yield. But if the conditions are fulfilled she always offers herself as an object. Prostitution proper only brings in a commercial element. By the care she lavishes on her toilet, by the concern she has for her beauty set off by her adornment, a woman regards herself as an object always trying to attract men's attention. Similarly if she strips naked she reveals the object of a man's desire, an individual and particular object to be prized.

Nakedness as opposed to the normal state is certainly a kind of negation. The naked woman is near the moment of fusion, her nakedness heralds it. But although she symbolises the contrary, the negation of the object, she herself is still an object. Hers is the nakedness of a limited being, even if it proclaims the imminence of her pride's surrender in the tumultuous confusion of the sexual spasm. The potential beauty of this nakedness and its individual charm are what reveal themselves in the first place—the objective difference, in fact, between the value of one object and that of another.

Religious prostitution

More often than not the object inciting male pursuit eludes it. That means not that the suggestion has not been made, but that the necessary conditions are not fulfilled. Even if they are, that first refusal which seems to deny the offer already made only enhances its value. This elusiveness is logically bound up with modesty. The object of desire could not answer male expectations, she could not invite pursuit and especially preference if, far from retreating, she did not make herself conspicious by her expression or her dress. Putting oneself forward is the fundamental feminine attitude, but that first movement is followed by a feigned denial. Only prostitution has made it possible for adornment to stress the erotic value of the object. Such adornment really runs counter to the second movement when a woman evades the attack. What happens is that the use of adornment implies that the wearer is a prostitute; or a pretence of evasion then sharpens desire. To begin with, prostitution is in harmony with this process. Feminine attitudes are made up of complementary opposites. The prostitution of some requires that others shall be elusive, and vice versa. But this interaction is spoiled by poverty. Prostitution is an open sore as soon as poverty alone puts a stop to the movement.

Certain women, it is true, never react by flight. They offer themselves unreservedly and accept or even solicit the gifts without which they would find it hard to show that they were available for men's pursuit. Prostitution is simply a consecration in the first place. Certain women become objects in marriage; they are the instruments of domestic work, of agriculture particularly. Prostitution made them into objects of masculine desire; objects which at any rate heralded the moment when in the close embrace nothing remained but only a convulsive continuity. When the commercial aspect of modern prostitution gained the upper hand this aspect was overshadowed. But if the prostitute received sums of money or precious articles, these were originally gifts, gifts which she would use for extravagant expenditure and ornaments that made her more desirable. Thus she increased the power she had had from the first to attract gifts from the richest men. This exchange of gifts was not a commercial transaction. What a woman can give outside marriage cannot be put to any productive use, and similarly with the gifts that dedicate her to the luxurious life of eroticism. This sort of exchange led to all sorts of extravagance rather than to the regularity of commerce. Desire was a fiery thing; it could burn up a man's wealth to the last penny, it could burn out the life of the man in whom it was aroused.

Sai kahu

Prostitution seems to have been simply a complement to marriage in the first place. A transitional step, the transgression in the marriage ceremony, led to an organised daily life, and labour could be shared between husband and wife. A transgression of this sort was no way of consecrating anyone to erotic life. Sexual relations continued overtly and the transgression that initiated them was not stressed after the first contact. With prostitution, the prostitute was dedicated to a life of transgression. The sacred or forbidden aspect of sexual activity remained apparent in her, for her whole life was dedicated to violating the taboo. We must look for coherence between the deeds and the words describing this vocation; we must see the ancient institution of sacred prostitution in this light. In any case, in a world before—or outside—Christianity, religion, far from opposing prostitution, was able to control its modalities as it could with other sorts of transgression. The prostitutes in contact with sacred things, in surroundings themselves sacred, had a sacredness comparable with that of priests.

Chika-matsu

Compared with modern prostitution, religious prostitution seems devoid of shame. But the difference is misleading. Surely it was in that she had retained if not a feeling of shame at least its simulacrum that the temple courtesan avoided the disgrace of the street whore of today? The modern prostitute is proud of the shame she is bogged down in and wallows in it cynically. The anguish without which shame cannot be felt is foreign to her. The courtesan had a certain reserve; she was not an object of scorn and was not so different from other women. Her personal modesty must have had some of the shine rubbed off it, but she maintained the principle of the first contact which requires that a woman shall be afraid of surrendering and a man shall expect the woman to try to escape.

In the orgy, fusion let loose abolished shame. Shame could be found in the consummation of marriage, but it disappeared with habit. In sacred prostitution it became a ritual matter and came to imply transgression. A man cannot usually feel that a law is violated in his own person and that is why he expects a woman to feel confused, even if she only pretends to do so; otherwise he would be unaware of any violation. Shame, real or pretended, is a woman's way of accepting the taboo that makes a human being out of her. The time comes when she must break the taboo, but then she has to signify by being ashamed that the taboo is not forgotten, that the infringement takes place in spite of the taboo, in full consciousness of the taboo. Shame only disappears entirely in the lowest form of prostitution.

We must not forget, however, that outside of Christianity the religious and sacred nature of eroticism is shown in the full light of day, sacredness dominating shame. The temples of India still abound in erotic pictures carved in stone in which eroticism is seen for what it is, fundamentally divine. Numerous Indian temples solemnly remind us of the obscenity buried deep in our hearts.[1]

Low Prostitution

It is not really payment that disgraces the prostitute. Payment could well be involved in the round of ceremonial exchanges without the degradation of a commercial exchange. In the earliest societies the gift of her body that the wife makes to her husband (the presentation of sexual service) may itself be the occasion of a gift in return. But the low prostitute, because she has become a stranger to the taboo without which we should not be human beings, falls to the level of the beasts; she generally excites a disgust like the one most civilisations claim to feel for sows.

The rise of low prostitution is apparently connected with the appearance of poverty-stricken classes whose unhappy

[1] See Max-Pol Fouchet, *L'Art Amoureux des Indes*, Lausanne, La Guilde du Livre, 1957, 4° (hors commerce).

plight absolved them from the need scrupulously to observe the taboos. I am not thinking of the working-class of today but of Marx's *Lumpen-proletariat*. Extreme poverty releases men from the taboos that make human beings of them, not as transgression does, but in that a sort of hopelessness, not absolute perhaps, gives the animal impulses free rein. Hopelessness is not a return to animal nature. The world of transgression which swallowed up humanity as a whole is essentially different from the animal world, and so is the restricted world of hopelessness. People who live side by side with taboos—with the sacred—and accept them in the profane world where they live their struggling lives have nothing animal about them, although others may often deny that they are human (they are in fact lower than the dignity of animals). The various objects of taboo evoke neither horror nor nausea in them, or too little at any rate. But without feeling them intensely themselves they know what other people's reactions are. The person who says that a dying man is going to "snuff it" sees that man as dying like a dog, but he is aware of the hopeless degradation his coarse words imply. The coarse expressions describing the organs, products or acts of sex are degrading in the same way. These words are prohibited. There is a general taboo upon naming those organs. To name them in a shameless manner is a step from transgression to the indifference that puts the most sacred on the same footing as the profane.

The lowest kind of prostitute has fallen as far as she can go. She might be no less indifferent to the taboo than animals are except that because what she knows about taboos is that others observe them, she cannot attain an absolute indifference; not only has she fallen but she knows she has. She knows she is a human being. Even if she is not ashamed of it, she does know that she lives like a pig.

Conversely, common prostitution as an institution complements the world of Christianity.

Christianity has created a sacred world from which everything horrible or impure has been excluded. In its turn, low prostitution has created the contemporary profane world where men have slumped into hopeless indifference before the unclean and from which the lucid precision of the working world has been shut out.

It is difficult to distinguish the workings of Christianity from the much vaster process exploited and given a coherent form by Christianity.

I have referred to the world of transgression and I said that one of its most obvious characteristics was its alliance with animal nature. The confusion of animal with human and animal with divine is the mark of very early humanity (and it persists with hunting peoples at least), but the substitution of human deities for animal ones came before Christianity. There was a slow progression of ideas rather than a revolution. Looked at as a whole, the transition from a purely religious society (and I connect the principle of transgression with the state of society) to the times when morality gradually established itself and gained predominance is a very difficult problem. It varies from country to country in the civilised world, and the victory of morality and the sovereignty of taboos were not everywhere as clear-cut as with Christianity. Nevertheless I think there is a perceptible link between the importance of morality and contempt for animals: contempt implies that man thinks he has a moral value that animals do not possess and which raises him far above them. In so far as "God made man in his own image", man had the monopoly of morality as opposed to inferior creatures and the attributes of deity vanished from the animal kingdom. Only the devil remained part beast, with his tail the sign first of transgression and then of degradation, of a hopelessness that is the counterweight of the affirmation of the Good and the duties imposed by the Good. Degradation would call forth moral indignation more readily and more whole-heartedly, of course: it is quite indefensible, whereas transgression is not. In any case Christianity's condemnation of degradation has also been responsible for the attitude that the whole of eroticism is something evil. The devil was a rebellious angel at the start, but the gaudy colours of revolt wore thin; rebellion was punished by despair, and what had been transgression turned into hopelessness. The anguish of transgression promised transcendental joy, but despair could only become more despairing. What had these fallen creatures left to hope for? They could only wallow like pigs in their own degradation.

Yes, like pigs. In this Christian world where morality and degradation are interdependent, animals are now disgusting. "This Christian world", for Christianity is morality pushed to its logical conclusion, the only form of morality in which the balance of potentialities could be achieved.

Eroticism, Evil and social degradation

The social basis of low prostitution is the same as that of morality and Christianity. It seems that social inequality and poverty, already the cause of one revolution in Egypt, were at the root of a disturbance in civilised countries about six centuries before our own era; the rise of the Hebrew prophets, among other movements, can be related to this disturbance. Seen in the light of degraded prostitution which can justifiably be assumed to have originated at this period in the Greco-roman world, the coincidence is ironic. The class of social outcasts almost certainly had no share in the desire to exalt the lowly and cast down the mighty from their seats: at the very bottom of the social ladder, they had no aims at all. The morality which exalted the lowly only served to oppress them further. The Church's curse fell most heavy upon those who were already down.

The religious side of eroticism was the one that mattered most to the Church, the one that called forth her full wrath. Witches were burnt, low-class prostitutes allowed to live. But the degradation of prostitution was stressed and used to illustrate the nature of sin.

The present situation results from the dual attitude of the

E*

Church, and its corollary, the dual attitude in men's minds. When the sacred and the Good were held to be identical, when religious eroticism was set outside the pale, the rational denial of Evil was the rejoinder. Then followed a world in which condemned transgression meant nothing and profanation itself almost lost its force. The only remaining escape-valve was hopeless degradation. Falling from grace was a dead-end for the fallen, but degraded eroticism was a sort of incitement without the satanic quality. For no-one believed in the devil now, and even to condemn eroticism as such was meaningless. Degradation at least continued to signify Evil, though no longer an Evil denounced by other people none too sure that they did in fact condemn it. Prostitutes fall as low as they do because they acquiesce in their own sordid condition. That may happen involuntarily, but the use of coarse language looks like a conscious decision; it is a way of spurning human dignity. Human life is the Good, and so the acceptance of degradation is a way of spitting upon the good, a way of spitting upon human dignity.

The sexual organs and the sexual act in particular are referred to by degrading names from the jargon of the dregs of society. Those organs and acts have other names, but some are scientific and others, more rarely used and shorter lived, belong to childhood or the shyness of lovers. The dirty words for love are closely and irrevocably associated with that secret life we lead concurrently with our profession of the loftiest sentiments. These unnameable names formulate the general horror for us, in fact, if we do not belong to the degraded class. They express it with violence, and are themselves violently rejected from the world of decency. No communication is conceivable between the two worlds.

The effects of this are useless to the world of the fallen by itself. Dirty language is an expression of hatred. But it gives decent lovers the same kind of feeling as transgression or profanation used to do. The decent woman saying to the man in her arms: "I love your——" might echo Bandelaire: "The unique, supreme pleasure of love lies in the certainty of doing wrong." But she already knows that eroticism is not wrong in itself. Evil is only evil when it leads to the abject condition of the thieving rabble and the lowest type of prostitute. This woman has nothing in common with such people and she detests their moral turpitude. She agrees that the organ named is not disgraceful in itself. But from the folk who range themselves hideously on the side of evil she borrows the word that reveals the truth at last: that the member she loves is accursed, that she only knows it for what it is in so far as it fills her with horror, yet that the horror is revealed even as she transcends it. She wishes to side with the free-thinkers, but rather than lose the sense of the elementary taboo without which eroticism cannot exist, she turns to those who deny all taboos, all shame, and who can only maintain the denial through violence.

CHAPTER XIII

BEAUTY

Man's fundamental contradiction

Thus the contrast between the bursting plethora of the being lost in continuity, and the will to survive of the separate individual, persists through many changes. If transgression is impossible, then profanation takes its place. Degradation, which turns eroticism into something foul and horrible, is better than the neutrality of reasonable and non-destructive sexual behaviour. If the taboo loses its force, if it is no longer believed in, transgression is impossible; but the feeling of transgression persists if only through sexual aberrations. That feeling has no comprehensible objective basis. How can it be understood, unless we go right back to the inevitable agony of the discontinuous creature doomed to die, that violence alone, blind violence, can burst the barriers of the rational world and lead us into continuity?

We define these barriers at all events, positing the taboo, positing God and even degradation. Yet always we step outside them once they have been defined. Two things are inevitable; we cannot avoid dying nor can we avoid bursting through our barriers, and they are one and the same.

But as we break through the barriers, as we die, we strive to escape from the terror of death and the terror that belongs even to the continuity glimpsed beyond those boundaries.[1]

---

[1] However on our way to death and continuity did we come to imagine God as a person concerned for our individual immortality, careful for the very hairs on a man's head? I know that this side sometimes disappears in the love of God and that violence is sometimes revealed beyond the conceivable and the conceived. I know that violence and the unkown have never excluded the possibility of knowledge and reason. But the unknown is not knowledge, discontinuity is not continuity which destroys and kills it. The world of discontinuity has the horrible power of imagin-

We invest the breaking of our barriers with some tangible form if necessary. We try to think of it as a thing. Left to ourselves, we jib at death and have to be forced to go the whole way. We are incessantly trying to hoodwink ourselves, trying to get at continuity, which implies that the boundaries have been crossed, without actually crossing the boundaries of this discontinuous life. We want to get across without taking the final step, while remaining cautiously on the hither side. We can conceive of nothing except in terms of our own life, and beyond that, it seems to us everything is wiped out. Beyond death, in fact, begins the inconceivable which we are usually not brave enough to face. Yet the inconceivable is the expression of our own impotence. We know that death destroys nothing, leaves the totality of existence intact, but we still cannot imagine the continuity of being as a whole beyond our own death, or whatever it is that dies in us. We cannot accept the fact that this has limits. At all costs we need to transcend them, but we should like to transcend them and maintain them simultaneously.

As we are about to take the final step, we are beside ourselves with desire, impotent, in the clutch of a force that demands our disintegration. But the object of our urgent desire is there in front of us and it binds us to the very life that our desire will not be contained by. How sweet it is to remain in the grip of the desire to burst out without going the whole way, without taking the final step! How sweet it is to gaze long upon the object of our desire, to live on in our desire, instead of dying by going the whole way, by

ing death, since in discontinuity knowledge is possible—death lying beyond knowledge and beyond the conceivable. So the distance between God, in whom violence and reason (continuity and discontinuity) co-exist, and the prospect of being torn asunder that confronts the intact personality (knowledge confronted by the unknown), is a slight one. But experience does show God as a means of escaping from the delirium rarely touched by God's love, it does show God as good, guarantor of social order and discontinuous life. What the love of God finally rises to is really the death of God. But on this point we can have no knowledge except to know that knowledge is finite. That does not mean that the experience of God's love does not give us the most truthful indications. We must not be surprised if theory does not invalidate possible experience. The quest is always for continuity to be reached through the "theopathic state". The paths of this endeavour are never straight ones.

yielding to the excessive violence of desire! We know that possession of the object we are afire for is out of the question. It is one thing or another: either desire will consume us entirely, or its object will cease to fire us with longing. We can possess it on one condition only, that gradually the the desire it arouses will fade. Better for desire to die than for us to die, though! We can make do with an illusion. If we possess its object we shall seem to achieve our desire without dying. Not only do we renounce death, but also we let our desire, really the desire to die, lay hold of its object and we keep it while we live on. We enrich our life instead of losing it.

Possession accentuates the objective quality of whatever may induce us to transcend our own limitations.[1] What prostitution puts forward as an object of desire (prostitution in itself is simply this offering of something as an object of desire), but fails to supply (if it is the prostitution of degradation and makes something foul of it), is there as something beautiful to be possessed. Beauty is its meaning, what gives it its value, and indeed the element that makes it desirable. This is chiefly so if desire is less concerned with an immediate response (the chance of transcending the limits) than with long and calm possession.

The contrast of purity and uncleanness in beauty

In speaking of the beauty of a woman I shall avoid referring to beauty in general[2]. I wish only to define the function of beauty in eroticism. On an elementary level it is just possible to see the effect of multi-coloured plumage and songs in the sexual life of birds. What the beauty of the feathers and songs means I shall not discuss. I do not contest their beauty, and I am even prepared to admit that animals are more or less beautiful as they more or less resemble the

[1] To deny ourselves as objects.
[2] I am fully aware that this section is incomplete. I have tried to give a coherent summary of eroticism, not an exhaustive description. Here I am concerned with feminine beauty in particular. There are many gaps in this book; this is only one of them.

ideal specimen of their kind. Beauty is none the less sub-jective, varying according to the inclinations of those assessing it. In certain cases we may believe that animals react to it as we do, but this is a risky supposition. I shall merely assume that human beauty is appreciated according to the current ideal. It varies, sometimes most unfortunately, on a central theme; there is not so very much room for personal preferences. However, it seems necessary to insist on one lowest common denominator applicable to man's appreciation of animal beauty as of human beauty. (Youth should also be included in this basic standard.)

Now there is a second element, less obvious but no less powerful, in assessing the beauty of a man or woman. The further removed from the animal is their appearance, the more beautiful they are reckoned.

This question is a difficult one and many considerations are bound up in it. I shall not examine it in detail but merely indicate that it arises. Any suggestion of the animal in the human form is unquestionably repugnant, and more par-ticularly the anthropoid shape is found disgusting. The erotic value of feminine forms seems to me to be bound up with the absence of the natural heaviness that suggests the physical use of the limbs and the necessity for the framework of bone: the more ethereal the shapes and the less clearly they depend on animal reality or on a human physiological reality, the better they respond to the fairly widespread image of the desirable woman. I shall discuss later the importance attached to hair which has a peculiar significance for human beings.

I think that what I have said is indubitably true. But the opposite, only secondarily obvious, also holds. The image of the desirable woman as first imagined would be insipid and unprovocative if it did not at the same time also promise or reveal a mysterious animal aspect, more momentously suggestive. The beauty of the desirable woman suggests her private parts, the hairy ones, to be precise, the animal ones. Instinct has made sure that we shall desire these parts.

But above and beyond the sexual instinct, erotic desire has other components. Beauty that denies the animal and awakes desire finishes up by exasperating desire and exalting the animal parts.

The final sense of eroticism is death

Together with an effort to reach continuity by breaking with individual discontinuity, the search after beauty entails an effort to escape from continuity. The twofold effort is never at an end: its ambiguity crystallises and carries onward the workings of eroticism.

Multiplication upsets the simplicity of existence, excess overturns the barriers and finally overflows in some way.

There is always some limit which the individual accepts. He identifies this limit with himself. Horror seizes him at the thought that this limit may cease to be. But we are wrong to take this limit and the individual's acceptance of it seriously. The limit is only there to be overreached. Fear and horror are not the real and final reaction; on the contrary, they are a temptation to overstep the bounds.

We know that once we are conscious of it, we have to react to the desire ingrained in us to overstep the limits. We want to overstep them, and the horror we feel shows to what excesses we shall be brought, excesses which, without the initial horror, would be unthinkable.

If beauty so far removed from the animal is passionately desired, it is because to possess is to sully, to reduce to the animal level. Beauty is desired in order that it may be befouled; not for its own sake, but for the joy brought by the certainty of profaning it.

In sacrifice, the victim is chosen so that its perfection shall give point to the full brutality of death. Human beauty, in the union of bodies, shows the contrast between the purest aspect of mankind and the hideous animal quality of the sexual organs. The paradox of ugliness and beauty in eroticism is strikingly expressed by Leonardo da Vinci in his Notebooks: "The act of coition and the members

employed are so ugly that but for the beauty of the faces, the
adornments of their partners and the frantic urge, Nature
would lose the human race." Leonardo does not see that the
charm of a fair face or fine clothes is effective in that that
fair face promises what clothes conceal. The face and its
beauty must be profaned, first by uncovering the woman's
secret parts, and then by putting the male organ into them.
No-one doubts the ugliness of the sexual act. Just as death
does in sacrifice, the ugliness of the sexual union makes for
anguish. But the greater the anguish—within the measure
of the partners' strength—the stronger the realisation of
exceeding the bounds and the greater the accompanying
rush of joy. Tastes and customs vary, but that cannot
prevent a woman's beauty (her humanity, that is) from
making the animal nature of the sexual act obvious and
shocking. For a man, there is nothing more depressing than
an ugly woman, for then the ugliness of the organs and the
sexual act cannot show up in contrast.

Beauty has a cardinal importance, for ugliness cannot be
spoiled, and to despoil is the essence of eroticism. Humanity
implies the taboos, and in eroticism it and they are transgressed. Humanity is transgressed, profaned and besmirched.
The greater the beauty, the more it is befouled.

The potentialities here are so numerous and so intangible
that the various aspects cannot be arranged to form a coherent whole. Repetitions and contradictions are inevitable. But
the main trend is clear enough. There is always the transition
from compression to explosion. The forms may alter but the
violence is constant, at once horrifying and fascinating.
Degraded, men are the same as animals, profanation is the
same as transgression.

I referred to profanation when I was discussing beauty;
I might just as well have talked about transgression, since
animal nature being ignorant of taboos has in our eyes the
significance of transgression. But the idea of profanation is
more readily comprehensible to us.

It has been impossible for me to describe without contradictions and without going over the same ground more than once a collection of erotic situations which are anyway nearer one another than these deliberate attempts to distinguish between them would have one suppose. I have been obliged to point these distinctions in order to make the central issue plain through many vicissitudes. There is no one form in which some aspect or another may not be apparent, however. All forms of eroticism are possible in marriage. There is something animal about human degradation, and in the orgy the object of desire may stand out with staggering clarity.

Similarly the need to make the fundamental truth evident obscures another fact, the reconciliation[1] of apparent opposites without which eroticism would not exist. I have been obliged to stress the twist given the original movement. In its vicissitudes eroticism appears to move away from its essence, which connects it with the nostalgia of lost continuity. Human life cannot follow the movement which draws it towards death without a shudder and without trying to cheat. I have shown it cheating, sneaking aside along the paths described.

---

[1] Of desire and individual love, of the persistence of life and the pull of death, of sexual frenzy and care of children.

PART TWO

SOME ASPECTS OF EROTICISM

CHAPTER I

KINSEY, THE UNDERWORLD AND WORK

> "Thence day-devouring idleness; for excesses in love
> demand both rest and food to restore lost energy.
> Thence the dislike of all work that forces these folk into
> quick ways of finding money."

Balzac: Splendours and Miseries of Courtesans.

*Eroticism is an experience that cannot be assessed from outside
in the way an object can*

It is possible for me to regard the study of man's sexual
behaviour with the interest of a scientist who observes
almost absently the play of light on the flight of a wasp. Of
course, human conduct can be the object of scientific study:
it is then observed with no more humanity than if it were
an insect's. Man is an animal before all else and he can study
his own reactions as he studies those of animals. Certain
reactions, however, cannot be entirely identified with
scientific data. These are the ones which sometimes reduce
men to the level of the beast by generally accepted standards.
More, these standards require them to be hidden, not to be
spoken of, and not to be wholly accepted in man's conscious
awareness. Ought the study of this sort of behaviour,
usually common to men and animals, be accorded a place
apart?

However low a man may sink he is in truth never just a
thing as an animal is. He conserves a certain dignity, a
fundamental nobility and even a sacred truth which attests
that he cannot be put to servile use (even when this abuse
occurs in practice). A man can never be regarded as a

means; even if this happens temporarily he conserves to some extent the sovereign importance of himself as an end in himself; in him persists the quality that makes it impossible to kill him and still less to eat him without horror. A man can always be killed and even eaten. But such acts are rarely insignificant for another man: at the very least nobody in his right senses could pretend that they are not charged with significance for other people. This taboo, this sacredness of human life is as universal as the taboos bearing on sexuality (like the one on incest, the one associated with menstruation and the varying but constant rules of decency).

In the world today only animals can be treated as things. A man can do whatever he likes with them; he is accountable to no-one. He may really be aware that the beast he strikes down is not so very different from himself. But even while he admits the similarity, his furtive act of recognition is immediately contradicted by a fundamental and silent denial. In spite of what may be believed to the contrary the feeling that assigns a spirit to man and the body to the beast is always disputed in vain. The body is a thing, vile, slavish, servile, just like a stone or a piece of wood. Only the spirit with its intimate and subjective truth cannot be reduced to a thing. It is sacred, housed in a profane body that only becomes sacred in its turn as death reveals the incomparable worth of the spirit.

So much is obvious at a first glance. What follows is not so simple and only becomes clear after lengthy consideration.

We are animals anyway. Men and spirits we may be, but we cannot help the animal in us persisting and often overwhelming us. Opposite the spiritual pole stands the pole of sexual exuberance demonstrating how animal life persists in us. Thus our sexual behaviour, belonging to the body, could in a way be regarded as a thing: the sexual organ is itself a thing (a part of that body which is itself a thing). This behaviour can be taken as the functioning of the sexual organ as an object. The member is really a thing just as a foot is (a hand can perhaps be regarded as human and the eye expresses the life of the spirit, but we have a sexual organ and feet in a very animal way). Besides, we consider that the delirium of the senses brings us down to the level of the beasts.

Yet if we conclude from this that the sexual act is a thing just like an animal in the hands of a vivisectionist, and if we think that it is outside the control of man's mind, we come up against a serious difficulty. If we are confronted by a thing our conscience is untroubled. The contents of our consciousness are easy for us to grasp if we tackle the objects they represent sideways on and consider the external aspect of such objects. But on the contrary, each time we can know the contents from within, without being able to relate them to their distinct and concomitant external manifestations we can only talk about them in a vague way[1].

Let us consider the Kinsey Reports in which sexual activity is treated statistically like external data[2]. Their authors have not really observed from the outside any of the inumerable facts they report. They were observed from the inside by the people whose experiences they were. Their methodical arrangement depends on intermediary confessions and accounts, relied upon by those who called themselves observers. The doubts which people have thought they ought to cast on the results or at least on their general value seem technical and superficial. The authors surrounded themselves with precautions that cannot be ignored (verification, repetition of the enquiry at long intervals, comparisons of graphs obtained in the same circumstances by different interviewers, etc.). The sexual behaviour of our fellows has ceased to be so completely hidden from us because of this gigantic enquiry. But the point is that what

[1] If I discuss *myself* clearly and distinctly, I do it by positing my own existence as an isolated reality, similar to that of other men whom I consider from outside and I could not distinguish other men clearly except in so far as they possess the absolute identity with themselves in their apparent isolation that I take things to have.

[2] Kinsey, Pomeroy and Martin, *Sexual Behaviour in the Human Male*, Saunders, Philadelphia and London, 1948.

Kinsey, Pomeroy and Martin, *Sexual Behaviour in the Human Female*, Saunders, Philadelphia and London, 1953.

this effort showed us was that the facts were not thought of as things before these machinations were put into practice. Before the Reports sexual life had the well defined reality of an object only on the lowest plane. Now, this reality is fairly clear if not very clear at all levels. Now it is possible to discuss sexual conduct as one discusses things. This is to some extent the originality of the Reports.

The first reaction is to dispute this strange and often senselessly clumsy business of bringing man's sexual life down to the level of objective data. But our intellectual operations are aimed only at immediate results. An intellectual operation is really only a transition: beyond the desired result lie consequences we did not anticipate. The Reports were based on the principle that the facts of sex are things, but supposing they were to make it obvious in the long run that the facts of sex are not things? Perhaps as a rule our consciousness demands a double process: the contents are to be envisaged as things as far as possible but they are never to be more clearly revealed or we made more aware of them than at that moment when their external aspect is seen to be inadequate and we turn back to their inner aspect. I shall now examine the mechanism of this reaction as far as sexual disorders may show it at work.

The reasons against observing genetic activity from outside are not only conventional ones. There is a contagiousness that rules out the possibility of dispassionate observation. It has nothing to do with that of germ-carried diseases. The contagion in question is like that of yawning or of laughter. A yawn makes one yawn, repeated gusts of laughter make one want to laugh, and if sexual activity is witnessed it is capable of rousing desire. It may also inspire disgust. Or we might put it that sexual activity even if only shown by a hardly perceptible agitation or by clothes in disarray easily induces in a witness a feeling of participation (at least if physical beauty lends significance to an incongruity of appearance). This is a disturbed state of mind, one which must normally bar methodical scientific observation. Seeing and hearing a man laugh I participate in his emotion from inside myself. This sensation felt inside me communicates itself to me and that is what makes me laugh: we have an immediate knowledge of the other person's laughter when we laugh ourselves or of excitement when we share it. That is why laughter or excitement or even yawning are not things: we cannot usually feel part of stone or board but we do feel part of the nakedness of the woman in our arms. The kind of man that Lévy-Bruhl called "primitive" could feel part of stone, it is true; but the stone was not a thing to him; it was living in his eyes just as he was himself. Lévy-Bruhl may well have been wrong to ascribe this way of thinking to primitive humanity alone. In poetry we only have to forget that stone is stone and talk about moonstones, the stone becomes part of my most intimate feelings for I have imperceptibly shifted ground even as I articulated the words to share in the intimacy of the moonstone. But if nakedness or excessive pleasure are not things, and if like moonstones they cannot be clearly grasped, the consequences are remarkable.

It is an odd thing to be demonstrating that sexual activity, usually treated on a par with meat to be eaten, as flesh that is, wields the same influence as poetry. It is true that poetry these days has questionable intentions and aims at scandalizing when possible. It is no less curious to observe that in sexual matters the body is not necessarily a thing and servile, but poetic and divine though animal. That is what the breadth and oddness of the methods used in the Reports make plain, revealing an impotence to treat their material as an object, as something that can be considered objectively. Any inquiry into the sexual life of subjects under observation is incompatible with scientific objectivity; but the necessarily very large number of appeals to subjective experience compensates for this in some measure. But the huge effort demanded by this means of compensation, this recourse to multiple examples which seem to cancel out the subjective aspect of the observations, brings out one irreducible element in sexual activity: the private feelings as opposed to things that the Reports suggest must exist beyond the graphs and curves. This element defies investigation from outside and cannot be classed under the headings of frequency, modality, age, profession and class. These things can be observed objectively but the essential thing eludes definition. We even ought to ask openly: Do these books discuss sexual life? Is it man we should be discussing if we simply gave numbers, measurements, classifications according to age and the colour of eyes? What man means to us transcends details of this sort; they invite consideration certainly, but all they do is furnish inessential data about something already known[1]. Similarly, true knowledge of man's sexual life is not to be found in these Reports; statistics, weekly frequencies, averages mean something only when we clearly have a picture of the surge of activity in question. Or if they really do enrich our knowledge, it is in the way I have mentioned, by giving us the feeling of something unamenable to description as we read. For example, and the apparently impossible incongruity is there before our eyes, we have to laugh on reading this title underneath the ten columns of a table: *Causes of Orgasm for the population of the United States* and these words under the columns of figures: *Masturbation, Petting, Intercourse, conjugal or otherwise, Animal Intercourse, Homosexuality.* These mechanical classifications, usually applied to things like tons of steel or copper, are profoundly incompatible with the realities of the inner being. Once at least the authors realised this, admitting that the enquiries, the sexual case histories at the basis of their analysis do sometimes appear as private matters in spite of everything; it is no business of theirs but these histories, they say, often imply the memory of deep wounds, frustrating pain, unsatisfied desire, disappointments, tragic situations and utter catastrophe. The un-

---

[1] Even the essentials of somatic anthropology means something only when they clarify what is already known and define the place of human beings in the animal kingdom.

happiness lies outside the inner meaning of the sexual act but it is seen to be felt very deeply and it cannot be extricated and isolated without losing its truth. Thus the authors themselves knew what abyss yawned beneath the facts they report. Though they may have sensed that much, the difficulties could not deter them. Their bias and their weakness are nowhere more apparent than in a case where they make an exception to their general rule of going by the subject's own account and not by direct observation. Without having personally witnessed the cases, they publish certain data furnished presumably by the objective observation of other parties. They have examined the time necessary—very short —for infants of six to twelve months to reach an orgasm through masturbation. These times, they tell us, were assessed either with a stopwatch or a chronometer. The incompatibility of the manner of observation and the fact observed, of the method suitable for things and an always embarrassingly intimate act goes beyond the point where it is laughable. There are more serious obstacles to the observation of adult practices, but the helplessness of the child and the immeasurable tenderness that disarms us in his presence make the trick with the watch a hurtful thing. In spite of the authors the truth will out; only a serious lack of understanding would confuse something completely different in kind, something sacred, with a mere thing; it is disturbing to transfer to the vulgarity of the profane world of things the momentous quality we sense in the secret violence of man or child. The violence of human sexuality, animal activity as it is, never fails to disarm us; to perceive it is to be deeply stirred.

Work binds us to an objective awareness of things and reduces sexual exuberance. Only the underworld retains its exuberance.

Let me return to the fact that theoretically animal nature can usually be treated as a thing. I cannot lay too great an emphasis on this; I shall endeavour to throw light on the problem by pursuing my analysis with the help of data from the Reports.

This data is abundant enough but its implications have not been worked out. We are faced with a voluminous collection of facts remarkably well assembled. The methods are reminiscent of those of the Gallup Institute and have been brought to a high pitch of efficiency, though it is harder to admire the theories they spring from.

For the authors sexuality is a normal and acceptable biological function in whatever form it appears. But religious principles restrict this natural activity[1]. The most interesting series of statistics in the first report shows the weekly frequency of the orgasm. Varying according to age and social category it is generally well below seven; above seven is classed at a high rate. But the normal rate for anthropoids is classed at a high rate. But the normal rate for anthropoids is once a day. Man's normal rate, the authors assure us, could be as high as that of the great ape but for the restrictions imposed by religion. They rate this stand on the results of their enquiry. They have classified the replies of people of different religious faiths by contrasting practising and non-practising members. 7.4% of pious Protestants as against 11.7% of nominal Protestants reach or exceed the rate of seven per week; similarly with 8.1% of pious Catholics as against 20.5% of the not so pious. These are remarkable figures. Obviously the practice of religion does put the brake on sexual activity. But our observers are impartial and indefatigable. They are not too content to produce data favourable to their theories. They pursue their researches in all directions. The frequency rates are given for each social class: labourers, factory workers, white collar workers, professional classes. The working population as a whole gives a figure of 10% at the high rate of frequency. Only the underworld reaches 49.4%. These are the most remarkable figures. The fact that they indicate is less uncertain than piety (think of the cults of Kali and Dionysos, Tantrism and

---

[1] An American critic, Lionel Trilling, is singularly right to insist on the ingenuousness of the authors who thought they had said all there was to be said when they used the word "natural".

all the other erotic forms of religion): that factor is work, whose nature and use have nothing ambiguous about them. By work man orders the world of things and brings himself down to the level of a thing among things; work makes a worker a means to an end. Human work is essential to mankind, is alone in its unequivocal opposition to animal nature. These statistics separate off the world of work and worker; these can be reduced to the level of things; they cut out the entire and unassailable privacy of sex.

There is a paradox in the contrast shown by these figures. Separate scales of values are associated in an unexpected way. Already we have seen how animal exuberance cannot be treated as a thing. Here the most careful attention is called for.

What I said in the first place showed how the fundamental opposition between man and thing could not be formulated without implying that animals could be regarded as things. On the one side is the external world, the world of things, of which animals are a part. On the other is the world of man, an inner world, a subjective world, a world of the spirit. But if the animal is nothing but a thing, if that is what sets it apart from man, it is still not a thing in the same way as an inert object is, a paving stone, say, or a shovel. Only the inert object, especially if it is manufactured and the product of work, is the thing proper, entirely void of mystery and subordinated to ends outside itself. Whatever has no meaning for itself is a thing. In this sense animals are not in themselves things but man treats them as such; they are things in so far as they are worked with as herds of sheep or cattle or as beasts of burden. If the animal enters the cycle of useful activity as a means and not as an end it is reduced to the status of a thing. Yet this reduction denies its real nature. The animal is only a thing while man is able to deny its true nature. If we no longer had that power, if we were no longer in a position to act as though the animal were a thing, if, for instance, a tiger should leap out upon us, the animal would not be essentially a thing, it would not be an object pure and simple, it would be a subject with its own inner reality.

Similarly the animal quality that persists in man, his sexual exuberance, could only be thought of as a thing if we had the power to abolish it and to go on living as if it did not exist. We do indeed deny it but vainly. Sexuality, thought of as filthy or beastly, is still the greatest barrier to the reduction of man to the level of the thing. A man's innermost pride is bound up with his virility. The connection is not with the animal denied but with the deep and incommensurable element of animal nature. This is also why we cannot be reduced as oxen are to a mere source of energy, to instruments, to things. In man as opposed to the animals there is indisputably an element that cannot be forced to work or treated as a thing. It is categorically impossible for man to be enslaved and suppressed to the same extent as the animals. But this is only evident at a second glance; man is first of all a working animal, submitting to work and thence obliged to renounce some of his exuberance. There is nothing arbitrary in sexual restrictions: each man has only a certain amount of energy and if he devotes some of it to work he has to reduce his sexual energy by that much. So humanity, seen from the human, anti-animal standpoint of work, is that within us which reduces us to things and our animal nature preserves the values of our subjective existence.

It is worth formulating this exactly.

Animal nature, or sexual exuberance, is that which prevents us from being reduced to mere things.

Human nature, on the contrary, geared to specific ends in work, tends to make things of us at the expense of our sexual exuberance.

Work as opposed to sexual exuberance is the condition of objective awareness

The statistical data of the first Kinsey Report echo these principles with startling accuracy. In the underworld alone, where no work is done and where behaviour in general adds up to a denial of humanity do we find 49.4% for the high rate of frequency. The authors of the Report think that on the average this is the normal frequency in nature—the animal nature of the anthropoids. But this figure is unique and contrasts with the generality of truly human behaviour which varies according to the groups but ranges from rates of 16.1% to 8.9%. The distribution is worth examining closely. By and large the rate varies with the degree of "humanisation"; the more humanised men are the more their exuberance is diminished. Here are the details: the high frequency rate occurs with 15.4% of labourers, 16.1% of semi-skilled workers, 12.1% of skilled workers, 10.7% of lower white collar workers, 8.9% of upper white collar workers.

There is one exception however: from the upper white collar workers to the professional or managerial classes the figure goes up by more than 3% to reach 12.4%. But the drop from labourers to upper white collar workers is fairly regular and the difference of 3.5% between the latter and the professional class represents an increase of about 30%: the rate goes up by about two or three orgasms a week. It is quite easy to understand why the figures go up again suddenly for the dominant class. This class enjoys a certain amount of leisure compared with the others, and its wealth does not always involve an exceptional amount of work on the average; clearly it has more spare energy than the working classes. This compensates for the fact that it is more humanised than any other class.

The exception of the dominant class has a clearer meaning however. When I pointed out that animal nature had its divine aspect and human nature its servile one, I had one reserve to make: there must nevertheless be something in human nature that cannot be treated as a thing and forced to work, so that it is absolutely impossible to enslave man as animals can be enslaved. This element is found at all levels of society but belongs chiefly to the ruling class. It is easy to see how being reduced to the level of a thing can only ever be a relative matter. Being a thing means being somebody's thing; and in that object, an animal or a man may be things, but they are things belonging to some man. A man especially can only be a thing belonging to another man, he to another and so on, but not indefinitely. The time comes when humanity is bound to assert itself, even if it has seemed to be enslaved, when, a certain man being dependant on no-one, the subordination of the masses derives significance in the person of the man who profits from it but who cannot himself be subordinated to anything. This happens with the dominant class, upon whom the duty generally devolves of freeing mankind in the persons of its own members from the bonds that make it a thing.

To that end, what is more, this class is usually dispensed from the need to work and if sexual energy can be measured it must usually have had as much to spend as the American underworld today.[1] American civilisation has moved away from that principle because the bourgeoisie, the single dominant class from the beginning, is hardly ever idle; (it retains some upper class privileges for all that). This accounts for the relatively low figure indicating sexual vigour.

A classification of the Kinsey Report founded on the frequency of orgasms is a simplification. It is not entirely meaningless but it leaves out one important factor. It does not take into account the length of time required for the sexual act. Now the energy spent in sexual activity is not just that used up for the emission. Sexual play consumes a far from negligible sum of energy in its own right. The expenditure of energy of an anthropoid whose orgasm is over in about ten seconds is obviously less than that of an educated man whose sexual play goes on for hours. But the art of making it last is itself unevenly distributed among the various classes. On this point the Report fails to give its usual wealth of careful detail. Nevertheless it is clear that

[1] In one sense, what is the ruling class but a lucky set of thieves, secure in the assent of the mass of the population? The most primitive peoples tend to reserve polygamy for their chiefs.

prolonged play is a characteristic of the upper classes. Men of the under-privileged classes are content with rapid encounters that though less brief than those of animals do not always enable their partner to achieve a climax. The 12.4% class is about the only one to have carried preliminary play and the art of making it last as far as it will go.

My intention is certainly not to defend the sexual honour of educated men, but these considerations help to make clear what the above statistics mean and to state what the inner-most urges of life require.

What we call the human world is necessarily a world of work, of reduction, that is to say. But labour does not only mean something painful. It is also the road to awareness that led man away from the beasts. Work endowed us with a clear and distinct consciousness of objects and science has always gone hand in hand with technology. Sexual exuberance, on the other hand, leads us away from awareness; it diminishes our perceptive powers, and anyway sexuality given free rein lessens our appetite for work, just as sustained work lessens our sexual appetite. An undeniably rigorous incompatibility, then, exists between awareness bound up with work and sexual activity. As far as man has made himself what he is by work and awareness he has had not only to moderate but also to refuse to acknowledge and even to curse his own super-abundant sexual energy. In one way this refusal has limited man's awareness of himself if not of objects. He has come to know the exterior world but he remains ignorant of his own nature. But if he had not first awoken to awareness through work he would know nothing at all; animal darkness would still hold sway.

The awareness of eroticism, unlike that of external objects, belongs to a darker side; it leads to a silent awakening

We thus achieve awareness only by condemning and by refusing to recognise our sexual life. Eroticism is not the only thing to be brushed aside: we have no direct awareness of anything within us that cannot be reduced to the simplicity of things, of solid objects. In the first instance we are clearly conscious only of things, and anything less sharply defined than a physical object is not clearly perceived at first. It is only later that analogy provides us with concepts not possessing the simplicity of the solid object.

In the first place such concepts are held in the manner of the Kinsey Reports; for the sake of clarity things which are not in the least amenable to treatment as grossly material objects are nevertheless taken to be such. That is how the realities of the inner life enter our appraising consciousness. So it is generally true to say that the realities of our inner experience escape us. Indeed, if we take them for what they are not, we only misjudge them further. We reject the truths implicit in our erotic life if we only regard it as a natural function, when we fail to see its significance, and denounce the absurdity of the laws which hinder its free course. If we affirm that guilty sexuality can be regarded as innocently material, our awareness, far from seeing sexual life as it is, neglects entirely those disturbing aspects which do not fit in with a clear picture. A clear picture is actually a first requirement but because of this the truth escapes notice. Such aspects, felt to be accursed, remain in the twilight where we are a prey to horror and anguish. By exonerating our sexual life from every trace of guilt science has no chance of seeing it for what it is. Our ideas are clarified but at the cost of being blinkered. Science with its emphasis on precision cannot grasp the complexity of the system in which a few factors are pushed to extremes when it rejects the blurred and indistinct realities of sexual life.

To get at the innermost depths of our nature we no doubt can and should go the long way round by way of the objects that purport to represent those intimate depths. If the experience envisaged does not look as if it can be entirely explained in terms of things or even trivial mechanisms, this is when the inner truth is revealed; it is revealed in so far as its accursed aspect is felt. Our secret experience cannot enter directly the field of our conscious awareness, but at least our consciousness can know just when it shifts out of the way the thing it condemns. So our deepest truths come up to consciousness as something accursed and condemned, as sins in fact. Consciousness can and must inevitably maintain a reaction of fear and repugnance to sexual life as long as it recognises the subordinate significance of this fear in favourable circumstances. (We do not have to accept as true the explanation in terms of "sin".) The precious lucidity of methodical knowledge through which man achieves mastery over things, the lucidity that is destroyed by sexual turbulence (or by which, if it comes out victorious, sexual turbulence is suppressed) is always able to admit its limitations if for practical reasons it has to ignore some part of reality. Would it be true lucidity if even while it enlightened us it could not help drawing a veil over some part of the truth? On the other hand would the man perturbed by desire fully apprehend his situation if that desire compelled him to hide his agitation in the dark night that besets him? But in the rending tumult of passion we can at least perceive the tumult and hence focus our intention beyond mere objects on the deepest truths of our passion.

The enormous statistical labour of the Kinsey Report supports this viewpoint, although it does not match their principles and even denies them outright. The Kinsey Report corresponds with the naive and often moving protest against the survivals of a first partly irrational civilisation. But naivety is a limit we do not wish to be bound by. On the contrary we follow the endless movement whose meanderings in the end bring us silently to the awareness of our secret life. The various forms of human life have superseded each other and we finally see how the last step must be taken. A gentle light, not the full glare of science, shows us a reality difficult to come to terms with compared with the reality of things; it makes possible a silent awakening.

CHAPTER II

DE SADE'S SOVEREIGN MAN

Those who are not bound by reason: thieves and kings

There is nothing on our world to parallel the capricious excitement of a crowd obeying impulses of violence with acute sensitivity and unamenable to reason.

Nowadays everyone has to take responsibility for his actions and obey the law of reason in everything. Leftovers from the past do persist but only the anti-social underworld preserves a quantity of energy that does not go into work; this happens on quite a large scale since there is no check on its underhand violence. This is so in the New World anyway, more stringently under the control of cold reason than the Old. (Of course Central and South America are different from the United States, and in another way the Soviet sphere of influence is different from the capitalist countries of Europe—but the facts given in the Kinsey Report are not yet available, and will not be for some long time, for the rest of the world as a whole. There are people who turn up their noses at these statistics, but for all their imperfections can they not see how valuable a Soviet Kinsey Report would be ?)

In the world as it used to be, men used not to renounce their exuberant eroticism for reason's sake as they do now. At any rate they wanted mankind personified by one of their fellows to escape the bonds to which the masses were subject. Everybody agreed that the sovereign should enjoy the privilege of riches and leisure, and the youngest and loveliest girls were reserved for him. Moreover, wars opened up greater possibilities than work for the conquerors. The conquerors of old enjoyed the privileges that are now the prerogative of the American underworld (and this very underworld is nothing but a shoddy leftover). Slavery prolonged the effects of wars and persisted certainly up to the Russian and Chinese revolutions, but the rest of the world still enjoys these effects, or suffers from them, according to one's point of view. In 'the non-communist world North America is indubitably the place where the remoter consequences of slavery are least important as far as social inequality is concerned.

Some sovereign rulers are still with us but for the most part they are domesticated and docile; the autocrats have gone and we are berefit of the vision of the "whole man" desired by a humanity unable to imagine equal personal success for everybody. Tales that have come down to us about the splendid extravagances of kings show us how meagre in comparison are the excesses of the American gangster or wealthy European. What is more, the spectacular apparatus of royalty has disappeared. This is the worst of it. In olden days the spectacle of royal privilege made up for the poverty of common life, just as tragedy on the stage counterbalanced the placidity of common existence. Now the frightening thing is the dénouement, the last act of the comedy the old world lived out.

In literature the idea of absolute and sovereign liberty occurs after the revolutionary denial of the monarchic principle

It was rather like a shower of firework stars, but so bewildering and so dazzlingly bright that it blinded the watchers. The show of pomp had by then long ceased to satisfy the masses. Were they weary of it? Did each man hope to achieve his own satisfactions?

Egypt by the third millennium had ceased to tolerate a state of affairs justified only by the Pharaoh; the rebellious masses demanded a share in those exorbitant privileges and the immortality that had been until then the sovereign's alone. In 1789 the French mob had demanded to live on their own account. The spectacle of the pomp of the aristocracy, far from satisfying them, drew forth louder angry murmurs. One isolated individual, the Marquis de Sade, took advantage of this to develop the system to its logical consequence under a pretence of criticising it.

The Marquis de Sade's system perfects as much as it criticises a certain way of bringing the individual in to the full excercise of all his potentialities above the heads of the goggling crowd. In the first place de Sade tried to use the privileges conferred on him by a feudal régime to further his passions. But the régime was by that time tempered sufficiently with reason (indeed, it almost always had been) to oppose the potential abuse of these privileges by a great lord. De Sade's abuse was apparently no worse than that of other lords of the same times, but he was careless and clumsy and blessed with a rather powerful mother-in-law. His privileges vanished when, a victim of chance, he became a prisoner in Vincennes and then in the Bastille. He was an enemy of the *ancien régime* and fought against it. The excesses of the Terror he condemned but he was a Jacobin and the secretary of a section. He worked out his criticism of the past along two lines: in the one he sided with the Revolution and criticised the monarchy, but in the other he exploited the infinite possibilities of literature and propounded to his readers the concept of a sovereign type of humanity whose privileges would not have to be agreed upon by the masses. The privileges de Sade visualised were outrageous compared with those of kings and lords. They were such as wicked kings and nobles might be expected to possess with impunity in their omnipotence according to the romantic idea. The gratuitous character of this notion and its value as a spectacle gave much more scope than institutions which responded feebly at best to the need for an existence freed from all limits.

Solitude in prison and the terrifying truth of an imaginary moment of success

It had formerly been the general wish that the erotic whims of some outstandingly exuberant personality should be unstintingly satisfied. Yet there were limits, and de Sade outstripped them to a staggering degree. De Sade's sovereign individual is no longer a man encouraged to his extravagance by the crowd. The kind of sexual satisfaction that suits everyone is not for de Sade's fantastic characters. The kind of sexuality he has in mind runs counter to the desires of other people (of almost all others, that is); they are to be victims, not partners. De Sade makes his heroes uniquely self-centred; the partners are denied any rights at all: this is the key to his system. If eroticism leads to harmony between the partners its essential principle of violence and death is invalidated. Sexual union is fundamentally a compromise, a half-way house between life and death. Communion between the participants is a limiting factor and it must be ruptured before the true violent nature of eroticism can be seen, whose translation into practice corresponds with the notion of the sovereign man. The man subject to no restraints of any kind falls on his victims with the devouring fury of a vicious hound.

The events of de Sade's real life lead one to suspect an element of braggadocio in his insistence on sovereignty seen as a denial of the rights and feelings of others. But the boasting was essential if he was to work out a system completely free from human weakness. In his life de Sade took other people into account, but his conception of fulfilment worked over and over in his lonely cell led him to deny outright the claims of other people. The Bastille was a desert; his writing was the only outlet for his passions and in it he pushed back the limits of what was possible beyond the craziest dreams ever framed by man. These books distilled in prison have given us a true picture of a man for whom other people did not count at all.

De Sade's morality, says Maurice Blanchot[1] "is founded on absolute solitude as a first given fact. De Sade said over

[1] *Lautréamont et Sade*. Editions de Minuit, 1949, pages 220-221. Maurice Blanchot's study is not only the first coherent account of De Sade's thought; in the author's words, it helps man to understand himself by helping to modify the conditions of all understanding.

and over again in different ways that we are born alone,
there are no links between one man and another. The only
rule of conduct then is that I prefer those things which affect
me pleasurably and set at nought the undesirable effects of
my preferences on other people. The greatest suffering of
others always counts for less than my own pleasure. What
matter if I must purchase my most trivial satisfaction through
a fantastic accumulation of wrongdoing? For my satisfaction
gives me pleasure, it exists in myself, but the consequences
of crime do not touch me, they are outside me"

Maurice Blanchot's analysis faithfully matches de Sade's
basic thinking. This thinking is doubtless artificial. It fails
to take into account the actual make-up of every real man,
inconceivable if shorn of the links made by others with him
and by him with others. The independence of one man has
never ceased to be any more than a boundary to the inter-
dependence of mankind, without which there would be no
human life. This is of cardinal importance. But de Sade's
doctrine is not so wide of the mark as all that. It may deny
the reality on which life is based, yet we do experience
moments of excess that stir us to the roots of our being and
give us strength enough to allow free rein to our elemental
nature. But if we were to deny those moments we should fail
to understand our own nature.

De Sade's doctrine is nothing more nor less than the
logical consequence of these moments that deny reason.

By definition, excess stands outside reason. Reason is
bound up with work and the purposeful activity that incar-
nates its laws. But pleasure mocks at toil, and toil we have
seen to be unfavourable to the pursuit of intense pleasure. If
one calculates the ratio between energy consumed and the
usefulness of the results, the pursuit of pleasure even if
reckoned as useful is essentially extravagant; the more so in
that usually pleasure has no end product, is thought of as an
end in itself and is desired for its very extravagance. This is
where de Sade comes in. He does not formulate the above
principles, but he implies them by asserting that pleasure is

more acute if it is criminal and the more abhorrent the crime the greater the pleasure. One can see how the excesses of pleasure lead to the denial of the rights of other people which is, as far as man is concerned, an excessive denial of the principle upon which his life is based.

In this de Sade was convinced that he had made a decisive discovery in the field of knowledge. If crime leads a man to the greatest sensual satisfactions, the fulfilment of the most powerful desires, what could be more important than to deny that solidarity which opposes crime and prevents the enjoyment of its fruits? I can picture this violent truth striking him in the loneliness of his prison. From that instant he ceased to have any truck with anything, even in himself, that might have invalidated his system. Had he not been in love himself, just like anyone else? When he had run off with his sister-in-law, had not that helped to get him locked up by arousing his mother-in-law's wrath so that she procured the fatal *lettre de cachet*? Latterly was he not to adopt political views based on concern for the welfare of the masses? Was he not horror-struck to see from his window, in the prison to which his opposition to the methods of the Terror had brought him, the guillotine at work? And finally did he not shed "tears of blood" over the loss of a manuscript in which he had striven to reveal—to other men, observe—the truth of the insignificance of other people?[1] He may have told himself that none the less the truth of sexual attraction is not fully apparent if consideration for other people paralyses its action. He refused to contemplate anything he could not experience in the interminable silence of his cell where

---

[1] *The Cent Vingt Journées de Sodome* is the first work in which he describes the sovereign life, the life of crime of licentious scoundrels dedicated to unlawful pleasure. A day or so before July 14th, 1789, he was moved to another prison for having tried to stir up the passers-by to rebellion by shouting out of his window "People of Paris, they are cutting the prisoners' throats!" He was not allowed to take anything with him and the manuscript of the *Cent Vingt Journées* was stolen in the looting that followed the fall of the Bastille. Scroungers picked over the piles of assorted objects littering the courtyard for anything they thought might be of us or value. In 1900 the manuscript was recovered from a German bookseller. De Sade himself said he had wept tears of blood for a loss which did indeed affect other people; it affected humanity in general.

only visions of an imaginary world bound him to life.

The mortal disorder of eroticism and "apathy"

The very extravagance of his affirmations stands in the way of getting them accepted at all easily. But by taking his affirmations as a starting point, it is possible to understand that tenderness has no effect on the interaction of eroticism and death. Erotic conduct is the opposite of normal conduct as spending is the opposite of getting. If we follow the dictates of reason we try to acquire all kinds of goods, we work in order to increase the sum of our possessions or of our knowledge, we use all means to get richer and to possess more. Our status in the social order is based on this sort of behaviour. But when the fever of sex seizes us we behave in the opposite way. We recklessly draw on our strength and sometimes in the violence of passion we squander considerable resources to no real purpose. Pleasure is so close to ruinous waste that we refer to the moment of climax as a "little death". Consequently anything that suggests erotic excess always implies disorder. Nakedness wrecks the decency conferred by our clothes. But once we have ventured along the path of sensuous disorder it takes a good deal to satisfy us. Destruction and betrayal will sometimes go hand in hand with the rising tide of genetic excess. Besides nudity there is the strangeness of half-clothed bodies; what garments there are serve to emphasise the disorder of the body and show it to be all the more naked, all the more disordered. Brutality and murder are further steps in the same direction. Similarly prostitution, coarse language and everything to do with eroticism and infamy play their part in turning the world of sensual pleasure into one of ruin and degradation. Our only real pleasure is to squander our resources to no purpose, just as if a wound were bleeding away inside us; we always want to be sure of the uselessness or the ruinousness of our extravagance. We want to feel as remote from the world where thrift is the rule as we can. As remote as we can:—that is hardly strong enough; we want a world turned upside down and inside out. The truth of eroticism is treason.

De Sade's system is the ruinous form of eroticism. Moral isolation means that all the brakes are off; it shows what spending can really mean. The man who admits the value of other people necessarily imposes limits upon himself. Respect for others hinders him and prevents him from measuring the fullest extent of the only aspiration he has that does not bow to his desire to increase his moral and material resources. Blindness due to respect for others happens every day; in the ordinary way we make do with rapid incursions into the world of sexual truths and then openly give them the lie the rest of the time. Solidarity with everybody else prevents a man from having the sovereign attitude. The respect of man for man leads to a cycle of servitude that allows only for minor moments of disorder and finally ends the respect that their attitude is based on since we are denying the sovereign moment to man in general.

From the opposite point of view, "the centre of de Sade's world" is, according to Maurice Blanchot, "the demands of sovereignty asserted through an enormous denial". Unfettered freedom opens out into a void where the possibilities match the intensest aspirations at the expense of secondary ones; a sort of heroic cynicism cuts the ties of consideration and tenderness for others without which we cannot bear ourselves in the normal way. Perspectives of this order place us as far from what we usually are as the majesty of the storm is from the sunshine or from the drearily overcast sky. In fact we do not possess the excessive store of strength necessary to attain the fulfilment of our soveriegnty. Actual soveriengty, however boundless it might seem in the silent fantasy of the masses, still even in its worst moments falls far below the unleashed frenzy that de Sade's novels portray. De Sade himself was doubtless neither strong enough nor bold enough to attain to the supreme moment he describes. Maurice Blanchot has pinpointed this moment which dominates all the rest and which de Sade calls apathy. "Apathy", says Maurice Blanchot, "is the spirit of denial applied to the man who has elected to be sovereign. It is in some ways the cause and principle of energy. De Sade seems to reason somewhat after this manner: the individual of today possesses a certain amount of strength; most of the time he wastes his strength by using it for the benefit of such simulacra as other people, God or ideals. He does wrong to disperse his energy in this way for he exhausts his potentialities by wasting them, but he does worse in basing his behaviour on weakness, for if he puts himself out for the sake of other people the fact is that he feels he needs to lean on them. This weakness is fatal. He grows feeble by spending his strength in vain and he spends his strength because he thinks he is feeble. But the true man knows himself to be alone and accepts the fact; he denies every element in his own nature, inherited from seventeen centuries of cowardice, that is concerned with others than himself; pity, gratitude and love, for example, are emotions that he will destroy; through their destruction he regains all the strength he would have had to bestow on these debilitating impulses, and more important he acquires from this labour of destruction the beginnings of true energy. It must be clearly understood indeed that apathy does not consist in ruining 'parasitic' affections but also in opposing the spontaneity of any passion no matter what. The vicious man who indulges his vice immediately is nothing but a poor doomed creature. Even debauchees of genius, perfectly equipped to become monsters, are fated for catastrophe if they are content to follow their inclinations. De Sade insists that for passion to become energy it has to be compressed, it must function at one remove by passing through a necessary phase of insensibility; then its full potentiality will be realised. Early in her career Juliette is always being scolded by Clairwill: she commits crime only in the flush of enthusiasm, she lights the torch of crime only at the torch of passion, she sets lewdness and heady pleasure above all else. This is easy and dangerous. Crime is more important than lewdness; crimes committed in cold blood are greater than crimes carried out in the heat of the moment; but the crime 'committed when the sensitive part has been hardened, that dark and secret crime is the most important of all because it is the act of a soul which having destroyed everything within itself has accumulated immense strength, and this can be completely identified with the acts of total destruction soon to come.' All the great libertines who live only for pleasure are great only because they have destroyed in themselves all their capacity for pleasure. That is why they go in for frightful anomalies, for otherwise the mediocrity of ordinary sensuality would be enough for them. But they have made themselves insensitive; they intend to exploit their insensitivity, that sensitiveness they have denied and destroyed, and they become ferocious. Cruelty is nothing but a denial of oneself carried so far that it becomes a destructive explosion; insensibility sets the whole being aquiver, says de Sade: 'The soul passes on to a kind of apathy that is metamorphosed into pleasures a thousand times more wonderful than those that their weaknesses have procured them.' "[1]

The triumph of death and pain

I have quoted that passage in full for it throws great light on the central point where being is more than just presence. Presence is sometimes almost sloth, the neutral moment when, passively being means indifference to being, already on the way to meaninglessness. Being is also the excess of being, the upward surge towards the impossible. Excess leads to the moment when transcendent pleasure is no longer confined to the senses, when what is felt through the senses is negligible and thought, the mental mechanism that rules pleasure, takes over the whole being. Without this excess of denial pleasure is a furtive, contemptible thing, powerless to keep its real place, the highest place, in an awareness that

[1] Maurice Blanchot, op. cit. page 256-258.

is ten times as sensitive. Clairwill, the heroine Juliette's companion in debauch, says "I'd like to find a crime that should have never ending repercussions even when I have ceased to act, so that there would not be a single instant of my life when even if I were asleep I was not the cause of some disorder or another, and this disorder I should like to expand until it brought general corruption in its train or such a categorical disturbance that even beyond my life the effects would continue".[1] To reach such impossible peaks is indeed no less formidable an undertaking than the ascent of Everest; no one can do it without a colossal concentration of energy. But in the concentration that leads to the summit of Mount Everest there is but a limited response to the desire to excel. If we start from the principle of denying others posited by de Sade it is strange to observe that at the very peak of unlimited denial of others is a denial of oneself. Theoretically, denial of others should be affirmation of oneself, but it is soon obvious that if it is unlimited and pushed as far as it can possibly go, beyond personal enjoyment, it becomes a quest for inflexible sovereignty. Concern for power renders real, historical sovereignty flexible. Real sovereignty is not what it claims to be; it is never more than an effort aimed at freeing human existence from the bonds of necessity. Among others, the sovereign of history evaded the injunctions of necessity. He evaded it to a high degree with the help of the power given him by his faithful subjects. The reciprocal loyalty between the sovereign and his subjects rested on the subordination of the latter and on their vicarious participation in his sovereignty. But de Sade's sovereign man has no actual sovereignty; he is a fictitious personage whose power is limited by no obligations. There is no loyalty expected from this sovereign man towards those who confer his power upon him. Free in the eyes of other people he is no less the victim of his own sovereignty. He is not free to accept a servitude in the form of a quest for wretched pleasures, he is not free to stoop to that! The remarkable

[1] Op. cit. page 244.

thing is that de Sade starts from an attitude of utter irresponsibility and ends with one of stringent self-control. It is
the highest satisfaction alone that he is after, but such satisfaction has a value. It means refusing to stoop to a lower
degree of pleasure, refusing to opt out. De Sade describes
for the benefit of other people, his readers, the peak that
sovereignty can attain. There is a movement forward of
transgression that does not stop before a summit is reached.
De Sade has not shirked this movement; he has accepted it
in all its consequences and these go further than the original
principle of denying others and asserting oneself. Denying
others becomes in the end denying oneself. In the violence
of this progression personal enjoyment ceases to count, the
crime is the only thing that counts and whether one is the
victim or not no matter; all that matters is that the crime
should reach the pinnacle of crime. These exigencies lie
outside the individual, or at least they set a higher value on
the process begun by him but now detached from him and
transcending him, than on the individual himself. De Sade
cannot help bringing into play beyond the personal variety an
almost impersonal egotism. We are not bound to consider
in terms of real life his entirely imaginary situations. But we
can see how he was forced in spite of his principles to accept
the transcendence of the personal being as a concomitant
of crime and transgression. What can be more disturbing
than the prospect of selfishness becoming the will to perish
in the furnace lit by selfishness? De Sade incarnated this
progression in one of his most perfect characters.

Amélie lives in Sweden. One day she goes to see Bor-
champs . . . This man, hoping for a monster execution, has
just turned over to the king all the members of a conspiracy
which he himself has plotted, and this betrayal delights the
young woman. "I love your ferocity," she tells him, "swear
to me that one day I also shall be your victim. Since I was
15 my imagination has been fired only at the thought of
dying a victim of the cruel passions of a libertine. Not that
I wish to die tomorrow—my extravagant fancies do not go

as far as that; but that is the only way I want to die; to have my death the result of a crime is an idea that sets my head spinning." A strange head, that one, and well deserving of the answer: "I love your head madly, and I think we shall achieve great things between us . . . rotten and corrupt it is I grant you!" Thus "for the whole man, man in his entirety, no evil is possible. If he inflicts hurt on others, the pleasure of it! If others hurt him, what satisfaction! Virtue pleases him because it is weak and he can crush it, and so does vice, for the disorder it brings even at his own expense gives him satisfaction. If he lives there is no event in his life that will not seem to him fortunate. If he dies his death is a greater happiness yet, and conscious of his own destruction he sees in it the crown of a life only justified by the urge to destroy. Thus the man who denies is the ultimate denial of all else in the universe, a denial which will not even spare him. Doubtless the strength to deny confers a privilege while it lasts, but the negative action it exerts is the only protection against the intensity of a huge denial"[1].

An impersonal denial, an impersonal crime!

Tending towards the continuity of beings beyond death!

De Sade's sovereign man does not offer our wretchedness a transcendent reality. At least his aberration points the way to the continuity of crime! This continuity transcends nothing. It cannot overtake what is lost. But in Amélie de Sade links infinite continuity with infinite destruction.

[1] Op. cit. page 236-237.

CHAPTER III

DE SADE AND THE NORMAL MAN

Pleasure is paradox

Jules Janin wrote of de Sade's books[1] "There are bloody corpses everywhere, infants torn from their mothers' arms, young women with their throats slit after an orgy, cups full of blood and wine, unimaginable tortures. Cauldrons are heated, racks set up, skulls broken, men flayed alive; there is shouting, swearing, blasphemy; hearts are ripped from bodies; all this on every page and every line. What an indefatigable scoundrel he is! In his first book[2] he shows us a poor girl at bay, lost, ruined, shrinking under a rain of blows, led by inhuman monsters through one underground vault after another, from graveyard to graveyard, beaten, broken, devoured alive, wilting, crushed . . . When the author has committed every crime there is, when he is sated with incest and monstrosities, when he stands panting above the corpses he has stabbed and violated, when there is no church he has not sullied, no child he has not sacrificed to his rage, no moral thought on which he has not flung the foulness of his own thoughts and words, then at last this man pauses, looks at himself, smiles to himself and is not frightened. On the contrary . . ."

If this examination is far from exhaustive, at least it describes in appropriate language a figure intentionally cut by de Sade: the horror and the ingenuousness of the feelings

---

[1] In *Revue de Paris*, 1834.

[2] The book referred to is *Justine*, or more precisely *La nouvelle Justine*, the freer version, that is, published by the author in 1797 and reissued by Jean-Jacques Pauvert in 1953. The first version was published in the Editions Fourcade in 1930, by Maurice Heine, published in the Editions du Point du Jour in 1946 with a preface by Jean Paulhan, and published again by Jean-Jacques Pauvert with a different version of the present study as a preface in 1954.

respond to a deliberate provocation. We are at liberty to think what we will of this attitude, but we know what men are with their particular circumstances and their limitations. We know in advance that generally speaking they cannot fail to judge de Sade and his writings in the same way. It would be useless to attribute Jules Janin's execration to his ineptitude, or that of people who agree with him. Janin's lack of understanding is in the order of things; it is that of'mankind in general; it comes from their lack of strength and their feeling of being threatened. The figure of de Sade is certainly unsympathetic to people moved by need and by fear. The sympathies and the dreads—the cowardice too, one must add—which determine men's usual behaviour are diametrically opposed to the passions responsible for the sovereignty of the voluptuary. But this sovereignty is significant because of our wretchedness, and one would be mistaken not to see in the reactions of an anxious man—an affectionate and cowardly man—an immutable necessity; to put it precisely, pleasure itself demands dread as a proper reaction. Where would pleasure be if the anguish bound up with it did not lay bare its paradoxical aspect, if it were not felt as unbearable by the very person experiencing it ?

All this is true and must be stressed first of all. The criticisms that de Sade defied were well founded. He was not against the fool and the hypocrite as much as against the decent man, the normal man in all of us, so to speak. He was less concerned to convince than to challenge. We should be underestimating him if we did not see that he carried defiance to extremes and turned truth upside down. His challenge would have no meaning, value or consequences without that boundless lie, and if the positions he attacked were not unshakable. The sovereign man of de Sade's imagination did not only exceed the possible. The idea of him never even disturbed the sleep of the just for more than a moment.

For these reasons, the opposite attitude to his, that of commonsense, that of Jules Janin, is the one to have when one discusses de Sade. I am addressing the anxious man whose first reaction is to de Sade as his daughter's potential murderer.

To admire de Sade is to diminish the force of his ideas

It is in any case a paradox to talk about de Sade at all. Whether or not we are, tacitly or openly, playing the proselyte is not important: is the paradox any less striking if we applaud the apologist of evil rather than the evil itself? The inconsistency is even greater if we do no more than admire de Sade: such admiration exalts his victims and transfers them from the world of physical horror to a realm of wild, unreal, sheerly glittering ideas.

Certain minds are fired by the thought of turning the most securely established values topsy-turvy. They are thus able to say gaily that the most subversive man who ever lived— the Marquis de Sade—was also the man who rendered the greatest service to humanity. Nothing to their mind could be more certain; we shiver at the thought of death and pain (even the death and pain of other people), tragic or unspeakable events cut us to the quick, but that which inspires us with terror is like the sun, no less glorious if we turn our weak eyes away from its blaze.

Like the sun at least in being intolerable to the naked eye, the figure of de Sade fascinated and terrified his contemporaries: was not the very idea that the monster was alive revolting? In our day and age, however, an apologist for his ideas is never taken seriously, and no one thinks them at all significant. His fiercest opponents regard them either as braggadocio, or else as simple, gleeful impertinence. His protagonists help to bolster up the ethic of the Establishment, in so far as they themselves subscribe to it: they imply that it is useless to try to shake it, it is sturdier than it looks. That would not matter if only de Sade's ideas did not in the process lose their essential value: namely, that of being incompatible with the ideas of reasonable beings.

De Sade asserted these unacceptable values in book after

book. Life, he maintained, was the pursuit of pleasure, and the degree of pleasure was in direct ratio to the destruction of life. In other words, life reached its highest intensity in a monstrous denial of its own principle.

Such a strange doctrine could obviously not be generally accepted, nor even generally propounded, unless it were glossed over, deprived of significance and reduced to a trivial piece of pyrotechnics. Obviously, if it were taken seriously, no society could accept it for a single instant. Indeed, those people who used to rate de Sade as a scoundrel responded better to his intentions than his admirers do in our own day: de Sade provokes indignation and protest, otherwise the paradox of pleasure would be nothing but a poetic fancy. I repeat that I prefer to discuss him only with people who are revolted by him, and from their point of view.

In the foregoing study, I spoke of how de Sade came to endow the excesses of his own imagination with a value which he saw as absolute, one which was a denial of the reality of other people.

I must now look for the significance which this value nevertheless possesses for those people whose reality it denies.

The divine is no less paradoxical than the vicious

The anxious man revolted by de Sade's remarks finds it nevertheless no easy matter to reject out of hand a principle that tends in the same direction as intense life bound up with the violence of destruction. At all times and in all places men have been fascinated and appalled by the notion of divinity. The words "divine" and "sacred" have carried undertones of an inner secret animation, a deep-seated frenzy, a violent laying hold of an object, consuming it like fire, leading it headlong to ruin. This animation was thought to be contagious, and passing from one object to another it brought with it a miasma of death. There is no greater peril, and if the victim is the object of a cult to be held up for veneration, we must admit straight away that this cult has a certain ambiguity. Religion certainly tries to glorify the sacred object and turn a destructive principle into the mainspring of power and all that is valuable, but on the other hand it is careful to restrict its scope and separate its limited field of influence by an insuperable barrier from the world of normal or profane life.

This violent and deleterious aspect of divinity was generally manifested in sacrificial rites. Often moreover the rites were extravagantly cruel: children were offered to monsters of red-hot metal, gigantic wicker figures crammed with human beings were set alight, priests flayed living women and clad themselves in the streaming bloody spoils. Acts as horrifying as these were rare; they were not essential to the sacrifice but they underlined its significance. The ordeal of the Cross itself links Christian conscience to the frightfulness of the divine, though blindly. The divine will only protect us once its basic need to consume and to ruin has been satisfied.

Such facts are properly referred to here. They have one advantage over de Sade's fantasies: no one can find them acceptable but every reasonable person will admit that they respond in some way to one of humanity's needs; if one considers the past one even finds it difficult to deny the universal and sovereign nature of this need; and on the other hand, the servants of these cruel gods were careful deliberately to set a limit to their ravages; they never scorned necessity nor the orderly world it rules.

So there had formerly been a solution in the destructiveness of sacrifice, to the double difficulty I have referred to in de Sade. Anxious life and intense life—fettered and unleashed activity—were protected from each other by religious practices. The profane world would continue, founded on useful activity, for there could be no food and no consumer goods without it. The opposite principle was no less valid for all that, with no attenuation of its disastrous effects in the feeling of horror felt along with the sacred presence.

Anguish and joy, intensity and death, met and were one in the celebrations. Fear gave meaning to exuberance and useful activity was utterly consumed in the end. But the two were kept apart; there was nothing to bring about the confusion between two opposite and irreconcilable principles.

The normal man considers the paradox of sacredness or eroticism as unhealthy

Considerations like these of a religious order have their limits nevertheless. It is true that they are aimed at the normal man and that it is possible to formulate them from his point of view, but they bring in an element which lies outside his field of consciousness. The sacred world is an ambiguous reality for modern man. Its existence is undeniable and its history can be written, but it is not a reality that can be grasped. That world is founded on human behaviour, human behaviour in circumstances no longer obtaining and we can no longer grasp the way it used to work. We know well enough what this behaviour was, and we can doubt neither its historic truth nor that it used to have what seems to be a sovereign and universal significance, as I have said. But certainly those concerned did not know what it meant and we can have no clear knowledge of it: no interpretation to date can be unquestioningly accepted. A reasonable man with habits of calculation instilled by hard nature and his own anguish could only be interested in a well-defined reality that such behaviour might correspond with. As long as he cannot see the reason behind them, how can he take the horrors of religion in the past at all seriously? He cannot be rid of them as easily as he can be rid of de Sade's fantasies, but he cannot put them in the same category as the needs which rule conduct according to reason, like cold or hunger. The meaning behind the word "sacred" is not of the same order as food or warmth.

We may put it in this way. The reasonable man is above all an aware man, but as the facts of religion only touch his consciousness from without, he acknowledges them reluctantly and whereas he is obliged to admit that in the past they carried the weight they did in fact carry, he is not going to allow them a single right in the present, or at least unless the element of horror is excised. One ought even to add at the same time that in one way it is easier to be receptive to de Sade's eroticism than to the religious demands of old. No-one today could deny that impulses connecting sexuality and the desire to hurt and to kill do exist. Hence the so-called sadistic instincts enable the ordinary man to account for certain acts of cruelty, while religious impulses are explained away as aberrations. By describing these instincts in masterly fashion then, de Sade has contributed to man's slow-growing awareness of himself—in philosophical terminology "consciousness of self"; The expression "sadistic", in universal use, is in itself clear proof of his contribution. In this sense what I call the Jules Janin attitude has been modified; it remains that of the reasonable and anxious man, but it no longer turns its back so ruthlessly on the significance of the name of de Sade. The instincts described in *Justine* and *Juliette* have their own charter now, and the Jules Janins of today acknowledge them. They no longer hide their eyes and indignantly refuse to try to understand them; but they classify them as pathological.

The history of religion, then, has given our consciousness but little assistance in its reassessment of sadism. The definition of sadism, however, has shown us that religious experience and behaviour need not be regarded as something bizarre and inexplicable. Sexual instincts to which de Sade gave his name will account for the horrors of sacrifice, and the whole horror-evoking complex is called pathological.

I have already said that I have no quarrel with this point of view. Short of a paradoxical capacity to defend the indefensible, no one would suggest that the cruelty of the heroes of *Justine* and *Juliette* should not be wholeheartedly abominated. It is a denial of the principles on which humanity is founded. We are bound to reject something that would end in the ruin of all our works. If instinct urges us to destroy the very thing we are building we must condemn those instincts and defend ourselves from them. But there remains this question. Would it be possible wholly to avoid the denial of humanity implicit in these instincts? May this denial perhaps depend on external factors, a sickness not essential to man's nature that could be cured, for example, or on individuals or collective groups that in theory could and should be suppressed,—in short, on elements that could be cut out of human kind? Or does man bear within himself the stubborn and persistent denial of the quality, call it reason, utility or order, upon which humanity is based? Is our being ineluctably the negation as well as the affirmation of its own principle?

Vice is the deep truth at the heart of man[1]

It might be that we wear our sadism like an excrescence which may once have had a meaning in human terms but has now lost it, which can easily be eradicated at will, in ourselves by asceticism, in others by punishment. This is how the surgeon treats the appendix, the midwife the after-birth, and the people their kings. Or are we concerned on the contrary with a sovereign and indestructible element of man-kind, yet one that evades conscious appraisal? Are we concerned, in short, with the heart of man, not the muscular organ, but the surge of feelings, the intimate reality that it symbolises?

If the first of these alternatives holds, the reasonable man would be justified; man will produce instruments for his own well-being indefinitely, he will subdue all nature to his laws, he will be free from war and violence without having to heed the fateful propensity which has hitherto bound him to misfortune. That propensity would be nothing but a bad habit, easy and necessary to mend.

The second alternative would seem to show that the

---

[1] This is no new proposition; everybody has heard it. So much so that it is popularly repeated over and over again without calling up the slightest protest, "There is a sleeping pig in every man's heart" (*Tout homme a dans son coeur un cochon qui sommeille*).

suppression of this habit would affect mankind at a vital point.

The proposition needs to be formulated with precision. It is far too momentous to be left vague for a single instant.

Firstly it presupposes in man an irrestible excess which drives him to destroy and brings him into harmony with the ceaseless and inevitable annihilation of everything that is born, grows, and strives to last.

Secondly, it bestowes a kind of divine or, more accurately, sacred significance on that excess and that harmony. Our desire to consume, to annihilate, to make a bonfire of our resources, and the joy we find in the burning, the fire and the ruin are what seem to us divine, sacred. They alone control sovereign attitudes in ourselves, attitudes that is to say which are gratuitous and purposeless, only useful for being what they are and never subordinated to ulterior ends.

Thirdly, the proposition implies that a humanity which considered foreign to itself the attitudes rejected by the first stirrings of reason would languish and sink into a state rather like that of old men (this does tend to happen, but not only in our own day) if it did not now and then behave in a way utterly opposed to these principles.

Fourthly, it is connected with the need of the normal man of today to become aware of himself and to know clearly what his sovereign aspirations are in order to limit their possibly disastrous consequences; to accept these if it suits him but not to push them any further than he needs, and resolutely to oppose them if his self-awareness cannot tolerate them.

The two poles of human life

Our proposition differs radically from de Sade's provocative assertions in that although it could not pass for the opinion of the average man (he usually thinks the opposite and believes that violence can be eliminated) it can be reconciled with the latter's attitude and if he accepted it he would find nothing there that could not be made to fit in with his point of view.

When one considers the most striking manifestations of the principles enunciated, one cannot fail to observe mankind's double nature throughout its career. There are two extremes. At one end, existence is basically orderly and decent. Work, concern for the children, kindness and honesty rule men's dealings with their fellows. At the other, violence rages pitilessly. In certain circumstances the same men practise pillage and arson, murder, violence and torture. Excess contrasts with reason.

These extremes are called civilisation and barbarism—or savagery. But the use of these words is misleading, for they imply that there are barbarians on the one hand and civilised men on the other. The distinction is that civilised men speak and barbarians are silent, and the man who speaks is always the civilised man. To put it more precisely, since language is by definition the expression of civilised man, violence is silent. Many consequences result from that bias of language. Not only does "civilised" usually mean "us", and barbarous "them", but also civilisation and language grew as though violence was something outside, foreign not only to civilisation but also to man, man being the same thing as language. Yet observation shows that the same peoples are alternately barbarous and civilised in their attitudes. All savages speak and by speaking they reveal their solidarity with the decency and kindness that are the root of civilisation. Conversely all civilised men are capable of savagery. Lynch law belongs to men who rate themselves as among the most highly civilised of our age. If language is to be extricated from this impasse, we must declare that violence belongs to humanity as a whole and is speechless, and that thus humanity as a whole lies by ommission and language itself is founded upon this lie.

Violence is silent and de Sade's use of language is a contradiction in terms

Common language will not express violence. It treats it as a guilty and importunate thing and disallows it by denying it any function or any excuse. If violence does

occur, and occur it will, it is explained by a mistake somewhere, just as men of backward civilisations think that death
can only happen if someone makes it by magic or otherwise.
Violence in advanced societies and death in backward ones
are not just given, like a storm or a flood; they can only be
the result of something going wrong.

But silence cannot do away with things that language
cannot state. Violence is as stubbornly there just as much as
death, and if language cheats to conceal universal annihilation, the placid work of time, language alone suffers, language
is the poorer, not time and not violence.

Useless and dangerous violence cannot be abolished by
irrational refusals to have any truck with it, any more than
the irrational refusals to treat with death can eliminate that.
But the expression of violence comes up against the double
opposition of reason which denies it and of violence itself
which clings to a silent contempt for the words used about it.

It is difficult of course to consider this problem in theoretical terms. Here is a concrete example. I remember that I
once read a story told by a deportee and this depressed me.
But I imagined the story told the other way round, by the
torturer whom the witness had seen lashing out. I imagined
the wretch writing and myself reading as follows: "I flung
myself upon him with insults and as he could not retaliate
with his hands tied behind his back, I rammed my flailing
fists into his face; he fell down and my heel finished off the
work; disgusted, I spat into a swollen face. I could not help
bursting into loud laughter: I had just insulted a dead man!"
Unhappily these few stilted lines do not ring false. But it is
unlikely that a torturer would ever write like that.

As a general rule the torturer does not use the language of
the violence exerted by him in the name of an established
authority; he uses the language of the authority, and that
gives him what looks like an excuse, a lofty justification. The
violent man is willing to keep quiet and connives at cheating.
On his side the willingness to cheat leaves the way clear for
violence. Inasmuch as men want to see torture inflicted, the

function of the legally constituted office of torturer provides a way. If he bothers with his fellow men at all, he talks the language of the State to them. And if he is under the sway of passion himself, his sly silence gives him the only pleasure geared to his needs.

The characters of de Sade's novels have a slightly different attitude from that of the torturer I have arbitrarily made to speak out. His characters do not speak to man in general, as literature does even in the apparent discretion of the private journal. If they speak at all it is to someone of their own kind. De Sade's twisted libertines talk to each other. But they indulge in long speeches to show they are right. As often as not they believe they are obeying the dictates of Nature. They boast that they are the only people who conform to her rules. But although their opinions may correspond with de Sade's philosophy, taken as a whole they have no coherence. Sometimes they are stirred by a hatred for Nature. At any rate, what they insist upon is the overriding value of violence, excesses, crimes and tortures. In this way they fall short of the profound silence peculiar to violence, for violence never declares either its own existence or its right to exist; it simply exists.

To tell the truth, these disquisitions upon violence which keep interrupting the accounts of infamous cruelties that make up de Sade's books do not belong to the violent characters into whose mouths they are put. If such people had really lived, they would probably have lived in silence. These are de Sade's own ideas, though he never really tried to shape them into a logically coherent whole, and he uses this means to address other people.

Thus de Sade's attitude is diametrically opposed to that of the torturer. When de Sade writes he refuses to cheat, but he attributes his own attitude to people who in real life could only have been silent and uses them to make self-contradictory statements to other people.

A paradox underlies his behaviour. De Sade speaks, but he is the mouthpiece of a silent life, of utter and inevitably speechless solitude. The solitary man for whom he speaks pays not the slightest heed to his fellows; in his loneliness he is a sovereign being, never called to account, never needing to justify himself to anyone. He never pauses at the fear that the wrongs he inflicts on others will recoil upon himself; he is alone and never subject to the bounds that a common feeling of weakness imposes on other people. All this calls for enormous moral energy, but such energy is in fact the point at issue. Describing the implications of this moral loneliness, Maurice Blanchot shows how the solitary man proceeds step by step towards total negation: denial of other people first, and then by some monstrous logic denial of himself. In his own ultimate negation the criminal, as he perishes a victim of the sea of crimes he has brought about, rejoices still in the triumph that crime, now somehow sacred, celebrates over the criminal himself. Violence bears within itself this dishevelled denial, putting an end to any possibility of speech.

It may be objected that de Sade's language is not common parlance, not addressed to all comers, but intended for those rare spirits capable of attaining to superhuman solitude in the very bosom of humanity.

The man who speaks, however blind he may be, has nevertheless broken out of the solitude to which his condemnation of other people has condemned him. From his point of view, violence is the opposite of the solidarity with other people implicit in logic, laws and language.

How shall we define that contradiction in terms, de Sade's monstrous utterance?

It is a language which repudiates any relationship between speaker and audience. In true solitude there could be no semblance even of solidarity. There is no room for a forthright, honest language, as de Sade's is to some extent. The paradoxical solitude in which de Sade uses it is not what it seems; it seeks to cut itself off from human kind and its purpose is the denial of humanity. Yet it does have a purpose! There is no limit to the cheating of the lonely man that his

exuberant life and endless imprisonment made de Sade into,
except at one point. If he did not owe humanity his denial
of humanity, at least he owed it to himself; in the last analysis
I see very little difference.

De Sade's language is that of a victim

Here is something striking. In complete contrast with the
torturer's hypocritical utterances, de Sade's language is that
of a victim. He invented it in the Bastille when he wrote the
Cent Vingt Journées. At that time he had with other men the
relationship of a man cruelly punished with those who were
inflicting the punishment. I said that violence had no tongue.
But the man punished for a reason he believes unfair cannot
resign himself to silence—silence would imply acceptance.
In their impotence many men make do with contempt
mingled with hatred. The Marquis de Sade, rebellious in his
imprisonment, had to give his rebellion a voice. He spoke
out, as violence itself never does. In his rebellion he had to
defend himself, or rather to attack, seeking to fight on the
ground of the moral man to whom language belongs.
Language is at the bottom of punishment but only language
can dispute its justice. De Sade's letters from prison show
him as a man fierce in his own defence, emphasising now
the triviality of his misdeeds, now the thinness of the excuse
for his punishment—it was supposed to reform him but
instead it was corrupting him completely. But these pro-
testations are superficial. De Sade in fact made straight for
the heart of the matter. He had been tried; now he was
going to be the judge. He sat in judgment on the man who
had condemned him, upon God, and generally upon the
limits set to ardent sensuality. This led him to attack the
universe, Nature, everything that opposed the sovereignty of
his own passions.

De Sade spoke out in order to justify himself in his own eyes before other people

Thus, refusing to cheat, he was brought by the harsh

measures used against him to this insensate pass: he gave his solitary voice to violence. He was fast behind prison walls, but he meant to justify himself.

It does not follow that the timbre of this voice was to meet the exigencies of violence better than it did those of language.

On the one hand, this monstrous anomaly hardly seems to correspond with the intentions of a man who, as he spoke, forgot the solitude to which he was condemning himself more unreservedly than other people had done, for he was betraying this solitude. Normal men, standing for common necessity, obviously could not understand him. His plea could not have any meaning, so that this enormous work taught solitude in solitude; a century and a half passed before its message was spread, and it would not be properly understood yet if we did not first notice its absurdity! Misunderstanding and revulsion from the generality of mankind are the only results worthy of de Sade's ideas. But this lack of understanding at least keeps their essence intact, whilst the admiration accorded him today by some few people proves very little since it does not commit them to the voluptuary's solitude. True, this self-contradictory admiration today is an extension of de Sade's own self-contradictory position, but that does not get us out of the dilemma. We should never hear a voice from another world, the world of inaccessible solitude, if, conscious of the impasse, we were not bent on finding the answer to the riddle by guesswork.

De Sade's language takes us out of the field of violence

Finally we realise one last difficulty.

De Sade's expression of violence changes violence into something else, something necessarily its opposite: into a reflecting and rationalised will to violence.

The philosophical dissertations which interrupt de Sade's narrative at the least excuse make them exhausting reading in the long run. Patience and resignation are needed to get through them. One has to tell oneself that a way of speaking

so different from other people's, from everyone else's, makes
it worth going on to the bitter end. Moreover, this monstrous
utterance has a strength which imposes respect. We face
de Sade's books as a terrified traveller might once have
faced giddy piles of rocks. We flinch away, and yet . . . The
horror before us is not aware of us, yet by simply being there,
does it not hold some meaning for us ? Mountains are something that can only appeal to man in a roundabout way,
and the same with de Sade's books. But humanity has
nothing to do with the existence of those lofty peaks. On the
contrary, man is completely committed to an undertaking
which would not exist without him. Mankind excises his
crazy elements . . . But the rejection of folly is nothing but a
convenient and unavoidable attitude which must call for
second thoughts. De Sade's philosophy, anyway, is not to
be classed as madness. It is simply an excess, an excess
to make our heads reel, but the excess of our own extravagance. We cannot ignore this peak without ignoring our own
nature. If we fail to come nearer to the peaks, or at least
climb the lower slopes, we must live like frightened ghosts—
and it is our nature that makes us tremble with fear.

Let me revert to the long disquisitions that punctuate and
clutter up the tales of criminal debauchery and prove inter-
minably that the criminal libertine, and he alone, is right.
Analyses and ratiocinations, learned references to ancient or
savage customs, paradoxes of an aggressive philosophy, they
all take us far away from violence for all their unwearying
obstinacy and casual incoherence. For violence means being
beside oneself, and being beside oneself is the same thing as
the sensuous frenzy that violence results in. If we consciously
desire to profit from violence, we can no longer reach the
heights of frenzy and lose ourselves in it. Violence, the core
of eroticism leaves the weightiest problems unanswered. We
have achieved awareness by pursuing a course of regular
activity; every element has its place in the chain of consciousness and is distinct and intelligible. But by upsetting the
chain through violence we revert to the extravagant and

incomprehensible surge of eroticism. So we experience something blinding and overwhelming, more desirable than anything else, which defies the conscious appraisal we bestow on all the other facts of our experience. Human life, therefore, is composed of two heterogeneous parts which never blend. One part is purposeful, given significance by utilitarian and therefore secondary ends; this part is the one we are aware of. The other is primary and sovereign; it may arise when the other is out of gear, it is obscure, or else blindingly clear: either way it evades the grasp of our aware intelligence. Hence the problem has two sides. Conscious understanding wishes to extend its range to include violence, for such an important part of man's make-up must not be neglected any longer. And on the other hand violence reaches beyond itself to lay hold of intelligence, so that its satisfactions, brought to the surface of consciousness, may become profounder, more intense and more compelling. But in being violent we take a step away from awareness, and similarly by striving to grasp the significance of our own violent impulses we move further away from the frenzied raptures violence instigates.

For the sake of greater satisfaction de Sade strove to infuse violence with the orderly calm of awareness

In a conscientious enquiry which leaves nothing in the dark, Simone de Beauvoir[1] pronounces thus on De Sade: "The most characteristic thing is an effort of will that seeks to give full rein to the desires of the flesh without ever being lost in them." If by "the flesh" we understand the erotically charged symbol, that is true and incontrovertible. Of course, de Sade is not the only one to exert his will to such an end; eroticism is different from animal sexuality in that for a man aroused clear images surge up with the distinctness of

---

[1] She gives her study a rather provocative title: "*Must we burn Sade ?*" (*Faut-il brûler Sade ?*) It appeared first in *Les Temps Modernes* and forms the first part of *Privilèges*, Gallimard 1955, in 16° (Collection "Les Essais", LXXVI). Unluckily the biography of de Sade which accompanies the study is a bravura piece which occasionally exaggerates the facts. (An English translation by Annette Michelson, together with selections from de Sade's writings, has been published by the Grove Press, New York, 1953.)

objects; eroticism is the sexual activity of a conscious being. None the less its essence is never accessible through our consciousness. Simone de Beauvoir is right when to show one of de Sade's desperate efforts to make something solid out of an exciting image, she quotes his conduct in the only debauch of which we have a detailed account, one given by a witness before a court: "In Marseilles, he had himself whipped, but every couple of minutes he would dash to the mantelpiece and, with a knife, would inscribe on the chimney flue the number of lashes he had just received".[1] His own stories are also full of measurements; often the length of the penis is given, in inches and twelfths; sometimes a partner will like to measure it in the course of the orgy. The characters' speeches are certainly as paradoxical as I suggest, for they are a defence to justify a man under punishment. Their violence lacks a certain authenticity, but at the cost of their slow ponderousness de Sade manages at last to bring to violence an awareness that permits him to talk about his own delirium as if it were an external object. The process is slowed down by this excursion but his satisfaction in it is increased. The climax has to be postponed, of course, but only for a time, and the transferred fearlessness of consciousness has added to pleasure a sense of lasting possession—the illusion of everlasting possession in fact.

De Sade's perversion brings violence into the field of conscious experience

On the one hand de Sade's writings reveal the antinomy of violence and awareness, but also, and this is their peculiar value, they tend to bring men back to an awareness of something they have almost completely turned their backs on, looking for loopholes and postponing the moment for coming to terms.

They bring to man's thinking on the subject of violence the slow pace and the spirit of observation that characterise the conscious intelligence.

[1] *Privilèges*, page 42.
    Marquis de Sade, Grove Press, page 49.

They develop logically and with the vigour of a determination to achieve results to demonstrate how little justified was de Sade's punishment.

Such was the basis of the first version of *Justine* at any rate.

In this way we reach a violence possessing the calmness of reason. As soon as violence demands it, back will come the utter unreason without which the final burst of sensuous pleasure is impossible. But in the forced inactivity of prison, violence may avail itself at will of the clear-sightedness and the unfettered exploitation of the self which underlies knowledge and consciousness.

De Sade had two ways open to him in prison. Possibly no one has ever gone further than he in his taste for ethical monstrosities, and simultaneously he was one of the greediest for knowledge among the men of his time.

Maurice Blanchot says of *Justine* and *Juliette:* "It is true to say that nowhere else and at no other time has there been such a scandalous book in the whole of literature . . ."

The fact is that what de Sade was trying to bring to the surface of the conscious mind was precisely the thing that revolted that mind. For him the most revolting thing was the most powerful means of exciting pleasure. Not only did he reach the most singular revelations by this means, but from the very first he set before the consciousness, things which it could not tolerate. He himself spoke only of "irregularity". The rules we obey are usually intended to conserve life; hence irregularity leads towards destruction. It does not always have this fatal meaning, however; nakedness fundamentally is a kind of irregularity, but where pleasure is concerned it does not lead to real destruction. (Observe that nakedness can also exist within the rules; nakedness in a doctors' surgery or in a nudist camp has no exciting effects.) De Sade's works introduce one scandalous irregularity after another. He insists now and then on the irregular aspect of the simplest sort of erotic attraction, for example, a novel way of undressing the partner. According to the cruel characters he brings on to the scene, nothing heats the passions more than irregularity. De Sade's essential merit is to have discovered and effectively demonstrated one function of moral irregularity in carnal pleasure. This excitement should theoretically lead to sexual activity. But the effect of any irregularity at all is stronger than the immediate manoeuvres. De Sade finds it equally possible to seek satisfaction through murder or torture in the course of a debauch, or by ruining a family or a country, or even just by stealing.

Independently of de Sade, the sexual excitement of burglars has not escaped notice. But no one before him had grasped the general mechanism linking the reflex actions of erection and ejaculation with the transgression of the law. De Sade knew nothing about the basic interrelation of taboo and transgression, opposite and complementary concepts. But he took the first step. This general mechanism could not be completely comprehended until we finally and tardily arrived at an understanding of the paradox of taboo and transgression. De Sade expounded his doctrine of irregularity in such a way, mingled with such horrors, that no one paid any heed to it. He wanted to revolt our conscious minds, he would also have liked to enlighten them but he could not do both at the same time. It is only today we realise that without de Sade's cruelty we should never have penetrated with such ease the once inaccessible domain where the most painful truths lay hidden. It is not so easy to pass from the knowledge of mankind's curious beliefs and behaviour, in the field of religion, now linked with our knowledge of taboo and transgression, to that of the strangeness of his sexual behaviour. The deep-seated unity of our nature is the last thing to appear. And if today the average man has a profound insight into what transgression means for him, de Sade was the one who made ready the path. Now the average man knows that he must become aware of the things which repel him most violently—those things which repel us most violently are part of our own nature.

CHAPTER IV

THE ENIGMA OF INCEST

Under the somewhat hermetic title of *Elementary Structures of Relationship*[1] Claude Lévi-Strauss' considerable work tackles the problem of incest. The problem is one which indeed arises within the family framework; the taboo on sexual relationships or marriage between two individuals is always decided by a degree or more exactly by a form of relationship. Conversely relationships are determined by the possibilities of sexual connections among individuals; this couple may not marry, that couple may, and such and such a degree of cousinship denotes a highly favoured position, often one that bars marriage with anyone not in that position.

We are struck straight away with the universality of prohibitions where incest is concerned. In one form or another all mankind is aware of it though the modalities will vary. In one place one sort of relationship is under the taboo, like cousins who are the children of brother and sister; elsewhere on the other hand this is the most favoured relationship for marriage and the children of two brothers or of two sisters may not marry. The most highly civilised people simply forbid intercourse between parents and children, brothers and sisters. But as a general rule with primitive peoples we find the various individuals classed into distinct categories which decide which sexual unions are forbidden and which encouraged.

Moreover, two separate situations must be considered. In the first, treated by Lévi-Strauss under the heading "Elementary Structures of Relationship" the precise nature of the blood relationship is responsible for the rules determining

[1] *Structure Elémentaires de la Parenté*, Presses Universitaires de France, 1949.

illegitimacy and potential marriage. In the second, referred to by the authors as "complex structures" but not dealt with in his published book, the way in which the spouse is selected depends on "other factors, economic or psychological". The categories undergo no change but if some remain taboo, custom no longer decides from which the bride shall be chosen. This is unfamiliar ground, but Lévi-Strauss thinks that taboos cannot be considered on their own and that one cannot study them without also examining the privileges that complement them. No doubt this is why he avoids the word "incest" in the title of his book and emphasises, though somewhat obscurely, the system of interlinked taboos and privileges, of relationships forbidden and relationships encouraged.

Some answers that have been given to the problem of incest

Lévi-Strauss contrasts the state of nature with that of culture, roughly as animals are generally contrasted with man. This prompts him to say that the prohibition of incest (and of course he also has in mind the complementary rules of exogamy) "is the primary step thanks to which, through which, and especially in which, the transition from Nature to Culture is made".[1]

The horror of incest thus embodies a factor which makes humans of us and the problem it poses is the problem of man himself as far as he adds a human element to animal nature. In consequence all that we are is at stake in our decision to eschew the loose freedom of sexual conduct and the natural and unformulated life of the animals. The formula may well imply the final ambition that links with knowledge the desire to reveal man to himself and thus to take over the potentialities of the whole universe. Possibly Lévi-Strauss would hesitate before such far-reaching demands and remind the reader of the modest nature of his words. But the demands or the processes involved in man's least movement forward cannot always be limited, and the aim of solving the riddle

[1] *Structures Elémentaires de la Parenté*, page 30.

of incest is a particularly ambitious one, namely, to reveal what has hitherto been veiled. Anyway, if in the past a certain process made possible the transition from Nature to Culture, how should another process which makes plain the significance of the first fail to be of overwhelming interest?

To tell the truth, we are quickly bound to admit that there are grounds for humility. Claude Lévi-Strauss finds that he has to report the mistakes of his predecessors in this field. They give us little encouragement.

The finalist theory invests taboos with a eugenic significance: the race must be protected from the results of consanguineous marriages. This viewpoint has its distinguished protagonists; Lewis H. Morgan, for instance, is a recent one. Lévi-Strauss affirms that it does not appear anywhere before the nineteenth century[1] but it is still widespread; there is nothing more common today than belief in the degeneracy of the children of an incestuous union. The observed facts do not confirm this superstition in any way; none the less the belief is still very much alive.

For some people "the prohibition of incest is nothing but the projection or reflection on a social level of feelings or tendencies which the nature of man is completely adequate to account for". It is an instinctive repugnance, they say. Lévi-Strauss is at pains to show that the reverse is true as psychoanalysts agree. Incestuous relationships are a universal obsession as dreams and myths show. If this were not so, why should the taboo be so solemnly proclaimed? Explanations of this order have a fundamental weakness. The disapproval which does not exist with animals is a historical occurrence, a result of the changes that made human life what it is; it is not simply part of the order of things.

Historical explanations are advanced to meet this criticism.

McLennan and Spencer saw in exogamous practices a custom sanctifying the habits of war-like tribes who normally obtained their wives by capture.[2] Durkheim explained the

---

[1] Op. cit. page 14.
[2] Op. cit. page 23.

taboo against marriage within the tribe with blood relations by that associated with menstruation and the absence of a taboo on marriage with men of another tribe. Such interpretations may be logically satisfactory but their weakness lies in the fact that the connections thus established are fragile and arbitrary[1]. To Durkheim's sociological theory one might add Freud's psychoanalytical hypothesis which attributes the transition from animal to human to a postulated murder of the father by the brothers. According to Freud, the brothers, jealous of each other, maintain the taboos on relations with their mother or sisters that their father imposed in order to keep them for his own use. Really Freud's myth brings in the most fantastic guesswork yet it has the advantage over the sociologists of being an expression of living compulsions. Lévi-Strauss expresses it neatly:[2] "He gives a fair account not of the beginnings of civilisation, but of its present state: the desire for the mother or the sister, the murder of the father and the repentance of the sons does not perhaps correspond with a fact or group of facts having a fixed place in history. But they may well express in symbolical form an inveterate fantasy. And the power of this fantasy to shape the thoughts of men without their knowledge results from the very fact that the acts evoked were never committed because culture has at all times and in all places opposed them."[3]

The limited significance of the external factors forbidding or permitting marriages

The short answer, whether uninspired or brilliant, will not do. A dogged patience is called for, able to take in its stride the tangled data which at first glance is like nothing so much as a tough intellectual puzzle.

A monster game of patience this problem certainly is, and one of the hardest problems ever to have to be sorted out.

---

[1] Op. cit. page 25.
[2] Op. cit. pages 609-610.
[3] Lévi-Strauss, op. cit. page 609 (note 1) refers the reader to A. L. Kroeber, "*Totem and Taboo*" in *Retrospect*.

It goes on and on and alas, it is desperately tedious: roughly two-thirds of Lévi-Strauss's big volume are devoted to the detailed examination of the multiple permutations and combinations thought up by primitive humanity to resolve one problem, the problem of the distribution of women. The aim is to define their position in the midst of these intricate absurdities.

Regrettably I am myself obliged to enter this maze; for a clear conception of eroticism we must struggle out of the darkness that has made its significance so hard to assess.

"The members of one generation" says Lévi-Strauss, "are divided generally into two groups: on the one hand cousins of whatever degree who call each other brothers and sisters (parallel cousins), and on the other cousins born of collaterals of different sexes, again of whatever degree, who have special names for each other and among whom marriage is possible (cross cousins)". This is the definition of a simple yet fundamental distinction, having numerous variations and posing innumerable problems. The basic assumption here is a problem in itself. "Why," we are asked,[1] "should a barrier be erected between cousins born of collaterals of the same sex and those born of collaterals of different sexes when there is the same degree of blood relationship in each case? Yet between the two there is all the difference between incest (parallel cousins being regarded as brothers and sisters) and marriage—not only a possible marriage but even the kind of marriage most approved of, since cross cousins are referred to by the name given to potential married couples. This distinction is incompatible with our biological criterion of incest."

Complications set in of course in every direction, and very often the choice seems to be quite arbitrary and unimportant; yet in the multitude of variations one further discrimination gives certain relationships a yet more privileged position.

[1] Op. cit. page 127-128.

G*

There is not only the fairly usual privilege between cross cousins as opposed to parallel cousins, but there is a further privilege between matrilinear crossed cousins as opposed to patrilinear. Let me summarise as simply as I can. My paternal uncle's daughter is my parallel cousin; in the world of "elementary structures" we are exploring there is a strong chance that I shall be allowed neither to marry nor to have any sexual connection with her; I look on her as a sister and I call her sister. But the daughter of my paternal aunt, who is my cross cousin, is different from the daughter of my maternal uncle, who is also my cross cousin; the first is patrilinear, the second matrilinear. There is a fair chance that I might be able to marry either of them quite freely; this is acceptable in many primitive societies. (It could also happen in this case that the first, born of my paternal aunt, might also be my maternal uncle's daughter; that maternal uncle may very well have married my paternal aunt,—in a society in which marriage between cross cousins is not subject to some secondary consideration that is what usually happens,—in that case I say that my cross cousin is bilateral.) But there is also a chance that marriage with one or other of these cross cousins might be forbidden as incestuous. Certain societies encourage marriage with the daughter of the father's sister (patrilinear) and forbid it with the daughter of the mother's brother (matrilinear), while elsewhere the opposite holds good.[1] But my cousins are differently placed. There is a strong chance that marriage with the first would be opposed by a taboo and a much smaller one if it were the second that I wished to marry. Lévi-Strauss says[2] "If we look at the distribution of these two forms of unilateral marriage, we observe that the second type is far more widespread than the first".

Here then to begin with are the essential types of consanguinity underlying prohibited or favoured marriages.

The fog has only become thicker, of course, while we

[1] Op. cit. page 544.
[2] Ibid.

have been probing into these details. Not only are the distinctions between these separate kinds of blood relationship purely theoretical ones, quite meaningless, not only are we miles from the clear and specific difference between our parents and sisters and the rest of mankind, but 'the relationships mean opposite things in different places! What we are after is the reason for the taboo; and we naturally seek it in the specific situation of the people involved, their respective cirumstances in the field of moral behaviour, their relationships and the nature of these relationships. But we are dissuaded from this method by such unmistakable arbitrariness and Claude Lévi-Strauss himself says how disconcerting sociologists find it. He says that they "find it difficult to forgive the marriage of cross cousins when on top of the enigma of the difference between children of collaterals of the same sex and children of collaterals of different sexes comes the extra mystery of the difference between the daughter of the mother's brother and the daughter of the father's sister."

But the author is really only showing how involved the problem is in order to solve it better.

The question is on what level these apparently meaningless distinctions are matters of consequence. If there are different consequences according to the category in question, the significance of the distinctions will be made plain. Lévi-Strauss has shown the part played by a system of distributive exchange in marriage as constituted in primitive societies. To acquire a wife was to acquire wealth, and moreover her value was sacred. The distribution of the wealth constituted by the total number of women posed vital problems calling for certain regulations. It looks as if the kind of anarchy that reigns in contemporary societies would have been powerless to resolve them. Cycles of exchange in which rights are settled in advance are the only method of guaranteeing, sometimes rather inadequately but more often quite efficiently, the fair distribution of the women among the men wanting them.

The rules of exogamy, giving women away, and the need for a rule to share them out among the men

It is not easy for us to understand the logic of the situation in primitive society. Amid the casual ease of contemporary life with its numerous and undefined potentialities we cannot imagine the tension inherent in life in restricted groups kept apart by hostility. We have to make an effort to grasp the anxiety that calls for guarantees in the form of rules.

We must beware, then, of picturing arrangements similar to those dealing with wealth today. Even in the worst cases, the notion evoked by the words "marriage by purchase" is far removed from the realities of primitive life where exchange is not just a simple operation completely dependent on commercial values as it is today.

Claude Lévi-Strauss has given the institution of marriage a place in the overall movement of barter that animates primitive societies. He refers the reader to "the conclusions of the admirable 'Essai sur le Don' "[1] and says "in this now classic study Mauss has attempted to show firstly that barter in primitive societies is less a matter of commercial transactions than one of reciprocal gifts, secondly that such gifts occupy a far more important place in those societies than in ours, and lastly that this primitive form of exchange has not solely or essentially an economic character but brings us face to face with what he admirably describes as "a total social act", that is, one endowed with a significance at once social and religious, magic and economic, utilitarian and sentimental, juridical and ethical."

Generosity is the keynote of this kind of exchange and it always has a ceremonial character. Certain goods cannot be intended for private or utilitarian consumption. They are

[1] Op. cit. page 66. The *Essai sur le Don* by Marcel Mauss appeared first in the Année Sociologique 1923-24 and has recently been reprinted in a volume called *Sociologie et Anthropologie* (Presses Universitaires de France, 1950) that brings together some of the writings of that great sociologist, now dead. In *La Part Maudite* (Editions de Minuit, 1949) I have given an exhaustive account of the *Essai sur le Don*, seeing in it if not the basis for a new conception of economics, at least a sign of the introduction of a fresh attitude. The work has been translated by Ian Cunnison under the title *The Gift*, Cohen and West, London 1954.

generally luxury articles. Even today the latter have a basic
function in ceremonies. They are reserved for gifts, iecep-
tions and celebrations; like champagne, for instance.
Champagne is drunk on certain occasions when it is custo-
mary to provide it. Of course, the champagne consumed is
the subject of commercial transactions. The producers are
paid for the bottles. But when it is actually being drunk,
only part is drunk by the person who has paid for it; that is
the principle underlying the consumption of a product used
in celebrations which by its very presence shows that the
occasion is a special one, a product, moreover, that to satisfy
all expectations must or ought to flow like water, unstintingly.

Lévi-Strauss's thesis invites considerations of this order.
The father marrying his daughter, the brother marrying his
sister would be like the man with a cellar full of champagne
who drank it all up by himself and never asked a friend in to
share it. The father must bring the wealth his daughter
represents into a cycle of ceremonial exchanges. He must
bestow her as a gift but the cycle entails a number of rules
valid within a given social group just like the rules of a game.

Claude Lévi-Strauss has set down the principle underlying the rules governing this system of barter which does
not come under the heading of a strictly mercantile transaction. He writes[1]: "The gifts are exchanged immediately
for goods of equivalent value or else received by the bene-
ficiaries on the understanding that they will on a later
occasion reciprocate with further gifts which may well be
worth more than the first but which in their turn establish
the right to yet further gifts, again more sumptuous than
the last". The point to remember here is that the overt
purpose of these operations is not "to derive economic
benefits or advantages". Sometimes an affectation of
generosity will even make people destroy the proffered gifts.
Destruction pure and simple has great prestige value. The
production of luxury objects whose real significance is the

[1] Op. cit. page 67.

honour of those possessing, receiving or bestowing them is in any case destructive of useful work (it is the opposite of capitalism which accumulates the profits of work and uses them to create further profits). When certain objects are destined for ceremonial exchanges they are withdrawn from productive use.

In discussing marriage by barter one must stress that the principle is the opposite of the commercial attitude with its haggling and calculations. Marriage by purchase is itself part of this process. "It is simply a variation on the system so thoroughly analysed by Mauss[1]," says Lévi-Strauss. This type of marriage is admittedly remote from the one we regard as truly human and humane, for we require freedom of choice on both sides. But neither does it lower women to the level of commerce and calculation. Women rank on a level with celebrations. A woman given in marriage has after all the same sort of significance as champagne has in our customs. In marriage, says Lévi-Strauss, women "are not primarily a symbol of social status but a natural stimulus."[2] "Even after marriage, Malinowski has shown that among the Trobriand islanders the payment of the *Mapula* by a man represents a reward intended to recompense the woman for the services given by her in the shape of sexual gratification."[3]

Thus women seem primarily important as a means of communication in the strongest sense, the sense of effusion. Consequently they have to be objects of generosity on the part of their parents in whose gift they are. The parents must give them away, but this happens in a world where each act of generosity contributes to the cycle of generosity in general. If I give away my daughter I shall receive another woman for my son or my nephew. Thus throughout a limited group based on generosity there is an organic and pre-arranged communication like the multiple movements of a dance or a piece of orchestral music. With the taboo on

---

[1] Op. cit. page 81.
[2] Op. cit. page 82.
[3] Op. cit. page 81.

incest the denial derives from an affirmation. The brother giving away his sister is less concerned to deny the value of sexual union with somebody closely related to him than to assert the greater value of marriages that would unite his sister with another man or another woman with himself. The communication that takes place in an exchange based on generosity is more intense and certainly greater than its immediate enjoyment. More precisely, festivities entail an outward-goingness, a refusal to turn in upon oneself, and so the calculations of the miser, logical though they may be, are denied the highest value. The sexual relationship is itself a communication and a movement, it is like a celebration by nature, and because it is essentially a communication it provokes an outward movement in the first place.

When the violent movement of the senses has been accomplished, a retraction and a renunciation are called for. But the recoil also requires a rule to organise the merry-go-round and ensure the return of the forward movement.

The positive advantages of certain blood relationships in the system of gift and barter

Lévi-Strauss, it is true, does not emphasise this aspect. He stresses a quite different side of the value of woman, not inconsistent perhaps, but in direct contrast, to wit, their material utility. I believe that this is a secondary factor if not in the functioning of the system, where the material side must often be of first importance, at least in the play of emotions which originally set the system going. But if we fail to take it into consideration, not only would we not see the implications of the exchanges that take place but also Lévi-Strauss's own theory would be out of place and the practical consequences of the system would not be fully apparent.

Up to now this theory is nothing but a brilliant and fascinating hypothesis. The meanings of these mosaics of various taboos is still to be sought, and so are the meanings attached to the choice between forms of blood relationship whose differences are apparently insignificant. Lévi-Strauss has in fact endeavoured to sort out the various effects of the different forms of relationships on the exchanges and he has sought to provide his hypothesis with a solid foundation in the process. To this end he decides to concentrate on the most tangible aspect of the exchanges he has followed up.

Over and against the attractiveness of women already mentioned, and referred to by Lévi-Strauss himself, though he does not dwell on it, stand the material benefits to be calculated in services rendered, that the possession of a wife confers on her husband.

This material interest cannot be denied and indeed I do not think one could well investigate the process of handing women over in marriage without noticing it. Later on I shall try to resolve these two obviously contradictory points of view. The standpoint I suggest, is not incompatible with Lévi-Strauss's interpretation, just the opposite in fact; but I must first stress the aspect he himself stresses. "As has often been observed,"[1] he says "in the majority of primitive societies, as also to a lesser degree in the rural classes of our own society, marriage has an economic importance. The difference between the economic status of the bachelor and that of the married man in our own society is practically only that the former has to renew his wardrobe more often[2]. The situation is completely different among groups in which the satisfaction of economic needs depends entirely upon the man and wife relationship and the division of labour between the sexes. Not only do men and women not have the same specialised technical skills and consequently depend on each other for the manufacture of the objects necessary for the daily tasks, but they produce different types of food. If they are to receive a balanced diet and

[1] Op. cit. page 48.
[2] There is an obvious exaggeration here. These days circumstances vary enormously from one case to the next. Similarly we may ask whether the lot of the bachelor is constant even among primitive men. I personally think that Lévi-Strauss's theory is mainly based on the "generosity" motivation, although "self-interest" must lend considerable weight to the transactions.

particularly if they are to eat regularly they depend on what is really a production co-operative—their own partnership. When a young man is bound by economic necessity to marry this is a kind of social sanction. If a society organises the exchange of women badly real disorder follows. That is why, on the one hand, the operation must not be entrusted to chance, but involves rules that guarantee a fair exchange; on the other hand, however perfect the system may be it cannot meet all cases; frequent adaptations and alterations must take place."

The basic theory remains the same and defines the way the system must be made to work.

Of course "the negative aspect is only the restrictive aspect of the prohibition"[1]; it is important everywhere to define the set of obligations which puts the machinery of mutual or general generosity into motion. "The group within which marriage is forbidden immediately calls into mind some other group . . . within which marriage is either merely possible or else inevitable, as the case may be; the taboo on carnal knowledge of one's daughter or one's sister obliges one to bestow that daughter or sister in marriage on another man, and at the same time it creates a claim on the sister or daughter of that other man. Thus all the negative stipulations of the prohibition have their positive counter part."[2] Thenceforth "whenever I forego any claim to sexual union with one woman, who then becomes available for another man, somewhere else there is a man renouncing another woman who then becomes available for me."[3]

Frazer was the first to notice that "the marriage of cross cousins proceeds simply and directly and quite naturally from the exchange of sisters in view of intermarriage".[4] But he could not give a general explanation from this starting point and sociologists have failed to pursue this notion, satisfying as it is. While the group neither gains nor loses in

[1] Op. cit. page 64.
[2] Ibid.
[3] Op. cit. page 65.
[4] Op. cit. page 176.

the marriage of parallel cousins, the marriage of cross cousins
entails an exchange between two groups; for under usual conditions the girl will not belong to the same group as her
cousin. In this way "a reciprocal structure is built up, according to which the group that has gained must give back and
the one that has given up may make demands."[1] "Parallel
cousins come from families in the same kind of situation, one
of static equilibrium, while cross cousins come from families
in opposing situations, that is in dynamic disequilibrium[2]."

Thus the mysterious difference between cross and parallel
cousins is explained as a difference between the situation
favourable to exchange and one where stagnation would tend
to result. But in this simple case only two groups are involved
and the exchange can be described as restricted. If more than
two are involved we have to deal with generalised exchange.

In generalised exchange, man A marries woman B;
man B marries woman C; man C woman A. (This system may be extended to include more groups.) In these different conditions, just as cross cousins were in a privileged
position, now the marriage of matrilinear cousins opens up
possibilities of indefinite linking-up of groups because of the
structure of the exchange system. Lévi-Strauss says "It is
enough for a human group to proclaim the law of marriage
with the daughter of the mother's brother for a vast round
of reciprocity as harmonious and ineluctable as physical or
biological laws to ensure; while marriage with the daughter
of the father's sister cannot extend the chain of matrimonial
transactions and cannot in any dynamic way further the
extension of alliances and power always tied up with the need
to make exchanges."

*The secondary significance of the economic aspect of Lévi-
Strauss's theory*

We cannot be surprised at the ambiguity of Lévi-Strauss's
doctrine. On the one hand the exchange or rather the

[1] Op. cit. page 178.
[2] Ibid.

bestowal of women involved the material interest of the giver but he offers the gift expecting to receive a gift in return. On the other hand it is based on generosity. This fits the duality of the gift-exchange, the institution to which the name "potlatch" has been given: "potlatch" is calculation in the highest degree and at the same time calculated interests are loftily ignored. But it is rather a pity that Lévi-Strauss has paid so little attention to the bearing of eroticism on the potlatch of women.

Eroticism springs from an alternation of fascination and horror, of affirmation and denial. It is true that marriage often seems to be the opposite of eroticism, but we are drawing conclusions from what is perhaps a secondary aspect. It is possible to believe that when the rules governing taboo and suspension of taboo came into effect, they were really the determining force in sexual activity. Marriage seems to have come down from a period when sexual activity was essentially dependent upon them. Could a rigid system of sexual taboos and suspension of taboos have come into being if it had not had in the first place some other purpose than the setting up of a home in the most material sense? Everything suggests that these regulations deal with the play of deep seated impulses among individuals. How otherwise can the unnatural renunciation of near relations be explained? We have here a truly extraordinary process, to make imagination boggle: a sort of inner revolution of violent intensity, to judge by the terror felt at the mere idea of failing to conform. This movement is no doubt at the bottom of the potlatch of women, exogamy, that is; the paradox of giving away the coveted object. Why should the sanction of the taboo have been everywhere so compelling if it did not arise in answer to the difficulty of suppressing certain impulses, such as reproductive activity? Conversely, did not the very fact of the taboo turn its object into something desirable, right at first anyway? If the taboo was a sexual one did it not apparently emphasise the sexual value of its object? Or rather it conferred an erotic value on this object. That is precisely where men differ from animals. The bounds set on freedom of action give a fresh fillip to the irresistible animal impulse. The connection between incest and the obsessive value of sexuality for man is not so easy to define, but this value does exist and must certainly be associated with sexual taboos taken as a whole.

I believe indeed that this pattern of reciprocity is of the essence of eroticism. I agree with Lévi-Strauss that it is also the factor underlying the rules of exchange bound up with the taboo on incest. The link between eroticism and those rules is often difficult to pin down because the latter have marriage as their purpose and as we have said, marriage and eroticism are often in opposite camps. Economic partnership for reproduction has become the dominant aspect of marriage. The rules of marriage, if they are enforced, may in the past have governed the whole course of sexual life, but eventually they became confined to regulating the distribution of wealth. Fertility and work are all that women now signify.

Yet this contradictory development was inevitable. Erotic life could only be subject to rules for a period of time; the rules ended by driving eroticism out of the world of law and order. Once eroticism had been dissociated from marriage the latter took on a primarily material significance and Lévi-Strauss is right to emphasise its importance. The rules intended to share out women as objects of desire also guaranteed their distribution as a labour force.

Lévi-Strauss's propositions describe only one aspect of the transition from animal to man. This transition should be considered as a whole

Lévi-Strauss's doctrine seems to answer, and with an accuracy one would hardly dare hope for, the main questions raised by the often curious nature of the taboos on incest in archaic societies.

However, the ambiguity I have discussed restricts its immediate applicability if not its long range validity. It envisages essentially a business of exchanges within a total social phenomenon involving the whole of life. In spite of that, the economic explanation is concentrated on from one end of the book to the other as if it could be considered in isolation. Theoretically I have no objection to this, but first of all the specific code relating to incest is what is supposed to be based on economic activity, not the whole process of social evolution. The author himself may well have made the necessary reservations even if he has not made the contrary viewpoint explicit. All we have to do is to see in perspective how the whole picture will come together. Lévi-Strauss himself felt the need of an overall view and he gives one in the last pages of the book but we find no more than hints and suggestions. The analysis of the one aspect in isolation proceeds with something like perfection, but the overall picture into which this aspect has to be fitted is merely sketched in.

The horror of philosophy[1] which dominates the world of science, doubtless justifiably, may account for this. Yet I find it hard to tackle the transition from nature to culture from the limited attitude of scientific objectivity with its tendency to isolate and to abstract. An attachment to such limitations is evident in the habit of referring to nature, not animal nature, and to culture, not man. This is to go from one abstract view to another and to ignore the point where the totality of being is undergoing change. It seems to me to be difficult to comprehend the totality through a state or a series of states enumerated in turn, and the change which occurs as man comes on the scene cannot be separated from the state of becoming, of being in general, from what happens if man and animal nature confront each other as the totality of being is rent asunder. In other words, the only way we can

---

[1] Claude Lévi-Strauss does not seem to share this horror, but I am not certain that he is aware of all the consequences of the transition from thought applied to a specific and artificially isolated object (the scientific approach) to thought concerned with the whole, with the absence of a specific object, which is the province of philosophy (though the word philosophy often only covers a less narrow and more daring approach to specific questions).

comprehend being is historically; through changes and transitions from one state to another, not in the successive phases looked at in isolation. When Lévi-Strauss talks about nature and culture he is setting one abstraction beside another; while the transition from the animal to man implies not only those states as such but also their movement into opposite camps.

The specific qualities of man

The rise of work, taboos which can be grasped historically in a subjective way, long lasting repugnances and an insurmountable nausea mark the contrast between man and the animals so well that for all the remoteness of the event in time the facts are obvious. I think the following statement will hardly be contested: that man is the animal that does not just accept the facts of nature, he contradicts them. Thus he alters the exterior world of nature. Out of it he makes tools and manufactured objects which make up a new world, the human world. Similarly he contradicts his own nature, he educates himself, he refuses to give free rein to the satisfaction of his animal needs, needs that a true animal will satisfy without reservations. It must also be agreed that there is a connection between man's denial of the world as he finds it and his denial of the animal element in himself. It is not for us to give pride of place to one or the other, to enquire whether education (in the form of religious taboos) is the consequence of work, or whether work is the result of a mutation in the field of ethics. But in so far as man exists there exist also work on the one hand and denial of the animal element in man's nature on the other.

Man flatly denies the existence of his animal needs; most of his taboos relate to them and these taboos are so strikingly universal and apparently so unquestioned that they are never discussed. Ethnography does deal with the menstruation taboo, it is true, but only the Bible can really be said to specify a particular form of the general taboo on obscenity. It refers to the taboo on nudity, saying that Adam and Eve knew themselves to be naked. But nobody mentions the horror of excremental matter which belongs to man alone. The conventions regarding our bodily waste products are not given any conscious consideration by adults and are not even entered on the list of taboos. There is therefore an aspect of the transition from animal to human so radically negative that no one talks about it. We do not count it among men's religious reactions although we include the most absurd taboos under that heading. On this point the denial is so absolute that we think it beside the point to notice and to assert that here is something worthy of comment.

For the sake of simplicity I shall not now discuss the third specifically human element in man's nature touching the knowledge of death, apart from a reminder that this conception of the transition from animal to human is really Hegel's. Hegel, however, insists on the first and third aspects but avoids the second, himself obeying with his silence the perdurable taboos we all abide by. This is less awkward than it seems at first sight, for the elementary forms of the denial of animal elements come up again in more complex ones. But if incest in particular is the subject under discussion we cannot doubt that it is reasonable to ignore the common taboo on obscenity.

The variability of the rules about incest and the general variability of the subject of sexual taboos

How indeed could we not define incest with that as a starting point? We cannot say that such and such a thing is obscene. Obscenity is relative. There is no "obscenity" in the sense that there is "fire" or "blood", but only in the way that an "outrage to modesty" exists. Such and such a thing is obscene if this or that person thinks it is and says so; it is not exactly an object, but a relationship between an object and the mind of a person. In this sense we can define situations of which given aspects are or at least seem to be obscene. Moreover, these situation are unstable and always presuppose certain ill-defined elements; or else what stability they have has an arbitrary character. Similarly they often have to be adapted to fit the necessities of life. Incest is a situation of this kind which has its arbitrary existence only within the mind of man.

This way of seeing it is so necessary and unavoidable that if we were unable to affirm the universality of incest we should hardly be able to demonstrate the universal character of the taboo on obscenity. Incest is the first proof of the fundamental connection between man and the denial of sensuality, of the carnal and animal.

Man has never managed to shut out sexuality except superficially or through a lack of individual vigour. Even the saints at least have their temptations. We can do nothing about it except fence off certain areas to be kept free of sexual activity. Times, occasions and people are marked off in this way: every aspect of sexuality is obscene in this place, or in these circumstances, or in the presence of these people. The different aspects, just like the places, times and persons, are variable and always arbitrarily defined. Thus nakedness is not obscene in itself. It has become obscene almost everywhere but unequally so. Genesis refers to nakedness, linking the birth of modesty with the transition from the animal to the human and this is only the feeling of obscenity in other words. But actions which outraged modesty even at the beginning of our own century do so no longer today, or much less at any rate. The relative nakedness of women on the beach is still shocking in Spain but not in France; but in a town even in France bathing suits still upset a certain number of people. In the same way a low-cut dress will not do in broad daylight but is correct wear in the evening. And the most intimate kind of nakedness is not obscene in a doctor's surgery.

In the same sort of way the reservations affecting people may shift. Theoretically the sexual contacts of people living together are limited to the inevitable conjugal relationship of the father and mother. But like the taboos on aspects of sensuality, on times and places, the limits are very uncertain and very changeable. In the first place, the expression "living together" can be used on one condition only: it must never be given a precise meaning. In this domain there are to be found as much that is arbitrary and as many adaptations as we saw there to be with nakedness. In particular the importance of convenience must be stressed. Lévi-Strauss's analysis makes this very clear. The arbitrary division between relations with whom marriage is permissible and those with whom it is forbidden varies with the need to guarantee cycles of exchange. When these organised cycles cease to be of use the scope of incest diminishes. If utility no longer enters into consideration men will end by ignoring obstacles which have come to seem hopelessly arbitrary, but to counter this tendency, when the taboo has been firmly grounded it has gained in strength: its intrinsic power has been felt more forcibly. Each time it is convenient, what is more, the limits can be extended; thus with divorce proceedings in the Middle Ages where theoretical cases of incest with no basis in contemporary custom were used as a pretext for the legal dissolution of princely marriages. No matter; the point is always to set against the disorder of the animal world the essentially and unconditionally human: this mode is not without its resemblance to the English lady of Victorian days who affected to believe that the flesh and the animal urges did not really exist. Thorough-going social humanity cuts out the disorder of the senses altogether; it denies its own natural principle, it refuses to accept it as a fact and only admits the space of a clean and tidy house through which move worthy people at once naive and inviolable, tender and inaccessible. This symbol does not only indicate the boundaries that make the mother sacrosanct to the son, the daughter to the father. It is in a general way the image—or the sanctuary—of humanity unsexed, holding its values aloft safe from violence and sullying passion.

The essence of humanity is to be found in the taboo on incest and the gift of women resulting from it

Let us come back to the fact that these remarks are in no

sort of contradiction with Lévi-Strauss's theory. The idea of an absolute denial (as absolute as possible) of the carnal and animal is inevitably situated at the very point where the two avenues explored by Lévi-Strauss converge, where in fact marriage itself begins. In one sense marriage combines economic interest and purity, sensuality and the taboo on sensuality, generosity and avarice. But its first movement puts it at the other extreme; it is a gift. Lévi-Strauss has shed clear light on this point. He has analysed the process so well that his interpretations show clearly what the essence of a gift is. The gift itself is a renunciation, the refusal of an immediate animal satisfaction with no strings attached. Marriage is a matter less for the partners than for the man who gives the woman away, the man whether father or brother who might have freely enjoyed the woman, daughter or sister, yet who bestows her on someone else. This gift is perhaps a substitute for the sexual act; for the exuberance of giving has a significance akin to that of the act itself: it is also a spending of resources. But the renunciation based on taboo that allows this kind of expenditure is the one thing that makes such giving possible. Even if there is some relief in giving as there is in the sexual act it is not at all a physical, animal relief; its transcendent nature belongs essentially to man. For a close relation to renounce his right, to forego the enjoyment of his own property: this is what defines human beings in complete contrast to the greedy animals. As I have said, such renunciation enhances the value of the thing renounced. But this is also a contribution to the creation of the human world in which respect, difficulty and reservations are victorious over violence. It complements eroticism which heightens the value of the object of desire. Without the counterbalance of the respect for forbidden objects of value there would be no eroticism. (There would be no complete respect if the lapse into eroticism were not both possible and full of delightful promise.)

Respect is really nothing but a devious route taken by violence. On the one hand respect keeps order in the sphere

where violence is forbidden; on the other it makes it possible
for violence to erupt incongruously in fields where it has
ceased to be permissible. The taboo does not alter the
violence of sexual activity, but for disciplined mankind it
opens a door closed to animal nature, namely, the transgression of the law.

The sudden upsurge of transgression (or free eroticism)
on this side, and on that the existence of an environment
where sexuality is not allowed are the extreme forms of a
situation where there are many middle ways. In general the
sexual act is not taken to be sinful and the places in which
only husbands from outside can have anything to do with
the local women echoes a very old practice indeed. More
often than not moderate eroticism is tolerated and where
there is condemnation of sexuality, even when it appears to
be stringent, it only affects the façade, the act of transgression
itself being allowed as long as it is not made public. Yet only
the extremes have much significance. The essential point is
that circumstances do exist, however limited they may be,
when eroticism is quite unthinkable, and equally there are
moments of transgression when eroticism is a complete upheaval.

It would be difficult to imagine these two extremes without taking into consideration the constant flux of circumstances. Hence the element of giving that comes into
marriage—(since gifts are part and parcel of celebrations and
giving is a luxury, an exuberance, an absence of calculation)
—this element associated with the turbulence of the feast
has a strong flavour of transgression about it. But this side
has certainly become blurred. Marriage is a compromise
between sexual activity and respect. More and more it is
coming to mean the latter. The act of marriage, the transition,
has retained some of the quality of transgression it originally
possessed. But in a world of mothers and sisters conjugal life
stifles and to a certain extent neutralises the excesses of
reproductive activity. In the process the purity on which the
taboo is based, which is characteristic of the mother or the

sister, slowly passes on to the wife, now a mother. Thus the state of marriage enables man to live a human life in which respect for taboo contrasts with the untrammelled satisfaction of animal needs.

CHAPTER V

MYSTICISM AND SENSUALITY

From the breadth of the modern Christian attitude to the "fear of sex"

People who are interested to a greater or lesser extent in the problems arising from mystical experience, that ultimate in human potentialities, know of the remarkable review known as the *Etudes Carmélitaines* edited by a Discalced Carmelite, Father Bruno de Sainte-Marie. From time to time this review publishes special editions like the recent one dealing with the burning question of the relationship between mysticism and continence[1].

There is no better example of the breadth of outlook, the open-mindedness and the solid informativeness typical of the work published by the Carmelites. It is not in any sense a piece of propaganda but a collection of contributions from experts of every shade of opinion on the occasion of an International Congress. Jews, orthodox Catholics and Protestants were invited to put their point of view; and in particular a great deal of space was given to religious historians and psycho-analysts who were not particularly conversant with religious practices.

Certainly the subject matter of the book calls for a range of viewpoints as wide as this. A series of articles all in the same key, exclusively Catholic, the work of authors already vowed to continence, might have left the reader feeling uneasy. They could have only been directed at an audience of monks and priests anchored to their own immutable standpoint. The work published by the Carmelites, though, is distinguished

---

[1] *Mystique et Continence: Travaux du VIIe Congrès international d'Avon.* Desclée de Brouwer, 1952, in 8°, 410 pages. (31e année de la *Revue Carmélitaine*).

by their resolute intention to look straight at every issue and to go boldly forward in their scrutiny of the weightiest problems. To judge by appearances it is a far cry from Freud to the Catholic attitude; it is a remarkable thing to find men of religion today inviting psycho-analysts to discuss Christian continence.

One cannot but sympathise with such plain honesty—what is more sympathise rather than register astonishment. For there is really nothing in the Christian attitude that suggests a superficial view of the realities of sex. Nevertheless I ought to express some doubt about how appropriate is the attitude implied in this miscellany to the problems involved. I doubt whether the best approach is the detached one. The religious seem to have been mainly concerned to prove that fear of sexuality was not the mainspring of the Christian practice of continence. In the enquiry which heads the collection of essays Father Bruno de Sainte-Marie writes thus: "Although we know that it may be a vertiginous liberating force, may not continence be practised through fear of sex?"[1] and Father Philippe de la Trinité in the first article says: "The Catholic theologian must answer *no* to Father Bruno's question whether continence may result from a fear of sex."[2] And further on, "Continence does not result from the fear of sex, so much is certain"[3]. I shall not discuss the accuracy of such an unhesitating reply, indicative of the attitude of these these men under vows. What I should like to question is the idea of sexuality inherent in this absence of fear. I shall try here to examine the question (which may at first sight seem foreign to the guiding preoccupations of these essays) whether fear is not precisely what does underlie "sex"; and whether the connection between "mystic" and "sexual" has not something to do with the gulfs of terrifying darkness that belong equally to both domains.

[1] Op. cit. page 10.
[2] Op. cit. page 19 (author's italics.)
[3] Op. cit. page 26.

The sacred nature of sexuality and the sexual qualities said to characterise the mystic life

In a highly interesting study[1] Father Louis Beirnaert, considering the comparison implicit in the language of the mystics between the experience of divine love and that of sexuality, emphasises "the aptness of sexual union to symbolise a higher union". He is content to remind us of the horror always attendant upon sexuality without insisting on it: "We with our scientific and technical mentality," he says, "are the ones who have turned sexual union into a purely biological fact . . ." In his eyes a sexual union has the virtue of expressing "the union of ineffable godhead with humanity," the fact is that it "already possesses in human experience an intrinsic fitness for symbolising the sacred event". "The phenomenology of religions shows us that human sexuality had a religious significance in the first place." The deliberate use of the phrase "religious significance" contrasts in Father Beirnaert's eyes with the "purely biological fact" of the genital union. For the sacred world did not assume until quite late on the unilaterally lofty meaning it has for the religious man of today. It still had an uncertain duality in classical antiquity. For the Christian apparently, sacred things are necessarily pure and impurity is profane. But for the pagan sacred things could also be unspeakably foul.[2] And if one takes a closer look one must admit that Satan in Christianity is not so far off from the divine, and even sin could not be regarded as completely foreign to sacredness. Sin was originally a religious taboo, and the religious taboo of paganism is in fact sacred. The fear and trembling that modern man cannot rid himself of when faced with things sacred to him are always bound up with the horror inspired by a forbidden object. I think in the present instance that it would be a distortion to conclude thus: "The conjugal symbolism of our mystics does not have any sexual significance. Rather sexual union

---

[1] *La Signification du Symbolisme Conjugal* pages 380-389.
[2] See above, page 136.

already has a transcendental significance." Transcendental?
That means denying its horror, the horror connected with
earthy reality.

Let us be quite clear. Nothing is further from my thought
than a sexual interpretation of the mystic life such as Marie
Bonaparte and James Leuba have insisted on. Even if the
mystical effusion is in some way comparable with sexual
excitement, to assert as Leuba does that the feelings of bliss
described by contemplatives always imply a degree of
activity of the sexual organs is an unjustified over-simplifica-
tion[1]. Marie Bonaparte takes her stand on a passage from
St. Theresa: "In his hands I saw a long golden spear and at
the end of the iron tip I seemed to see a point of fire. With
this he seemed to pierce my heart several times so that it
penetrated to my entrails. When he drew it out I thought he
was drawing them out with it and he left me completely
afire with a great love for God. The pain was so sharp that it
made me utter several moans; and so excessive was the
sweetness caused me by this intense pain that one can never
wish to lose it, now will one's soul be content with anything
less than God. It is not bodily pain, but spiritual, though
the body has a share in it—indeed, a great share. So sweet
are the colloquies of love which pass between the soul and
God that if anyone thinks I am lying I beseech God, in His
goodness, to give him the same experience."

Marie Bonaparte concludes: "Such is St. Theresa's
famous transverberation; I should like to compare with it
something a friend of mine confessed to me once. She had
lost her faith, but when she was fifteen she had undergone an
intense mystical crisis and had wanted to become a nun.
Now she remembered that one day, on her knees before the
altar, she had felt such unearthly bliss that she thought God
himself had descended into her. It was only later when she
had given herself to a man that she realised that this descent

[1] Father Beirnaert refers (page 380) to J. Leuba, *La Psychologie des Mystiques
Religieux*, page 202. Dr. Parcheminey gives an account (page 238) of the theories of
Marie Bonaparte as set out in an article in the *Revue Française de Psychanalyse*
(1948) No. 2.

of God into her had been a violent venereal orgasm. Chaste Theresa never had a chance to make a comparison of this sort and yet it seems to be an explanation of her transverberation". Dr. Parcheminey put this in precise language: "Such considerations lead to the hypothesis that all mystical experience is nothing but transposed sexuality and hence neurotic behaviour". It would indeed be hard to prove that Theresa's "transverberation" does not justify Marie Bonaparte's comparison: there is nothing to prove that it was not a violent venereal orgasm. But that is unlikely. In fact Marie Bonaparte ignores the fact that the experience of contemplation was linked early on with the liveliest awareness concerning spiritual joy and sensual emotion. Father Beirnaert says: "Contrary to what Leuba says, mystics are perfectly aware of the physical sensations accompanying their experience. St. Bonaventure talks of those who 'in spiritualibus affectionibus carnals fluxus liquore maculantur'. St. Theresa and St. John of the Cross refer to it in explicit terms. But all this they regard as extrinsic to their experience; when this sensation occurs they ignore it and regard it without dread or fear. In any case contemporary psychology has shown that organic sexual urges are often at the root of a powerful emotion that spills over through every possible channel. It is thus comparable with the idea of 'redundantia' familiar to St. John of the Cross. Finally let us remember that movements of this sort occur at the beginning of mystical life but do not continue into the higher stages, into spiritual marriage particularly. In short, the existence of physical sensations in the course of the ecstacy does not mean in the least that the experience is a specifically sexual one". This summary may not answer every question that may be asked, but it does make a clear distinction between spheres whose fundamental characteristics might pass unnoticed by psychoanalysts, possibly unacquainted with any religious experience at all and certainly unvisited by mystical experience[1].

---

[1] They themselves are inclined to presuppose, however, that the psychiatrist's vocation demands a minimum number of neurotic characteristics.

There are staggering similarities and even corresponding or interchangeable characteristics in the two systems, erotic and mystical. But these connections can only be at all clearly perceived if the two kinds of emotion are actually experienced. It is true that psychiatrists deliberately leave their their personal experience behind while they are examining the sick whose shortcomings they cannot feel in any deep-seated way. On the whole if they dismiss the mystical experience without having known it they are reacting as they do before their patients. The result is inevitable: behaviour outside their own experience they regard a priori as abnormal: they identify the right they assume to make outside judgments with the pathological nature of whatever they are examining. In addition, those mystical experiences that are manifested in equivocal states of disturbance are the easiest to recognise and those which most clearly resemble sexual agitation. This leads to the superficial conclusion that mysticism is akin to a neurotic state of exaltation. But the greatest pain is not betrayed by cries, and so with mysticism, the furthest frontier of human experience perceived in man's innermost self. "Sensational" moments are not a matter of mature experience. In practical terms the states of mind which would save psychiatrists from drawing over-hasty conclusions do not come within their range, for we can only know them if we experience them personally. Descriptions of them by the great mystics should in theory mitigate our ignorance but the very simplicity of these descriptions renders them disconcerting—they present no symptoms like those of neuropaths, nor cries as of "transverberated" mystics. Not only do they offer little foothold for a psychiatrist's interpretation to establish itself but, moreover, their details are so intangible that the psychiatrist will usually miss them altogether. If we wish to say at what precise point the light can be thrown on the relationship between eroticism and mystical spirituality we must return to the inner life which Catholics under vows are practically the only ones to take as a starting point in this volume.

The morality of "dying to oneself" and the difference between this and ordinary morality

The religious who deal with mysticism have not all experienced exactly what they are talking about but as one of the contributors to this volume says[1], mysticism (the only kind regarded by the Church as authentic, of course) "is a constituent of every Christian life". "Living a Christian life and living a mystical life mean the same thing", and "all the elements we perceive in the highest states are already present in those which can be called lower". It is true that the religious do not seem to have been able to put their finger on the precise point where everything becomes clear. As I have suggested, they start from confused ideas about sexual and sacred matters. But the deviation due to a view I consider mistaken, is not so serious and in any case is worth pursuing, for at least it moves towards an enlightened understanding.

Father Tesson's views do not always seem entirely adequate to me but they are profound, and it will soon be clear, I hope, why I take them as a starting point. Father Tesson insists that where mystical states are concerned morality is the decisive factor. "The merit of the moral life" he says, "is what enables us to assess a man's religious and mystical value." "Morality judges and guides the mystical life."[2] Here is a remarkable thing. Father Tesson who takes morality to be the sovereign principle of the mystical life, far from attacking sensuality stresses its conformity with God's purpose. According to him "two forces attract us towards God: one, sexuality, is 'written into our nature'; the other one, mysticism, 'comes from Christ'." "Superficial disagreements may temporarily disrupt but cannot destroy the profound harmony between the two."

Father Tesson interprets the Church's doctrine saying

<hr>

[1] Father Tesson, *Sexualité, Morale et Mystique*, page 359-380. The same opinion is maintained by Father Philippe de la Trinité in *Amour Mystique, Chasteté Parfaite*, page 17-36 (introductory article).
[2] Father Tesson, *Sexualité, Morale et Mystique*, page 376.

that "the exercise of genital sexuality", allowed only in
marriage, is "neither a permitted sin nor an act of mediocre
value only just tolerated because of human weakness".
Within the bounds of marriage carnal acts are "part of the
marks of love exchanged by a man and a woman who have
bound themselves together for life and even longer".
"Christ intended that Christian marriage should be a sacra-
ment and he sanctified married life with a special grace".
Hence there is nothing to prevent these acts when "carried
out in a state of grace" from being "meritorious". The union
is the more "humanised" in that the love is "elective" and
exclusive. What is more, "there is nothing to stop a conjugal
life including the acts we are discussing from being part of a
profound mystical life and even of a life of holiness".

Such an attitude, while of indisputable significance and
interest, must nevertheless be taken as incomplete from the
outset. It cannot prevent there being a secular conflict
between sensuality and mysticism whose sharper aspects
the authors of this collection have probably dwelt on only
in order to diminish their importance.

I must mention, but only in passing, that the author does
not fail to perceive some possibility of confusion in this
open minded attitude to sexual life to which the very volume
he is contributing to bears witness. He says: "Too much
emphasis has been laid in recent publications on the idea
that the sexual union of husband and wife is the greatest act
of love. The fact is that while the common habit of carnal
activity is an expression of love having deep emotional and
vital overtones, other manifestations of love are better suited
to showing those aspects belonging to the spirit and the will,
and more and more emphasis must be laid on these". Here
he reminds us of the evangelical law which also concerns
those choosing married life: "Man must die that he may
live".

There is a connection between this and Father Tesson's
morality that "judges and guides the mystical life". Indeed,
this morality with essentials arising from neither opposition

to sexuality nor from the necessities of life (these factors are associated), seems to be related to the fundamental proposition: man must die that he may live. It is thus based in a positive way on a certain value: divine life; it is not limited negatively to those precepts, essential merely, for safeguarding the life man already has. Divine life cannot be founded on the observation of these precepts alone though nothing is possible without them. Love alone is its truth and its strength. It may even not be in direct contrast with the evils the precepts are designed to counter. The sickness that may affect the divine life is rather that paralysing weight of "routine, superficial punctiliousness and Pharisaic conformity". None the less morality is dependent on the law which "the Church . . . may under no circumstances permit to be broken". But if the law is broken the theologian must not be in too great a hurry to pronounce judgment. "Recent work in psychology" has focused attention on "the state of mind of people with a rather vigorous inner life, a deep aspiration towards obedience and towards God, who meet obstacles and a lack of balance within themselves". "Psychoanalysis has shown us the powerful influence of subconscious motives in this field often masquerading as intentional"; "a serious revision of moral psychology" is therefore called for. "The obvious failures, however grave, in obligations that have been undertaken are perhaps not the most serious in the long run, for here the faults are clearly recognised as such. The thing most prejudicial to spiritual life is to sink into mediocrity or preen oneself in self-satisfaction and conceit; though of course these attitudes are not mutually exclusive." "Since outside the limits of his conscious mind a man is not necessarily responsible for his failure to obey the law, one must assume that this sort of failure, whether perceived as a failure or whether, when recognised, committed involuntarily, will be met with in subjects committed to the paths of perfection and mysticism and even in saints." This morality is not centred on the guarantee of social and individual life given us by the "main precepts" but on mystical passion leading man to die to himself in order to inherit eternal life. What it condemns is the dragging weight of attachment to the self, in the guise of pride and mediocrity and self-satisfaction. So Father Tesson's proposition which would have morality as the guide and the judge of the mystic life could be reversed and we might equally well say that mysticism guides and judges the moral life. Hence, and this is really self-evident, morality cannot be confined to keeping life going as it is; it calls for life to expand and blossom. I was going to say on the *contrary* it calls for this. For it is written that we must die that we may live.

The present moment and death in the "nuptial flight" and in the life of holy orders

The bond between life and death has many aspects. It can be felt equally in sexual and mystical experience. Father Tesson like most of the other contributors to the Carmelites' volume insists on the harmony between sexuality and life, but however it may be regarded, human sexuality is only ever admissible within certain limits, and outside these it is forbidden. There is everywhere in the long run a certain sexual impulse felt as unclean. From then on it is no longer a matter of beneficient sexuality "intended by God" but rather of malediction and death. Beneficent sexuality is close to animal sexuality, unlike eroticism which is man's own and only genital in its origins. Eroticism is a sterile principle representing Evil and the diabolic.

This is precisely where the final and the most significant relationship between sexuality and mysticism is to be sought. In the life of believers and persons under vows, which often manifests a certain disequilibrium, seduction is often aimed rather at the erotic than at the genital. This is what plainly emerges from the images associated with St. Anthony's temptation. The obsessive element in temptation is what the religious fears. His aspirations to divine life are translated into the desire to die to himself; thenceforth everything perpetually changes before his eyes, each element continually transforming itself into its opposite. Death desired by the holy man turns into divine life for him. He has set his face against the genital order, meaning life, and he is seduced by a form that spells death. But malediction or death as the temptation of sexuality presents them to him is also death seen from the point of view of divine life sought through the death of the self, so temptation is doubly significant of death. How should we fail to imagine that his movement leads the religious on to the "temple roof", from the heights of which the man who opens his eyes wide with no shadow of fear, will perceive the interrelation of all the contradictory potentialities?

I shall now endeavour to describe what he will *perhaps* see from that rooftop.

In the first place let me state this paradox. Is not the problem thus formulated already given in nature? Nature ties up life and death in genital matters. Let us take the extreme case of sexual activity bringing about the death of the animal giving birth. It is not wholly lacking in absurdity to speak of nature's intentions, yet the inevitable process of life wasting its substance is not only just that. At the very moment when it is poured out in extravagant profusion life has an aim that seems to contradict the losses it so feverishly makes sure of. It is only given up to this spendthrift waste of energy in so far as it is aimed at an increase. Whether with plants or with animals, the luxury of flowers or adornment may not be the luxury it appears. It may look like an end in itself. No doubt the splendour of flowers and animals is useless enough as far as function goes and to function our intelligence insensitively assigns it. It looks like an enormous fraud—just as if reproduction were the pretext for a tumultuous surge to spill forth independently. However blindly it seems to proceed, life must have needed some excuse for giving free rein to the extravagant festival it bears within itself—as if the mighty flood required an alibi.

This sort of approach is quite unsatisfactory. Anyway it leads us into a sphere where man's reflections have always progressed with an unjustifiable want of seriousness. Every-thing was going along so nicely that Schopenhauer's simpli-fications were readily accepted: the impulses of sexuality had one meaning only—Nature's purpose working through them. No one bothered to reflect that "Nature" behaved in a ridiculous way.

It is impossible to examine all the implications of a problem that forces me into an attitude of irony. I am con-tent just to suggest how far life which is an exuberant loss is at the same time directed by a contrary movement demand-ing increase.

Yet loss is the winner in the long run. Reproduction only multiplies life in vain, multiplies it in order to offer it up to death whose ravages alone increase when life tries blindly to spread further. I contend that the waste becomes greater and greater in spite of the need for an achievement in the opposite direction.

Let us return to a point I think important: the extreme case of the sexual act bringing about the animal's death. Here life persists in increasing and yet is lost. I could find no finer example of dying to oneself. I still intend not to adopt the attitude that would have the animals subordinated to the result. In this particular case the individual's lot goes far beyond consequences which are only important for the species. These consequences provide for the repetition of the process from one generation to the next, but indifference to the future, the striking and in a sense solar adhesion to the single instant of time may not be ruled out, as it must be if all we do is take those elements of the instant that make it less important than what follows after. No one could deny the animal's death to itself unless he had some preconceived beliefs about it; and it seems to me that by entering its death under the heading "care of the type", human thought is grossly over-simplifying the conduct of the male at the moment of the nuptial flight.

To return to eroticism in man, it would have the same significance for the religious undergoing temptation as death for the drone as it flies towards it, if the bee could decide freely as the monk can in full awareness of death in store. The religious cannot die a physical death; he will die to the divine life he desires. This is one of the "incidental disagreements" in Father Tesson's words which continually bring into conflict "the two forms of attraction which draw us towards God", the one "written into our nature"—sexuality the other mystical, "coming from Christ". I do not see how we can discuss the relationship of these two forms with any clarity if we do not take them when they are most strongly opposed, and also most markedly alike. Their "deep-seated harmony"? It may exist, but are we going to find it by attenuating the conflicting characteristics if they are at the same time precisely the ones that make them alike?

In Father Tesson's words, divine life requires that the seeker after it shall die. But no one has in mind a death that is merely passive absence of life. Dying can take on the active meaning of behaviour, behaviour that sets at nought the cautiousness inculcated by the fear of death. Animals themselves have reflexes of immobility or flight in the face of danger; they bear witness to a primary concern which has numerous manifestations in man. To live for the moment, no longer to heed these instincts for survival; this is dying to oneself, or at least it is living with death as an equal. Each man indeed prolongs through his whole life the effects of his attachment to himself. He is continuously bound to courses of action aimed at a result valid on the plane of the prolonged individual existence. In so far as he is willing to enslave the present to the future he is self-satisfied, conceited, and mediocre and prevented by selfishness from approaching the life Father Tesson called divine and which may also be more broadly called sacred. Father Tesson has summed up this life, I think, in the formula "to live the divine life, a man must die" Beyond pride and mediocrity we keep glimpsing a terrifying truth. The immensity of everything that is, unintelligible to the intelligence which explains everything in terms of acts, causes or aims, this immensity terrifies him

in so far as no place is left for the limited being who judges
the world through calculations, in which he relates to himself
and his own mediocre and conceited views parts, selected
from the totality they are lost in. Immensity, though, spells
death to the man it attracts; a kind of vertigo or horror siezes
him who sets himself and his precarious egotistic attitude
against those infinitely present deeps, infinitely absent too.
Like an animal threatened with death his reflexes of stupefied
immobility and flight, intolerably confused, nail him in
the attitude of a man under torture that we commonly call
anguish. But the danger that now holds the animal rooted to
the spot and now sends him off in headlong flight comes from
without; it is real, precise; while with anguish, desire for the
indefinable is what controls the reflexes of the animal in the
face of death. The being threatened with death like this
reminds us of the situation of a religious who sick in mind
tries out a carnal act, or in the animal kingdom the drone
about to die not by an enemy's act but from the fatal impulse
that drives him through the light towards the queen. Each
case shows at least the fulguration of one instant in which
the creature braves death.

The temptation of the religious and morose delectation

There is one point that can never be sufficiently stressed.
The taboo on sexuality which the religious of his own free
will carries to extremes, creates in temptation a state of affairs
abnormal certainly, but in which the erotic element, rather
than undergoing a change, stands out more sharply. If it
seems paradoxical to compare the temptation of the man in
holy orders with the nuptial and disastrous flight of the
drone, death is none the less the end of both, and I might
call the religious in his temptation a lucid drone, one who
knows that death would follow the satisfying of his desire.
Normally we ignore the similarity, for the reason that in the
human species the sexual act never entails real death and
men under vows of continence are almost the only ones to
see in it a promise of moral death. Yet eroticism is only

fulfilled, only exhausts all its potentialities if it brings some degradation in its train, the horror of which will suggest the simple death of the flesh.

The very differences between the drone and the religious show clearly the significance of the resemblance between them, and stress one characteristic of the sensual passions that relates them to mysticism in a closer way than their common vocabulary does.

I have said already that the lucidity of the religious is opposed to the blindness of the insect, but this difference is summed up in the contrast between man and animal. I wish now to bring up a question which transcends this problem and is a limited form of it. I am referring to the resistance of the man under a vow of chastity which is quite foreign to the drone and generally also to the human being. (It is true that feminine resistance is frequent, but however meaningful her behaviour may be, if a woman resists she is not always clearly aware of why; she resists like the females of animals. Only the religious in the throes of temptation gives his refusal its full significance.)

The struggle of the religious springs from his will to maintain a spiritual life, and that life would be mortally imperilled if he fell from grace. The sin of the flesh puts an end to the soul's soaring towards immediate freedom. We have seen that for Father Tesson as for the whole Church "man must die to live eternally". There is an ambiguousness of vocabulary here: apparently the death which strikes at eternal life is the contrary of the one which is the condition of eternal life. But this contrast is only apparent. Life must in any case be defended against harmful forces. The theme of keeping life going,—real life, material life, under cover of a spiritual truth—is not noticeably altered if the life of the soul is the one meant. In theory life destroyed by sin has an elementary value, it is Good. Life destroyed by divine life is perhaps Evil. But death always destroys a reality that wants to live on. If I die to myself I scorn the creature organised for duration and growth and similarly if through sin I destroy the spiritual life within me. The seductive, the marvellous, the ravishing wins every time over the need to organise things to last, over the resolute intention to become more powerful. What resists and changes, is now the interest of the selfish individual and now the ordering of the religious life. But the preoccupation with the future, sordid or not, puts a brake on immediate pleasures.

As we have seen Father Tesson speaks openly of the "two forms of attraction which draw us towards God", the sexual, belonging to Nature, and the mystical, coming from Christ. God—for me—means the lightning flash which exalts the creature above the concern to protect or increase his wealth in the dimension of time. Men of religion will say that I am leaving out the most important thing, that in temptation one of two conflicting forces ought to be loved and the other ought to be abhorred. That is not so, or at least only superficially. I must stress the following fundamental principle.

In temptation there is only an object of attraction of a sexual nature; the mystical element which restrains the tempted man has now no "immediate force"; its power derives from the fact that the religious, faithful to his decisions, prefers the safeguard of the equilibrium acquired through the mystical life to the delirium into which temptation would have him slide. The peculiar quality of temptation is that the divine in its mystical form has ceased to be directly accessible and can only be understood intellectually. The divine is at that moment directly accessible on the sexual plane, the demoniac plane, as it were; this demoniac-divine or divine-demoniac offers what God himself, as he is discovered through major mystical experience, offers, and offers it more compellingly since the religious would choose physical death to a lapse into temptation. I am aware of the satisfactions for the sordid ego promised by such a lapse, but the religious denies the ego that would take advantage of them, or rather he foresees the inner degradation of the self tied to order and the Church that might one day be plain for all to see, and it is for the sake of that self that he renounces his primary egotism.

The second self desires to lose itself in God, but when temptation assails him God is no longer *felt* in his mind, he no longer compels with the vertiginous power that is his essence; quite the contrary, for what is now the compelling force is the calculated advantage of the second self as discerned by the intellect. God is still a factor but only as understood by the conscious mind. Calculated interest wins, not burning desire.

Hence at the moment of temptation the resistance of a man under vows is to a dizzy rush into perdition. The religious who says no is in fact in the position of a drone who knows what will be the outcome of his headlong flight towards the queen.

But because of his fright and the refusal that springs from it, the thing that attracts the religious has no longer the same significance as the queen leading the insect on to its death in light. The thing refused is at once hateful and desirable. If sexual fascination has its fullest radiance, its beauty is so great that the religious is still enraptured by it. He is enraptured but he trembles too; there is a halo of death about it that makes its beauty hateful.

This ambiguous aspect of temptation is clearly evident in the prolonged form of temptation that the Church has named morose delectation.

In morose delectation the beauty of the object and its sexual attraction have vanished. Only the memory of them persists in the form of the halo of death I have mentioned. Thenceforward the object is less an object than the aura surrounding the state of the soul and it is impossible to say whether it is horror or fascination; there is a compelling feeling of death about this aura while the object of sensuality inspires fear and passes out of the field of consciousness. Naturally the similarity of morose delectation to the nuptial flight is more remote than that of temptation. It can be perceived nonetheless in spite of the slightly comical impotence of delectation. Delectation is a sort of paralysed nuptial flight; the compulsion is still there but now, though it may become painful, it is in blind darkness like the animal's. It is in fact a means of reconciling desire for the soul's salvation with desire to be lost in the mortal bliss of an embrace. But the desire for a desirable object is this time the desire for an object with no charm of its own; it is the unintelligible and unconscious desire for death or at least damnation.

Guilty sensuality and death

An analysis of delectation throws light on the hitherto inexplicable subject of man's sensuality. This is how it must be regarded if we are to see what links it to man's only pure experience, the mystical experience. I believe that to take human sensuality in its loftiest form, in the way the Carmelites' book does, as something intended by God and not dependent on the mistaken directions it has sometimes followed and which have sullied it, will lead us away from the illumination of mysticism. Limited sensuality with its permitted aspects covers up the mortal aspects that are seen in the flight of the drone or the temptation of the religious, whose meaning is more remotely evident in morose delectation. What is true is that the kind of genital activity intended by God, limited to marriage, and more generally the sort of sexuality thought of as natural and normal, as opposed on the one hand to unnatural deviations and on the other to experiences considered as guilty and sin-laden, and having a harsher flavour because of that—the lure of the forbidden fruit.

Mostly, for a pure soul, licit sexual desire would be absolutely pure. That is possible, but that partial truth hides a fundamental truth.

In spite of the common tendency to associate an element of shame with sexuality it is reasonable and in conformity with the Church's attitude to number sexuality as a function among the necessary activities. There is something to be praised and marvelled at in the lovers' embrace, quite the contrary of the element of shame I have discussed. The embrace is life's flowering and its most blissful form. The example of the drone whose embrace is a peak of experience with a fatal outcome is not appropriate here. All the same, some aspects of sensuality put us on our guard from the start. The orgasm is popularly termed "the little death". The reactions of women are comparable in principle with those of females trying to escape from the fatality of love; though different from those of the religious assailed by temptation, these reactions do reveal the existence of a feeling of dread or fright generally bound up with the idea of sexual contact. These aspects have a theoretical confirmation. The expenditure of energy necessary for the sexual act[1] is everywhere enormous.

One need look no further for the cause of the fear associated with sexual activity. Death is exceptional, an extreme case; each loss of normal energy is indeed only a little death compared with the death of the drone, but whether obscurely or clearly this little death is what is feared. On the other hand it is also desired (within human limits at least). No one could deny that one essential element of excitement is the feeling of being swept off one's feet, of falling headlong. If love exists at all it is, like death, a swift movement of loss within us, quickly slipping into tragedy and stopping only with death. For the truth is that between death and the reeling, heady motion of the little death the distance is hardly noticeable.

The desire to go keeling helplessly over, that assails the innermost depths of every human being is nevertheless different from the desire to die in that it is ambiguous. It may well be a desire to die, but it is at the same time a desire to live to the limits of the possible and the impossible with ever-increasing intensity. It is the desire to live while ceasing to live, or to die without ceasing to live, the desire

---

[1] I am not talking about the expenditure of "sexual energy". I agree with Oswald Schwartz (*Psychologie Sexuelle*, Gallimard 1951 page 9) in believing the concept of sexual energy to be a groundless fiction; however Schwartz seems to ignore the fact that a non-predetermined sum of physical energy, expendable in several directions, always enters into sexual activity.

of an extreme state that Saint Theresa has perhaps been the only one to depict strongly enough in words. "I die because I cannot die". But the death of not dying is precisely not death; it is the ultimate stage of life; if I die because I cannot die it is on condition that I live on; because of the death I feel though still alive and still live on. St. Theresa's being reeled, but did not actually die of her desire actually to experience that sensation. She lost her footing but all she did was to live more violently, so violently that she could say she was on the threshold of dying, but such a death as tried her to the utmost though it did not make her cease to live.

Sensuality, tenderness and love

The longed-for swoon is thus the salient feature not only of man's sensuality but also of the experience of the mystics. We are returning to the comparison between mysticism and guilty eroticism but we have moved away from idyllic or licit sexuality. We have come upon an aspect of sensuality, however, whose mode is close to the temptation of the religious and to morose delectation because of a fundamental ambiguity. In each case it is hard to say whether the object of desire is the incandescence of life or of death. The incandescence of life means death; death means an incandescence of life. In speaking of the temptation of the religious I was not able to make this ambiguity absolutely clear. Yet the turbulence and disastrousness of sexuality are of the essence of temptation. Temptation is the desire to fall, to fail, to faint and to squander all one's reserves until there is no firm ground beneath one's feet. Later on I shall take that as a starting point to investigate the way that sexual and mystical experience are linked. But I must first show how forms of sexual activity so varied and often so bluntly contradictory, harmonise in the nostalgia for a moment of disequilibrium.

The ambiguity I have referred to looks at first as if it leads if not to ruin (for the loss of energy involved can be made good, the breathless rush that sends us careening over is only temporary) at least to a loss of balance. This is of course not a lasting loss; it generally occurs at intervals during phases of balanced activity; these ensure that it shall recur and also that the damage done can be made good. But the strong and healthy phases during which sexual disequilibrium rights itself hides its deeper significance.

One of the most important purposes of sexual reorganisation is the anxiety to find a place for the disorders of love-making in an orderly pattern covering the whole of human life. Such order is founded upon the tender friendship of a man and a woman and upon the bonds which unite them with their children. There is nothing more important for us than placing the sexual act at the basis of the social edifice. Civilised order is not to be founded on the deepest sexuality, on disorder, that is; limits are to be set to this disorder by connecting it with order, by merging the path of disorder with that of order and by trying to subordinate the former to the latter. That operation is doomed to failure since eroticism never cedes it sovereign power except by degrading itself to the level of animal activity. Balanced forms within which eroticism is possible lead only to a fresh unbalance in the end or to the ageing that precedes the final disappearance.

The most significant manifestation of the necessity for this alternation of balance and lack of balance is the violent and tender love of one being for another. The violence of love leads to tenderness, the lasting form of love, but it brings into the striving of one heart towards another the same quality of disorder, the same thirst for losing consciousness and the same after-taste of death that is found in the mutual desire for each other's body. In essence, love raises the feeling of one being for another to such a pitch that the threatened loss of the beloved or the loss of his love is felt no less keenly than the threat of death. Hence love is based on a desire to live in anguish in the presence of an object of such high worth that the heart cannot bear to contemplate losing it. The fever of the senses is not a desire to die. Nor is love the desire to lose but the desire to live in fear of possible loss, with the beloved holding the lover on the very threshold of a swoon. At that price alone can we feel the violence of rapture before the beloved.

The ridiculous thing about this urge towards transcendence in which concern for the preservation of life is scorned is the almost immediate transition to the wish to organise it in a lasting way, or at least a way intended to be lasting, with the disequilibirium of love protected—if possible—from disequilibrium! For the lover not to erect against the loss of the beloved conventions that destroy liberty is not derisory, nor is it for him not to subordinate love in essence capricious to setting up a home and a family in the physical sense. Neither does the absence of love make nonsense of a home (the absence of love, take it whatever way you like, is simply nothing at all). But confusing love with material organisation, enmeshing the sovereignty of passion in the purchase of a few bits of ironmongery—these are ridiculous. (Certainly, unless one is incapable of doing so, it is no less ridiculously pretentious to refuse to organise a life together.)

These contrasts are the more disconcerting in that love is already different from sensual eroticism and belongs to the pretexts which sensuality finds for the disorders of desire to show them to be a power for good. The same ambivalence occurs at all levels. On the one hand the love of the sexual partner (a variant of marriage as inserted into the order of active society and often coinciding with it) changes sexuality into tenderness; tenderness attenuates the violence of nocturnal pleasures, and sadistic actions are here more common than might be supposed; it is possible for tenderness to take on a balanced form. On the other hand the fundamental violence that makes us lose control always tends to disturb a relationship of tenderness—to make us find in that relationship that death is near, and death is the symbol of all sensuality, even that modified by tenderness. Here is the violence of lovemaking without which sexual love could not have lent its vocabulary as it has done to describe the ecstasies of the mystics.

The underworld, sexual cynicism, and obscenity

The extension to fields where disorder seems unjustifiable of an ambivalent desire to lose control is in line with the tendency that dominates human life. We are always striving to duplicate strong and viable forms which can contain and limit our disequilibrium with unstable ones not likely to last which emphasise the lack of balance. In the simple disorder of a passion it is true that this tendency is involuntary: disorder is held to be wrong and the spirit struggles against it. But in the cynical and impudent degradation of the kind of life I now propose to discuss, want of order is an accepted principle. The desire to fall headlong to which we yield in spite of ourselves is completely and unrestrainedly accepted. Thereafter its power vanishes, for people living in a state of permanent disorder only know moments of sullen disequilibrium. Prostitutes and men who live off them, together make up a class; they often succumb and find a dull pleasure in yielding and in letting themselves go. They do not always slip to the bottom of the slope; besides, they find it necessary to create a rudimentary and limited organisation to protect their common interests against the widespread equilibrium of a society whose order they refuse to adhere to and which they are bent on destroying. They cannot carry their refusal right to the bitter end, being anyway far from insensitive to the maintenance of a cynically egotistical life. But the advantages of insubordination allow them to supply their wants with ease; they can cheat all the time and this gives them as much leisure as they want for indulging in the delights of a life of perdition. They yield completely to the essential disorder of destructive sensuality and ceaselessly impel human life down the slope towards degradation and death. In the heart forsaken by anguish, free rein is given to a huge and squalid derision. All one has to do is to steal or kill if necessary in a lazy way, keep alive with the minimum of effort and in any case live at other people's expense.

All this is basically a question of a revolting lowering of standards, of a vulgar abortiveness. The life of the underworld is not to be envied. It has lost a certain vital resilience without which humanity could sink too low. All it does is exploit a complete loss of self-control, unimaginatively and in a way that minimises apprehension for the future. Having submitted unrestrainedly to the pleasure of losing self-control it has made lack of control into a constant state with neither savour nor interest.

Seen in itself, within the limits of the people who live in this way, this degradation of sensuality would be practically insignificant. But it has far-reaching overtones. It has meaning not only for those who let themselves go completely; a lack of restraint, insipid for the people practising it, has the sharpest tang for those who witness it, if they continue to practise moral restraint in their own life. The obscenity of the conduct and language of prostitutes is thin stuff for people whose daily experience it is. But for others who have remained pure here is the possibility of a vertiginous fall. Low prostitution and obscenity taken together constitute a sharply defined and significant form of eroticism. They distort and darken the picture of sexual life but are not responsible for any profound change in its meaning. Sensuality is indeed the field of derision and imposture; it is essentially a wish to lose one's footing but without falling irrevocably, and this could not be so without a certain fraudulence for which we are blindly responsible but which takes us in nevertheless. To live our sensual life we always have to act out a naive comedy for our own benefit, and the most ridiculous one is the obscenity of prostitutes. So the gap between the indifference found inside the world of obscenity and the fascination that world exercises on the world outside is far from being as unstable as it seems at first sight. There is a lack of balance, but only a sensual lack of balance; the bitterness of the comedy or the feeling of degradation bound up with payment add a pleasurable element for the man who gives in to his desire to lose control.

The unity of mystical experience and eroticism

The importance of obscenity in the succession of key images of sexual activity is finally responsible for the gulf separating religious mysticism and eroticism. Because of its importance the contrast between divine and carnal love is a very marked one. The comparison one is finally bound to make between manifestations of uncontrolled obscenity and the holiest of ecstasies is thought scandalous, and this from the first day when psychiatry as a science took to meddling somewhat heavy-handedly in the explanation of mystical states. Scientists know nothing about these states on principle, and the reaction of those who to defend the Church have protested against their conclusions has often been dictated by their outraged feelings, so that they have failed to see beyond the errors and over-simplifications to the basic truth put forward, albeit in a distorted form. People on both sides have taken to confusing the issue in the clumsiest way. But it must be admitted that this volume of the Carmelites is an appreciable step in the direction of open mindedness: in spite of everything Catholic minds have come to admit that comparisons are possible and the psychiatrists do not deny the difficulties they are up against.

One must go further. I think the position must be clearly outlined before we pick up the threads of the problem again.

Let me repeat that I believe that it is not enough to recognise that there may be links between the two spheres; this is what the Carmelites and the others in holy orders who have collaborated with them have done in obedience to an old tradition. We must avoid two reefs: we must not try to diminish the experiences of the mystics for the sake of comparison, as psychiatrists have done albeit unintentionally. Neither must we spiritualise the domain of sexuality to exalt it to the level of ethereal experiences. I feel bound to

define point by point the meaning of the different forms of
sexuality, only giving a secondary place to the hybrid ones
that spring from an effort to moderate or to purify, but proceeding from the most easily assimilated to that which is
characterised by a refusal to be integrated into the social
order. In particular the question posed by the latter must be
elucidated. The domain of obscenity bound up with prostitution in the first place is what has lent a scandalous tinge to
sensuality. The most important thing of all is to show how
the spiritual content of obscenity iself repeats the basic
layout of the whole domain. Obscenity is repugnant, and it
is natural that timid minds should see nothing more to it
than this unpleasantness, but it is easy to see that its ignoble
sides are connected with the social level of the people who
create it, people whom society vomits forth in the same way
that they in turn vomit up society. No matter: the fact
remains that this repugnant sexuality is really nothing but a
paradoxical way of giving greater point to an activity which
in essence must lead to loss of control; that leaving out
everybody whose social degradation causes it, the attraction
of obscenity for those who are perturbed by it as an outside
factor has nothing to do necessarily with their low personal
qualities: how many indisputably high-minded and dis-
interested men and women have only looked on it as a way
of losing control almost completely?

All this leads one to say at long last that once the constant
factor of sex has been understood in these various manifestations there is nothing to prevent the relationship of sex
and mysticism being grasped as well: all that is needed is to
find the common factor in the fascination of such apparently
contradictory experiences as obscenity and idyllic love,
morose delectation and the mating of the drone. The trances,
the states of rapture and the theopathic states prolifically
described by mystics of every religious discipline—Hindu,
Buddhist, Moslem or Christian, not to mention the rarer
ones who have no religion—all have the same significance:
non-attachment to ordinary life, indifference to its needs,

anguish felt in the midst of this until the being reels, and the way left open to a spontaneous surge of life that is usually kept under control but which bursts forth in freedom and infinite bliss. The difference between this experience and that of sensuality is only a matter of confining these impulses to the domain of inner awareness, without the intervention of real and intentional physical activity, (or if the body does come into play it is in a minimal fashion, even in the breathing exercises that Hindus deliberately practise for certain effects). Conscious thought, conscious decisions, even negative ones, for at such a time the only aim of conscious reflection is to destroy its own subtleties, are the most important factors in this sphere, at first glance apparently so remote from the sphere of eroticism. If love for some personal being is the form taken by mystical effusion—for Christ in Europe, for the Kali in India, for example, and to some extent for God everywhere—this person exists in the mind. It is doubtful whether inspired beings like Christ were ever the subject of true mystical contemplation during their lifetime.

At any rate the two spheres are obviously close. Mysticism has often traced its path through love for a certain individual although it tends to transcend such love; for ascetics it may be both a convenient way and a jumping-off ground. It is not easy to ignore the accidents that happen to mystics during their exercises, at least in the early stages. As we have seen, men pursuing the paths of mysticism not infrequently find that they are "sullied with the liquid of the carnal flux", as St. Bonaventure puts it. Father Louis Beirnaert, quoting St. Bonaventure[1] tells us "That is something that mystics consider intrinsic to their experience". I do not imagine they are mistaken; these accidents show nevertheless that basically sensuality and mysticism are akin. If my reasoning has been followed it will be apparent that with intentions and key images analogous in both spheres, a mystical impulse of thought may always set off involuntarily the same reflex

[1] Op. cit. page 386.

that an erotic image would. If this is so the converse must also be true. Indeed Hindus do base their exercises in tantrism on the possibility of inducing a mystical crisis with the help of sexual excitement. They choose a suitable partner, young, beautiful and of a lofty spirituality, and being careful to avoid the final spasm they pass from the carnal embrace to spiritual ecstasy. There is no reason to believe that their experiences are not genuine and straight forward, according to people who know such practitioners. It must always be possible no doubt to devitate from the original purpose but this probably happens seldom and one would not be justified in denying that this method can lead to states of pure rapture. It seems therefore that communication is always possible between sensuality and mysticism, obedient as they are to the same motive force[1].

Continence and the condition of an unconditioned moment

Such communication, though, is not necessarily desirable. The physical spasms of men vowed to continence are not intentional. It is doubtful whether the systematic transition from sensuality to spirituality is appropriate if the aim is to reach the remoter areas of completely detached spiritual experience. Certainly the effort is of decisive significance at the peak of human questings. It is free from anxiety about specific occasions dependent on complex material conditions which act as a painful drag on erotic life (among the various reasons given by mèn under vows to justify continence this is the least easy to dispute). On the other hand mystical experience takes place (or at least can take place) in the very field where the final efforts of the questioning intelligence are made; on this level it is impossible to ignore the fact that because of the movement towards death that is its essence

---

[1] The same is not true of other areas of human potentialities. There is no sexual excitement in philosophical or mathematical research or even poetic creation. Though fighting or criminal activities, theft or burglary may just possibly have that effect. Sexual excitement and ecstasy are always connected with an active sense of transgression.

that experience comes into play at the dénouement, that is at the moment of greatest tension.

In assessing the importance of mystical experience one fact must be stressed. It entails a complete detachment from material conditions. Thus it meets man's need to be independent of factors not chosen by himself but imposed from without. The aim is a state that can be called sovereign. Erotic experience, at least at a first glance, is subordinated to the event; mystical experience sets man free from the event. In the sphere of mysticism we reach complete sovereignty; particularly in states described by theology as theopathic. Such states which may be provoked independently of their Christian forms are quite different not only from erotic states but also from minor mystical states; their distinguishing mark is the high degree of indifference to what happens. In the theopathic state there is no more desire; the subject becomes passive and suffers what happens to him with a kind of immobility. In the inert beatitude of this state, when each object and the whole universe have become utterly transparent, hope and dread have both vanished. The object of contemplation becomes equal to *nothing* (Christians would say equal to God), and at the same time equal to the contemplating subject. There is no longer any difference between one thing and another in any respect; no distances can be located; the subject lost in the indistinct and illimitable presence of the universe and himself ceases to belong to the passing of time. He is absorbed in the everlasting instant, irrevocably as it seems, with no roots in the past or hopes in the future, and the instant itself is eternity.

With this in mind we might say that sensuality is to mysticism as a clumsy try is to a perfect achievement, and no doubt we ought to ignore what is after all a wrong turning on the spirit's road to sovereignty.

Yet I should dispute the notion that sensuality ought to be dismissed where the mystical state is concerned. I will only call attention in passing to the fact that the Moslem mystics, the Sufis, found contemplation compatible with marriage. It is a pity that the Carmelites' book does not mention this. By and large the Catholics under vows who have contributed to it admit this as a possibility, but they would distinguish between a principle (fairly remote from reality as far as Christianity is concerned) and the description of an actual experience. The criticism I would offer has nothing to do with the interesting possibility that these two experiences may coincide, however. The factor that I think ought to militate against the rejection of eroticism has nothing to do with the question whether it is *useful* to renounce sexual life in order to attain the most desirable ends. I merely wonder whether a calculated resolve and a renunciation at that is compatible with the state of indifference that is the out-standing characteristic of mysticism. I do not say that the path of calculated resolve will not lead us to that state. But what I am convinced of is that if a person does reach it, he does so in spite of his calculations and in spite of his resolve.

We have already seen how in temptation resistance is based on the need to maintain life and to last out, together with the organisation that makes it possible to do so. But surely the gift of the self and the refusal to work in servile fashion for a result that shall transcend the present moment would call for a truer indifference than that of a monk or a dedicated man *striving* to reach a state of indifference?

That makes no difference to the conditional and subordinate character of eroticism, though.

Very likely not.

But where others may see a trap, I see the sovereignty of chance.

Chance, inescapably the final sentence, without which we are never sovereign beings.

At some moment or another I must either abandon myself to chance or keep myself under control, like the religious vowed to continence. The intervention of will, the decision to keep clear of death, sin, and spiritual anguish, makes nonsense of the free play of indifference and renunciation.

Without such free play, the present instant is subordinated to preoccupation with the time to come.

No doubt preoccupation with the future can be consistent with the freedom of the present moment, but with temptation the contradiction is flagrant. Eroticism may certainly stray into some overwhelmingly depressing modes, but on the other hand the calculations of a tempted religious must be stressed, for they confer a miserliness, a poverty, a dismal discipline on the ascetic life of no matter what religion or sect.

That is only true in theory.

Yet even if the most far-reaching experiences are still possible for all that in the orderly and regulated life of the monk, I cannot forget, as I strive to grasp the significance of the flights of mysticism that constraint in the face of temptation is the key. If our aim is to explore the farthest potentialities of being, we may well opt for the disorderliness and randomness of love. In spite of what appears on the surface, the simplicity of the instant belongs to the man who, spontaneously bewitched, is laid open to anguish.

CHAPTER VI

SANCTITY, EROTICISM AND SOLITUDE

Today I wish to discuss sanctity, eroticism and solitude.[1] Before I come to lay certain ideas coherently before you, let me say a word about my intention, which you may find surprising. The word "eroticism" is ambiguously suggestive. I should like just to say why I have decided to discuss eroticism, sanctity and solitude in the same breath.

My starting point is that eroticism is a solitary activity. At the least it is a matter difficult to discuss. For not only conventional reasons, eroticism is defined by secrecy. It cannot be public. I might instant some exceptions but somehow eroticism is outside ordinary life. In our experience taken as a whole it is cut off from the normal communication of emotions. There is a taboo in force. Nothing is absolutely forbidden, for there are always transgressions. But the taboo is sufficiently active for me to be able to say by and large that eroticism, perhaps the most intense of emotions, is as if it did not exist as far as our existence is present for us in the form of speech and language. These days the taboo has been attenuated somewhat—otherwise I could not be talking to you today—but I think that just the same, since this hall belongs to the world of speech, eroticism must remain something exterior as far as we are concerned. Talk about it I shall, but as something beyond our present set of experiences, as a beyond accessible on one condition only, that we leave the world we now inhabit to shut ourselves up in solitude. Particularly it seems to me that to reach this beyond, we must renounce the philosophical attitude. The philosopher can speak of everything he feels. Erotic experience will commit us to silence.

[1] Lecture given to the *Collège Philosophique*, Spring 1955.

This is not true of an experience possibly very close to it the experience of sanctity. The emotions felt in that experience can be expressed in a speech or form the subject of a sermon. Yet erotic experience is possibly close to sanctity.

I do not mean that eroticism and sanctity are of the same nature, and anyway that subject falls outside my scope. All I mean is that both experiences have an extreme intensity. When I speak of sanctity I am referring to the life that the presence of a sacred reality within us informs, a reality that may completely overwhelm us. Just now I shall be content to look at the emotion of sanctity on the one hand and at the emotion of eroticism on the other, in so far as each has extreme intensity. My meaning is that with these two emotions one brings us closer to other men and the other cuts us off from them and leaves us in solitude.

That is the starting point of the argument I want to lay before you. I shall not speak from the philosophical standpoint as it is usually understood. Let me affirm here and now that the philosophical experience as such excludes both these emotions. I agree that the philosopher's experience is a separate one, untouched by other experiences—a specialist's experience, in fact. Emotions put it out of joint. I have long been struck by one thing. The true philosopher must devote his life to philosophy. In the practice of philosophy there is no serious reason why we should not find the weakness common to all cognitive activity—superiority in one field bought at the expense of relative ignorance in other fields. The situation gets worse every day; every day it becomes harder to acquire the sum of human knowledge since this sum is always and unendingly on the increase. The principle that philosophy should be this sum of knowledge treated not simply as a juxtaposition of facts in the memory but as a synthesising operation is still retained, but with great difficulty; every day philosophy becomes a little more of a specialised discipline like the others. It is not my purpose today to discuss the impossibility of constructing a philosophy independent of political experience, except to say that this is a characteristic orientation of contemporary philosophy. On this point philosophy has opened its doors to experience. But once this principle has been admitted, philosophy is still commonly studied in a vacuum. I mean that it is difficult to live and to philosophise simultaneously. I mean that humanity is made up of separate experiences and philosophy is only one experience among others. Philosophy finds it harder and harder to be the sum of knowledge, but it does not even aim at being the sum of experiences, in the specialist's peculiar narrow-mindedness. Yet what significance can the reflections of mankind upon himself and on being in general have, if they take no account of the intense emotional states? Obviously this implies the specialisation of something which by definition may on no account be allowed to be anything but total and universal. Obviously philosophy can only be the sum of the possibles in the sense of a synthesis, or nothing.

I repeat: philosophy is the sum of the possibles in the sense of a synthesis, or nothing.

This, I think, is what it was for Hegel. Erotic experience, at least in the first forms of his dialectic construction, had an overt share in the elaboration of the system, but it is not impossible to believe that it secretly had a deeper influence. Eroticism can only be envisaged dialectically, and conversely the dialectician, if he does not confine himself to formalism, necessarily has his eyes fixed on his own sexual experience. However that may be (and I do admit that one may hesitate faced with this somewhat obscure point), it seems that in part at least Hegel drew his peculiar dialectic from his theological knowledge as well as from his knowledge of Meister Eckhart and Jacob Boehme. But I have not brought Hegel into the discussion in order to insist on the value of his philosophy. On the contrary, in spite of my reservations I intend to assign Hegel deliberately to specialised philosophy. Besides, I only need to remind you how strongly he opposed that tendency of contemporary romantic philosophy to assert that anyone could be a philosopher with no special preparation. I do not say that he was wrong to blame impro-visation in the sphere of philosophy; that would be out of the question. But Hegel's practically inpenetrable system, even if it were the ultimate in philosophy, certainly has this quality of specialised discipline. It assembles ideas, but at the same time cuts those assembled ideas off from experience. That no doubt was his ambition, for in Hegel's mind the immediate is bad, and Hegel would certainly have identified what I call experience with the immediate. Nevertheless, without embarking on a philosophical discussion I should like to stress the fact that Hegel's argument rings like a specialised activity. I do not think that he can have helped feeling this himself. In order to counter objections in advance he contended that philosophy was a development in time, a speech delivered in successive phases. Everybody can agree with this, but it means making a special moment subordinate to the others out of each moment of philosophy. Thus we only abandon specialisation to slumber with the specialist, this time without recall.

I do not say that each of us, nor anybody, is entitled to wake up. This sum of the possibles seen as a synthesis may exist only in my imagination. I feel quite free to fail. I am uneasy at the thought of taking a failure for a success. Above all I do not yet see the need for limiting the potentialities before me by imposing a specialised piece of work upon myself. What I have in mind is a choice which faces each one of us at each moment. At this very minute I have the choice between obedience to the theory I have undertaken to expound to you and a response to some whim or other that might seize me. I get out of this with some difficulty by telling myself that what I am saying coincides with the direction of the whim; I do not give in to the wish to yield to it but I recognise the greater value of the whim, the opposite of specialisation. Specialisation is the condition of efficiency, and the search for efficiency is characteristic of anyone who feels what he lacks. In this there is an admission of impotence, a humble submission to necessity.

True enough, there is a regrettable weakness in wanting such and such a result and not taking the steps that would bring it about. But there is a strength in not wanting this result and refusing to take the road that leads to it. At this intersection, sanctity is just as much of a possible choice as eroticism. Sanctity is at first on the side of caprice as far as specialised effort goes. The saint is not after efficiency. He is prompted by desire and desire alone and in this resembles the erotic man. The point is whether desire corresponds, better than the specialisation of a project, better than the specialisation that ensures a project's efficiency, with the essence of philosophy, if philosophy is first of all, as I contend it is, the sum of the possibles seen as an operation of synthesis. To put it another way: can that operation be thought of through the simple process of calculation ending in specialisation? Or again, can the sum of the possibles be thought of through the predominance of interest over whim, the other name for desire?

Before going any further I shall try now to make the essential point about eroticism in spite of the difficulty of talking about it.

In the very first place eroticism differs from animal sexuality in that human sexuality is limited by taboos and the domain of eroticism is that of the transgression of these taboos. Desire in eroticism is the desire that triumphs over the taboo. It presupposes man in conflict with himself. The taboos against human sexuality really have specialised forms; for example they affect incest or menstruation, but they can also be thought of in a general way, as for example a way which certainly did not exist in the earliest times (during the transition from the animal to the human), a way even now called into question—nakedness. In fact the taboo on nakedness is to-day simultaneously very strong and in question. Everybody realises the absurd relativity, the gratuitousness of the taboo on nakedness, the fact that it has been conditioned by historical events; everybody realises also that the taboo on nakedness and the transgression of that taboo make up the general stuff of eroticism, I mean sexuality turned into eroticism (the sexuality peculiar to man, the sexuality of a creature with the gift of tongues). With so-called neurotic complications and with vice of one sort or another; this notion is always significant. Vice can be thought of as the art of giving oneself the feeling of transgression in a more or less maniac way.

Perhaps I should remind you of the curious origin of the theory of taboo and transgression. We find it in the oral teaching of Marcel Mauss whose work is certainly the least questioned contribution to the French school of sociology, but it was followed up by nothing in print. Mauss had a certain distaste for formulating his ideas and giving them a definitive and printable shape. I can even quite believe that the most remarkable results must have been an embarrassment to him. The basis of the transgression theory does indeed appear in his written work, but only in the form of a brief indication; it is not dwelt upon. Thus in the *Essai sur le Sacrifice* he says in a couple of sentences that the Greeks regarded the sacrifice of the Bouphonia as the crime of the sacrificer. He does not generalise. I myself did not follow his oral teaching, but as far as transgression is concerned Marcel Mauss' doctrine is set forth in a little book by one of his pupils, *L'homme et le Sacré*, by Roger Caillois. As luck would have it Roger Caillois, far from being a mere compiler, was himself capable not only of setting out the facts in a compelling fashion but of giving his arguments the strength of active and personal thinking. Caillois' theories may be summed up as follows. For the peoples with whom ethnography is concerned man's time is divided into profane time and sacred time, profane time being ordinary time, the time of work and of respect for the taboos, and sacred time being that of celebrations, that is in essence the time of transgressing the taboos. As far as eroticism goes, celebrations are often a time of sexual licence. As far as religion goes, it is particularly the time for sacrifice, for the transgression of the taboo on murder.

I have given a formal exposition of this doctrine with my personal elaborations in a work dealing with the Lascaux cave paintings, paintings made by the first men, that is, when art was born, when man had really made the step from animal to human[1]. I felt impelled to connect the taboo with work. Work certainly existed before the beginnings of art. We have traces of work in the shape of stone tools preserved in the earth whose relative dates we can ascertain. I decided that work must have implied from the beginning the existence of a world of work from which sexual life and murder and death in general were excluded. Sexual life on the one hand, murder, death and war on the other are grave if not overwhelming disturbances where work is concerned. I cannot see that there is any doubt that such moments must have been radically banished from working time, when men must soon have been co-operating with each other. When it was a question of work the creation and suppression of life must have been put aside, for work itself, in comparison with moments of intense emotion where life and death were at stake and asserting themselves, was a neutral time, a sort of annulment.

The point I am making must I think by now be plain enough. I do not say that non-specialised philosophy is possible. But philosophy in so far as it is a specialised undertaking is work. That is to say that it excludes without even deigning to notice them the moments of intense emotion I referred to earlier. Hence it is not that sum of the possibles seen as a synthesising operation that I take to be of cardinal value. It is not the sum of the possibles, the sum of possible experiences, but only the sum of certain well-defined experiences aimed at knowledge. It is only the sum of knowledge. With a clear conscience, even with a feeling of getting rid of a foreign body, getting rid of some muck, or at least of a source of error, it leaves out the intense emotion bound up

---

[1] *Lascaux ou la naissance de l'art* ("Les grands siècles de la peinture") Geneva, Skira 1955. I say "the first men", but only in so far as the men of Lascaux cannot have been so very different from the first men. The Lascaux cave paintings are obviously later than the date that can be assigned accurately enough to the "birth of art".

with birth, with the creation of life as with death. I am not the first to feel surprised at this disappointing consequence of philosophy, the expression of average humanity become foreign to extreme humanity, that is to the convulsions of sex and death. It even seems to me as if a reaction against this cold and rigid aspect of philosophy is characteristic of modern philosophy as a whole from, say, leaving out Kierkegaard, Nietzsche to Heidegger. Naturally, or so it seems to me, philosophy is in a parlous condition. It has no common ground with a certain extravagant bohemianism of thought which I may well incarnate for some of you. In this it is fully justified. Philosophy is nothing if it is not an effort and hence a disciplined effort, but when it brings in concerted effort and discipline, does not philosophy also fail in its deepest purpose, at least if it is as I have said, "the sum of the possibles seen as a synthesising operation?" The final point I want to make is that philosophy finds itself in an impasse; without discipline it could accomplish nothing and yet in that it cannot embrace the extremes of its subject, the extremes of the possible as I have called them, the outermost reaches of human life, it is doomed to failure. If it is to be fundamental even a philosophy of death must turn away from its subject. But this is not to say that philosophy is still possible if it becomes absorbed in it, losing itself in the final vertigo, or only if at the summit philosophy denies philosophy and sneers at philosophy. Supposing indeed that philosophy really sneered at philosophy; that would entail at once discipline and the abandonment of discipline; at such a moment the sum of the possibles is at stake in its entirety, and the sum is a synthesis, not merely an addition, since it ends in that synthetic view where human effort shows its impotence and relaxes in the feeling of its impotence with no regrets. Without discipline this point could not have been reached, but discipline itself can never go the whole road. This is the truth of experience. All the time the mind, the brain of man is reduced to the state of a container overflowing with, burst by its contents—like a suitcase into which objects keep being put which stops being a suitcase in the end, since it ceases to enclose the objects entrusted to it. And above all, extreme states bring an element that cannot be subjected to calm reflection into the sum of the possibles.

I will try to give an accurate description of this overflowing that we may experience.

We are faced with the necessity of making a choice. First we must make a quantitative choice. If we see them as homogeneous the possibles are too numerous. For example, given the limited span of life, we must forego reading such and such a book in which we might perhaps have found fundamental principles and the answer to the question we are asking ourselves. Then we must tell ourselves that we cannot reach the possibles described in that book.

If the experience of extreme states of being is in question, this time the choice is a qualitative one. For such an experience dislocates us and excludes calm reflection, its essence being to put us "beside ourselves". It is difficult to imagine the life of a philosopher continually or at least fairly often beside himself. We come back to the essential human experience dividing time into working time and sacred time. The fact of remaining open to possibilities bordering on madness (which is what happens with any possibility concerned with eroticism, with the threat, or more often the presence, of death, or with sanctity) keeps the work of reflection continually subordinate to something else, and just here reflection comes to an end.

In practice we do not reach an absolute impasse, but what is the heart of the matter? More often than not we forget that philosophy is as competitive as any game. The idea is to get as far on as one can. Humiliatingly enough we are in the position of a man trying to set up a record. The palm may be awarded to developments in various directions according to various points of view. From the point of view of professorial philosophy, the palms obviously go to the man who works and holds aloof from the possibilities offered by transgression. I am deeply suspicious, I admit, of

superiority in the opposite direction, where the winner would
be the refuser, the ingenuous mouthpiece of laziness and
pretention. In agreeing to compete I have personally felt it
necessary to accept the difficulties of both paths, the path of
transgression as well as the path of work. The limit occurs
when it is plainly impossible to respond satisfactorily in both
directions at the same time. It is no good persisting. I think
the only answer to the question I have put is a feeling of
oppression and impotence. We are obviously faced with the
impossible. It is not necessary to be resigned but we must
realise that the absence of resignation delivers us from
nothing. One temptation I must admit to feeling, however.
At least with transgression, coinciding as it does with laziness, I can see the advantage of apparent inferiority. But
even that is a lie, I cannot deny it; the competition is open
and I have entered my name. The fact that my participation is for me inevitably bound up with disputing the
principles of the superiority in question has nothing to do
with it. One must still advance as far as possible and my
indifference is beside the point. Even if I refuse to be
involved my refusal is not entire and that is enough.
I am committed just the same. Today in any case here I am
speaking to you, and that means that solitude is not enough
for me.

Let us now push this enquiry to its logical conclusion and
try to show the significance of Christianity in relation to the
questions I have put forward. Not that I think that I ought to
discuss specifically Christian sanctity when I refer to sanctity. But whatever my intentions are there is no practical
difference in the minds of my hearers between sanctity and
Christian sanctity, and I have not brought up this point in
order to balk the issue. To return to the ideas I was trying to
put over just now, I must emphasise the fact that in the
Christian system what I call transgression is called sin. Sin
is a fault, it is that which ought not to have happened. Take
first the death on the Cross: it is a sacrifice, a sacrifice whose
victim is God himself. But although the sacrifice redeems us,

although the Church sings its paradoxical *Felix Culpa!*—
happy error—to the underlying fault, that which redeems
us is also that which ought not to have taken place. For
Christianity the taboo is absolute and transgression of any
kind is condemned out of hand. Yet the condemnation is
relaxed because of the very fault most to be condemned, the
worst transgression imaginable. The transition from eroticism to sanctity makes very good sense. It is the transition
from that which is damned and rejected to that which is
fortunate and blessed. On the one hand eroticism is the
solitary fault, the thing which saves us only by separating
us from everybody else, the thing that saves us only in the
euphoria of an illusion, since when all is said and done that
which in eroticism bears us to pinnacles of intensity also lays
the curse of solitude upon us at the same time. On the other
hand sanctity delivers us from solitude but on the condition
that we accept the paradox of the happy error, the Felix
Culpa! whose very extravagance redeems us. Under such
circumstances we can only return to our fellow men by
evading the issue. This evasion is doubtless worthy of the
name "renunciation" since in Christianity we cannot simultaneously perform a transgression and enjoy its fruits—only
others can enjoy them in damnation and solitude. Harmony
with his fellows is not recovered by the Christian unless he
foregos the enjoyment of the means of his redemption, of
that which is still never anything but transgression and the
violation of the taboos upon which civilisation is founded.

If we follow the path marked out by Christianity, it is
true, we can not only escape from solitude but also achieve
a kind of equilibrium which avoids the primary disequilibrium of my starting point, preventing us from reconciling
discipline and work with the experience of the ultimate.
Christian sanctity at any rate opens up the possibility of
pushing as far as it will go the experience of that final convulsion ultimately leading to death. Sanctity and the transgression of the taboo concerning death are not to be completely identified. War particularly is the transgression of

this taboo. But sanctity is none the less placed on a level with death; in this, sanctity resembles the heroism of the warrior lived out by the saint as if he were dying. What a bewildering twist of direction, though! He lives as though he were dying, but in order to achieve eternal life! Sanctity is always a project. Perhaps not in essence. St. Theresa used to say that even if Hell were to swallow her up she could not but persevere. Anyway, the intention to gain eternal life is connected with sanctity as if with its opposite. Just as if in sanctity only a compromise allowed the saint to make common ground with the mob, with the rest of humanity. With the mob and with philosophy, which comes to the same thing—common ideas, in fact.

The oddest thing is that agreement has been reached between deliberate transgression and the other kinds on the understanding that it shall be a tacit one. This agreement occurs in all forms of archaic religions. Christianity invented the only path of transgression that still permitted discussion. Here let us recognise simply that discussion freed from Christian principles tends to deny anything that looks like transgression and to deny at the same time anything that looks like a taboo. On the sexual level, take the aberration of nudism, which is a denial of the sexual taboo, a denial of the transgression which the taboo necessarily engenders. If you like, discussion is the denial of that which distinguishes the human as opposed to the animal.

As far as I am concerned—it seems to me—as I have been speaking—that I have paid a kind of homage—a rather clumsy one—to silence. A homage to eroticism, too—perhaps. But at this point I should like to counsel my hearers the most extreme caution. I am really speaking a dead language. This language, I believe, is the language of philosophy. I will go so far as to say that in my opinion philosophy is also the death of language. It is also a sacrifice. The operation I spoke of that synthesises all the possibles is the suppression of every contribution of language which substitutes a neutral and indifferent atmosphere for the experience of springing life. I have cautioned you about language. I must therefore caution you at the same time against my own words. Not that I want to end upon a note of farce, but I have been trying to talk a language that equals zero, a language equivalent to nothing at all, a language that returns to silence. I am not talking about nothingness, which sometimes looks to me like a pretext for adding a specialised chapter onto speech; I am talking about the suppression of whatever language may add to the world. I realise that this suppression cannot be rigorously applied. Anyway the point is not to bring in another sort of duty. But I owe it to myself to put you on guard against an unfortunate use of what I have said. From this point anything that does not take us out of the world (in the sense that through the Church or against the Church a sort of sanctity takes men out of the world) would betray my purpose. I said that discipline, committing us to the ways of work as it does, moves us away from the experience of extremes. Agreed, at least in a general sense, but this experience has its own discipline. At any rate this discipline is primarily contrary to any form of verbal apology of eroticism. Eroticism is silence, I have said; it is solitude. But not for people whose very presence in the world is a pure denial of silence, a chattering, a neglect of potential solitude.

CHAPTER VII

A PREFACE TO "MADAME EDWARDA"

"Death is the most terrible thing of all, and the greatest strength is demanded to keep death's work going."

Hegel

The author of Madame Edwarda has himself drawn our attention to the seriousness of his book[1]. Nevertheless I think it should be stressed because of the frivolity with which books on sexual subjects are usually treated. Not that I have any hope—or intention—of altering that. But I would ask the reader of my preface to reflect for a moment on the traditional attitude to pleasure (which reaches its greatest intensity in the relationship of the sexes) and to pain (which death stills, it is true, but only after making it worse). Various factors contribute to give us a picture of man, of humanity, equally remote from extreme pleasure and extreme pain: the commonest taboos bear on sex and death, so that both have become sacred matters bound up with religion. The real difficulty began when the taboos connected with the circumstances of a being's disappearance became the only ones to be treated seriously and those connected with its appearance—the whole of genetic activity—came to be taken lightly. There is no question of protesting against the majority tendency, for fate has decreed that man shall laugh at his own reproductive organs. Yet even as this very laughter points the contrast between pleasure and pain, showing pain and death as deserving respect while pleasure is derisory and deserving of scorn, it indicates their essential common nature. Laughter may not show respect but it does

[1] Pierre Angélique, *Madame Edwarda* third edition J. J. Pauvert 1956.

show horror. Laughter is an attitude of compromise adopted by man when some repugnant but not apparently important factor confronts him. If eroticism is taken seriously or tragically it is overwhelming.

I must first make plain the futility of the common contention that sexual taboos are nothing but prejudice and it is high time we were rid of them. The embarrassment and shame that go hand in hand with a strong feeling of pleasure are supposed to be simply proofs of stupidity. We might just as well say that we ought to make a clean sweep of the whole business and get back to animal habits of eating anything and ignoring filth and excrement. Just as though our whole humanity did not spring from the reaction of horror followed by fascination linked with sensitiveness and intelligence. Yet though we may not wish to dispute the laughter roused by indecency we are at liberty to go back at least partially on the attitude for which such laughter is responsible.

For it is laughter that justifies a form of condemnation that dishonours us. Laughter takes us along the path that transforms prohibitions and inevitable necessary decencies into a blinkered hypocrisy and a lack of understanding of the issues at stake. Extremes of licence coupled with joking go hand in hand with the refusal to take erotic truth seriously, I mean tragically.

The preface to the little book in which eroticism is directly depicted as making the participants aware of a rending sensation gives me an opportunity of making a deliberately emotional appeal. Not that I find it surprising that the spirit should turn away from itself and with its back to itself, as it were, change into an obstinate caricature of its own truth. If man needs lies that is his own lookout when all is said and done. The man who perhaps has a spark of pride is submerged in the mass of humanity. Anyway, I shall never forget the wonder and violence of the determination to open my eyes, to look straight at what is happening, at what *is*. And I should not know what is happening if I knew nothing about extreme pleasure and extreme pain.

Let us be clear on this point. Pierre Angélique is careful to explain it. We know nothing and we are in the depths of darkness. But at least we can see what it is deceives us, what it is that hinders us from knowing our own distress, or more accurately from knowing that joy is the same thing as pain, the same thing as death.

What that loud and smutty laughter distracts us from is the oneness of extreme pleasure and extreme pain, the oneness of being and dying, of knowledge finishing with this dazzling prospect and final darkness. No doubt in the long run we might laugh at this truth, but it would be total laughter, not stopping at contempt for something repugnant but overwhelming us with disgust.

In order to reach the limits of the ecstasy in which we lose ourselves in bliss we must always set an immediate boundary to it: horror. Not only can pain, my own or that of other people, carry me nearer to the moment when horror will seize hold of me and bring me to a state of bliss bordering on delirium, but there is no kind of repugnance whose affinity with desire I do not discern. Horror is sometimes confused with fascination, but if it cannot suppress and destroy the element of fascination it will reinforce it. Danger has a paralysing effect, but if it is a mild danger it can excite desire. We can only reach a state of ecstasy when we are conscious of death or annihilation, even if remotely.

A man differs from an animal in that certain sensations affect him painfully and strike at his inmost being. These sensations vary with the individual and with ways of life. But the sight of blood, the stink of vomit evoke the horror of death in us and give us a feeling of nausea worse than pain. We find these feelings so close to the ultimate vertigo unbearable. Certain people would rather die than touch a snake, even a harmless one. A region exists where death means not only disappearance but also the intolerable feeling of disappearing against our will, when the thing to do is not to disappear at all costs. This "at all costs" and this "against our will" are precisely what distinguish the moment of utter bliss and the nameless though miraculous ecstasy. If there is nothing that transcends us, transcends us in spite of ourselves, something that at all costs ought not to be, we shall not attain the insensate moment towards which we are striving and which we are at the same time resisting with might and main.

Pleasure would be a poor enough thing without this aberrant transcendency, not confined to sexual ecstasy and experienced in the same way by mystics of various religions, the Christian religion foremost. We receive being in an intolerable transcendence of being, no less intolerable than death. And since in death it is given and taken away at the same time we must seek it in the feeling of death, in those unbearable instants where we seem to be dying because the being within us is only there through excess, when the fullness of horror and joy coincide.

Thought itself, reflection, that is, is only fulfilled in excess. What is truth, apart from the representation of excess, if we only see that which exceeds the possibility of seeing what it is intolerable to see, just as in ecstasy enjoyment is intolerable? What is truth, if we think that which exceeds the possibility of thought?[1]

When such emotional cogitations give out of their own

[1] I apologise for adding here that this definition of being and of excess cannot be given any solid philosophical foundation in that excess transcends its own foundations; excess is by very definition the factor that sets being beyond the limits of definition. Being no doubt also exists within limits, and they allow us to be articulate. (I too am being articulate at this moment, but in the process of speaking I do not forget that not only is the word destined eventually to elude my control, it eludes it as I speak. These methodically organised sentences are possible (and on the whole they are, since excess is exceptional, marvellously and miraculously exceptional, and excess indicates the attraction—fascination if not horror—of everything that is *more than that which is*) but their impossibility was originally postulated; consequently I am never confined within their logic but I retain a sovereign independence of which my death alone despoils me, proving how impossible it would have been to confine myself within the limits of an existence free of excess. I do not dispute the factor of conscious awareness without which I should not be writing, but the hand that writes is dying and through its death in store evades the limits accepted as it writes (accepted by the writing hand, rejected by the dying hand.)

accord, one last cry, and they are engulfed because they can
be borne no longer, we come back to God. That is the significance and the enormity of this insensate little book: the story
brings in God himself with all his attributes; yet this God is a
whore exactly like all other whores. But what mysticism
cannot put into words (it fails at the moment of utterance),
eroticism says; God is nothing if he is not a transcendence
of God in every direction; in that of vulgar being, in that of
horror and impurity; even in that of nothing at all in the last
analysis. We cannot add to language without impunity the
word which transcends words, the word God. As soon as we
do so this self-transcending word vertiginously destroys its
own limits. That which it is shrinks from nothing. It is.
everywhere where it cannot be expected: it is an *enormity*
itself. Anyone with the least suspicion about it holds his
tongue forthwith. Or else seeking some issue and knowing
that he is caught he seeks within himself that which could
annihilate him and make him like God, like nothing.[1]

Along the indescribable path where what must be the most
incongruous of all books is our guide at first, there may well
be discoveries yet to be made.

Happiness, for example, we might say at random.

In that case joy would be present in the contemplation of
death (it masquerades as its opposite, sorrow).

I am not in the least inclined to think that physical pleasure
is the most important thing on earth. Man is not to be
identified with the organ of pleasure. Yet this unacknow-
ledgable organ teaches him a secret[2]. Since pleasure depends

---

[1] So here is the first theology suggested by a man alight with laughter who is
prepared not to put a limit to *that which does not know what the limit is*. If you have
paled over the texts of the philosophers, the day you read this will be a red letter
day! How is the man that can silence them to give utterance himself except in a
way they cannot conceive?

[2] I might well point out into the bargain that excess is the very principle of
sexual reproduction, for *divine providence* wished her secret to be plain in her
work! Could man be denied anything? The day he notices that the ground has
shifted beneath his feet he is told that this is providential. But even if he should be
punished for his blasphemy, it is by blaspheming and spitting on his own limitations
that the most miserable creature finds fulfilment, it is by blaspheming that he is
God. The fact is that creation is inextricable, and cannot be reduced to any other
impulse of the mind than to the certitude, being exceeded, of exceeding.

on a prospect seen as harmful, we should very likely cheat and try to get at joy whilst steering clear of horror as far as we can. The images which arouse desire or bring on the final spasm are usually shady and equivocal: if they are aimed at horror or death it is always in an underhand way. Even from de Sade's point of view death is diverted to the other partner and that partner is at first a delicious expression of life. The sphere of eroticism is inescapably destined to deceit. The object provoking the reaction of Eros gives itself out to be other than it is. Hence in erotic matters the ascetics are right.

They say that beauty is the snare of the devil; indeed only beauty can make tolerable the need for disorder, violence and indignity that lies at the root of love. This is not the place to examine the details of different kinds of delirium with their multiplicity of forms, the most violent of which are slyly revealed to us by pure love and bear the blind excess of life to the gates of death. The ascetics' condemnation may be coarse, cowardly and cruel but it is in harmony with the tremor without which the truth of darkness must escape us. There is no reason why sexual love should be invested with an importance that belongs only to the whole of life, but if we did not bring the light to the very point where darkness falls how should we know ourselves as we are, formed by the projection of being into horror? Supposing being is lost, supposing it sinks into the nauseous emptiness which it ought to have avoided *at all costs . . .*

Certainly there is nothing more ominous. How ridiculous the carvings of Hell on church porches ought to look to us! Hell is the feeble idea God involuntarily gives us of himself. But on the scale of unlimited loss we come again upon the triumph of *being*—whose only failure has ever been to be in tune with the movement that would have it perishable. Being joins the terrible syncopated dance of its own accord, the dance we must accept for what it is, conscious of the horror it is in key with. If our heart fail us there is no torture like it. And the moment of torment will always come:

how would we overcome it if it were to fail? But all of being
ready and open—for death, joy or torment—unreservedly
open and dying, painful and happy, is there already with its
shadowed light, and this light is divine: and the cry that
being—vainly?—tries to utter from a twisted mouth is an
immense *alleluia*, lost in endless silence.

CONCLUSION

If my readers' interest in eroticism is of the same order as their interest in separate problems, this book is of no use to them.

I do not say that eroticism is the most important thing of all. The problem of work is more urgent. But that is a problem within our means, whereas eroticism is the problem of problems. In that he is an erotic animal, man is a problem for himself. Eroticism is the problematic part of ourselves.

The specialist can never tackle eroticism.

Of all problems eroticism is the most mysterious, the most general and the least straightforward.

For the man who cannot escape his own nature, the man whose life is open to exuberance, eroticism is the greatest personal problem of all. At the same time it is a universal problem in a way that no other problem is.

The erotic moment is also the most intense of all (except perhaps for mystical experience); hence its place is at the loftiest peak of man's spirit.

If eroticism is to be placed so high, then so is the question with which I end my book.

But it is a philosophical one.

I believe that the supreme philosophical question coincides with the summits of eroticism.

This concluding summary is in one way foreign to the circumscribed subject-matter of my book. It takes us away from eroticism to philosophy; but then in my experience eroticism cannot be regarded as a mere off-shoot detached from the main course of life, as it is in the minds of many people, without being seriously misrepresented. Besides, philosophy itself cannot exist in isolation. The time comes when we have to take hold of conceptual data as a whole, the ideas upon which our existence hinges in this world.

This body of thought would clearly not be available to us if language had not made it explicit.

But if language is to formulate it, this can take place only in successive phases worked out in the dimension of time. We can never hope to attain a global view in one single supreme instant; language chops it into its component parts and connects them up into a coherent explanation. The analytic presentation makes it impossible for the successive stages to coalesce.

So language scatters the totality of all that touches us most closely even while it arranges it in order. Through language we can never grasp what matters to us, for it eludes us in the form of interdependent propositions, and no central whole to which each of these can be referred ever appears. Our attention remains fixed on this whole but we can never see it in the full light of day. A succession of propositions flickering off and on merely hides it from our gaze, and we are powerless to alter this.

Most men are indifferent to this problem.

It is not necessary to answer the riddle of existence; it is not even necessary to ask it.

But the fact that a man may possibly neither answer it nor even ask it does not eliminate that riddle.

If I were to be asked what we are, I should answer: 'We are the door to everything that can be, we are the expectation that no material response can satisfy, no trick with words deceive. We seek the heights. Each one of us can ignore this search if he has a mind to, but mankind as a whole aspires to these heights; they are the only definition of his nature, his only justification and significance.'

This peak, this supreme moment, is not the one philosophy has in view.

Philosophy cannot escape from the limits of philosophy, of language, that is. It uses language in such a way that silence never follows, so that the supreme moment is necessarily beyond philosophical questioning. At any rate it is beyond philosophy as far as philosophy claims to answer its own questions.

That is how the problem must be seen.

Questioning has meaning only as elaborated by philosophy. The supreme questioning is that to which the answer is the supreme moment of eroticism—that of eroticism's silence.

The philosophical moment prolongs that of work and of taboo. I will not go into this. But philosophy progresses, unable to stop, and sets itself up against transgression. If philosophy were to shift its ground from work and taboo with their complementary accord to take its stand upon transgression, it would be philosophy no longer but a mockery of itself.

Compared with work, transgression is a game.

In the world of play philosophy disintegrates.

If transgression became the foundation-stone of philosophy (this is how my thinking goes), silent contemplation would have to be substituted for language. *This is the contemplation of being at the pinnacle of being.* Language has by no means vanished. How should one reach the heights if language did not point the way? But descriptive language becomes meaningless at the decisive instant when the stirrings of transgression itself take over from the discursive account of transgression, and one supreme moment follows these successive apparitions. In the hushed silence of that one moment, that moment of death, the unity of being is revealed through the intensity of those experiences in which truth stands clear of life and of its objects.

In the introduction to this book I have tried—in terms of language—to make this supreme moment accessible to the understanding, and I have related it to the feeling of the *continuity* of being.

As I have mentioned, the introduction was actually the text of a lecture. Jean Wahl was present, and afterwards he raised the following objection. (I had attributed this feeling of continuity to the partners in erotic activity.)

Jean Wahl said: "One of the partners must be conscious of continuity. Bataille talks to us, Bataille writes, he is aware of what he is doing, and the moment that he is, the continuity can be broken. I don't know what Bataille will have to say about this, but I think there is a real problem here. Consciousness of continuity is no longer continuity, but there is no more speech for all that."

Jean Wahl had taken my meaning exactly.

I answered him straight off and told him that he was right, but that sometimes on the borderline continuity and consciousness draw very close together.

The supreme moment is indeed a silent one, and in the silence our consciousness fails us.

Just now I wrote: "In the hushed silence of that moment, the moment of death . . .

Where would we be without language? It has made us what we are. It alone can show us the sovereign moment at the farthest point of being where it can no longer act as currency. In the end the articulate man confesses his own impotence.

Language does not exist independently of the play of taboo and transgression. That is why if philosophy is to tackle all problems as a single whole it must start from an historical analysis of taboo and transgression. It is by taking issue over the question of origins that philosophy, changing into a transgression of philosophy, will attain to the pinnacle of being. The pinnacle of being stands revealed in its entirety only through the movements of transgression in which, thought founded on the development of awareness through work, at last transcends work in the knowledge that it cannot be subordinate to it.

BIBLIOGRAPHY

ANGÉLIQUE, PIERRE, *Madame Edwarda*, 3rd ed., Paris, Pauvert, 1956.

AYMÉ, MARCEL, *Uranus*, Paris, Gallimard, 1948.

BATAILLE, GEORGES, *Lascaux ou la Naissance de l'Art*, Paris, Skira, 1955.

La Part Maudite, Paris, Editions de Minuit, 1949.

BAUDELAIRE, CHARLES, *Fusées III* in *Journaux Intimes*, Paris, Georges Crès, 1919.

BEAUVOIR, SIMONE DE, *Marquis de Sade*, John Calder, 1961.

BEIRNAERT, FATHER LOUIS, *La Signification du Symbolisme Conjugal*.

BLANCHOT, MAURICE, *Lautréamont et Sade*, Paris, Editions. de Minuit, 1949.

BOSSUET, *Sermon sur la Mort* in *Oeuvres*, 2 vols., Paris, Cité des Livres, 1929-1930.

BREUIL, HENRI, *Quatre Cents Siècles d'Art Pariétal*, Paris, Montignac, 1952.

BRUNO DE SAINTE-MARIE, FATHER, *Mystique et Continence*, Revue Carmelitaine, 31st Year, 1952.

CAILLOIS, ROGER, *L'Homme et le Sacré*, 2nd ed., Paris, Gallimard, 1950.

CLAUSEWITZ, KARL VON, *On War* (Translated by A. M. E. Maguire), London, Clowes, 1909.

DAVIE, M. R., *The Evolution of War*, Yale University Press, 1929.

FOUCHET, MAX-POL, *L'Art amoureux des Indes*, Lausanne, La Guilde du Livre, 1957.

FRAZER, JAMES, *The Golden Bough*, London, Macmillan, 1911-1915.

FREUD, SIGMUND, *Totem and Taboo*, London, Hogarth Press, 1955.

GROUSSET, RENÉ and REGNAUD-GATIER, SILVIE, *Histoire Universelle*, Paris, Gallimard, 1955.

HERTZ, ROBERT, *Mélanges de Sociologie religieuse et de Folklore*, Paris, Alcan, 1928.

HUBERT, HENRI and MAUSS, MARCEL, *Esquisse d'une Theorie Generale de la Magie*, Annee Sociologique, 1902-1903.

HUYSMANS, J. K., *Là-Bas*, Paris, Crès, 1930.

JANIN, JULES, Article in *Revue de Paris*, 1834.

KINSEY, POMEROY and MARTIN, *Sexual Behaviour in the Human Male*, Philadelphia and London, Saunders, 1948. *Sexual Behaviour in the Human Female*, Philadelphia and London, Saunders, 1953.

KROEBER, A. L., *Totem and Taboo in Retrospect*.

LEIRIS, MICHEL, *Miroir de la Tauromachie*, Ed. G.L.M., 1938.

LEUBA, J., *La Psychologie des Mystiques Religieux*.

LEVY-BRUHL, LUCIEN, *Les Fonctions mentales dans les Sociétés Inferieures*, Paris, Alcan, 1910.

LEVI-STRAUSS, CLAUDE, *Les Structures Elementaires de la Parenté*, Paris, Presses Universitaires, 1949.

MAUSS, MARCEL, *Essai sur la Nature et la Fonction du Sacrifice*, Paris, Annee Sociologique, 1899. *Essai sur le Don*, Paris, Année Sociologique, 1923-1924. *Sociologie et Anthropologie*, Presses Universitaires de France, 1950.

and HUBERT, HENRI, *Esquisse d'une Théorie Generale de la Magie*, Paris, Année Sociologique, 1902-1903.

PARCHEMINEY, DR., Article in *Revue Française de Psychanalyse*, 1948, No. 2.

PHILIPPE DE LA TRINITÉ, FATHER, *Amour Mystique Chasteté Parfaite*.

SADE, MARQUIS DE, *Les Cent-vingt Journées de Sodome*, Oeuvres Completes, Paris, 1948. *La Nouvelle Justine*, Paris, Pauvert, 1954.

SCHWARTZ, OSWALD, *Psychologie Sexuelle*, Paris, Gallimard, 1951.

TESSON, FATHER, *Sexualité Morale et Mystique*.

VINCI, LEONARDO DA, *Notebooks*, 2 Vols., London, Cape, 1948.

WEIL, ERIC, *Logique de la Philosophie*, Paris, Vrin, 1951.

INDEX

THE LITERATURE OF
DEATH AND DYING

Abrahamsson, Hans. **The Origin of Death:** Studies in African Mythology. 1951

Alden, Timothy. **A Collection of American Epitaphs and Inscriptions with Occasional Notes.** Five vols. in two. 1814

Austin, Mary. **Experiences Facing Death.** 1931

Bacon, Francis. **The Historie of Life and Death with Observations Naturall and Experimentall for the Prolongation of Life.** 1638

Barth, Karl. **The Resurrection of the Dead.** 1933

Bataille, Georges. **Death and Sensuality:** A Study of Eroticism and the Taboo. 1962

Bichat, [Marie François] Xavier. **Physiological Researches on Life and Death.** 1827

Browne, Thomas. **Hydriotaphia.** 1927

Carrington, Hereward. **Death:** Its Causes and Phenomena with Special Reference to Immortality. 1921

Comper, Frances M. M., editor. **The Book of the Craft of Dying and Other Early English Tracts Concerning Death.** 1917

Death and the Visual Arts. 1976

Death as a Speculative Theme in Religious, Scientific, and Social Thought. 1976

Donne, John. **Biathanatos.** 1930

Farber, Maurice L. **Theory of Suicide.** 1968

Fechner, Gustav Theodor. **The Little Book of Life After Death.** 1904

Frazer, James George. **The Fear of the Dead in Primitive Religion.** Three vols. in one. 1933/1934/1936

Fulton, Robert. **A Bibliography on Death, Grief and Bereavement:** 1845-1975. 1976

Gorer, Geoffrey. **Death, Grief, and Mourning.** 1965

Gruman, Gerald J. **A History of Ideas About the Prolongation of Life.** 1966

Henry, Andrew F. and James F. Short, Jr. **Suicide and Homicide.** 1954

Howells, W[illiam] D[ean], et al. **In After Days;** Thoughts on the Future Life. 1910

Irion, Paul E. **The Funeral:** Vestige or Value? 1966

Landsberg, Paul-Louis. **The Experience of Death:** The Moral Problem of Suicide. 1953

Maeterlinck, Maurice. **Before the Great Silence.** 1937

Maeterlinck, Maurice. **Death.** 1912

Metchnikoff, Élie. **The Nature of Man:** Studies in Optimistic Philosophy. 1910

Metchnikoff, Élie. **The Prolongation of Life:** Optimistic Studies. 1908

Munk, William. **Euthanasia.** 1887

Osler, William. **Science and Immortality.** 1904

Return to Life: Two Imaginings of the Lazarus Theme. 1976

Stephens, C[harles] A[sbury]. **Natural Salvation:** The Message of Science. 1905

Sulzberger, Cyrus. **My Brother Death.** 1961

Taylor, Jeremy. **The Rule and Exercises of Holy Dying.** 1819

Walker, G[eorge] A[lfred]. **Gatherings from Graveyards.** 1839

Warthin, Aldred Scott. **The Physician of the Dance of Death.** 1931

Whiter, Walter. **Dissertation on the Disorder of Death.** 1819

Whyte, Florence. **The Dance of Death in Spain and Catalonia.** 1931

Wolfenstein, Martha. **Disaster:** A Psychological Essay. 1957

Worcester, Alfred. **The Care of the Aged, the Dying, and the Dead.** 1950

Zandee, J[an]. **Death as an Enemy According to Ancient Egyptian Conceptions.** 1960